W9-AIA-390

The real Dominic Lockhart had returned.

The man she had briefly seen, the one who could laugh, who could relax, even talk about how he felt, had once again become hidden behind that wall of superiority and reserve.

Well, so be it. She may have harbored ridiculous fantasies last night when they were side by side in bed, but that was all it could possibly be.

"Right, well, I for one have work to do today," Nellie said, standing quickly.

"I'm well aware of the long hours that servants work."

She stared at him for a moment, wanting to give him a lecture on the working conditions of most servants, but once again registered the bruising on his face, now turning various shades of green, blue and yellow. He did not need lectures from her. She'd accused him of being haughty, but if she hadn't been so haughty when they first met, if she hadn't been so determined to make him feel uncomfortable, he'd now be lying in his own bed, his face unscathed by fists and boots. Meeting her had caused him so much harm. He was right. He should return to his own world as soon as possible.

Author Note

Nellie Regan featured as a lady's maid in *Beguiling the Duke* and *Awakening the Duchess*. She was never happy being a secondary character in someone else's story and I had to work hard to stop her from taking over. Now she has her own book, where her big personality and even bigger aspirations take center stage.

The late Victorian era was a time when feisty women like Nellie were starting to challenge the status quo that kept people of her class and sex in their place. It was also a time of growth for the middle class and saw a rapid expansion of shops and businesses, such as Nellie's hairdressing parlor, which catered to this "new" money.

Mr. Dominic Lockhart is also one of the new men who emerged in the Victorian period—men with money but no real status in a society where having the right background often meant more than how wealthy you were.

I loved writing Nellie and Dominic's story and hope you enjoy reading *Aspirations of a Lady's Maid*.

EVA SHEPHERD

—

Aspirations of a Lady's Maid

HARLEQUIN
HISTORICAL

If you purchased this book without a cover you should be aware that this book is stolen property. It was reported as "unsold and destroyed" to the publisher, and neither the author nor the publisher has received any payment for this "stripped book."

HARLEQUIN®
HISTORICAL™

Recycling programs for this product may not exist in your area.

ISBN-13: 978-1-335-50567-5

Aspirations of a Lady's Maid

Copyright © 2020 by Eva Shepherd

All rights reserved. No part of this book may be used or reproduced in any manner whatsoever without written permission except in the case of brief quotations embodied in critical articles and reviews.

This is a work of fiction. Names, characters, places and incidents are either the product of the author's imagination or are used fictitiously. Any resemblance to actual persons, living or dead, businesses, companies, events or locales is entirely coincidental.

This edition published by arrangement with Harlequin Books S.A.

For questions and comments about the quality of this book, please contact us at CustomerService@Harlequin.com.

Harlequin Enterprises ULC
22 Adelaide St. West, 40th Floor
Toronto, Ontario M5H 4E3, Canada
www.Harlequin.com

Printed in U.S.A.

After graduating with degrees in history and political science, **Eva Shepherd** worked in journalism and as an advertising copywriter. She began writing historical romances because it combined her love of a happy ending with her passion for history. She lives in Christchurch, New Zealand, but spends her days immersed in the world of late Victorian England. You can follow her on evashepherd.com and Facebook.com/evashepherdromancewriter.

Books by Eva Shepherd

Harlequin Historical

Beguiling the Duke
Awakening the Duchess
Aspirations of a Lady's Maid

Visit the Author Profile page
at Harlequin.com.

To Dawn, Jamie and Fernando.
Thanks for making working in the
"broom cupboard" so much fun.
And to Hayley B, thanks for my beautiful
website and all the IT help.

Chapter One

England—1895

Just look at them...unbelievable. Nellie Regan shook her head and released a disdainful sigh. It was supposed to be a celebration, but you would think the assembled guests were attending a funeral. Although even a wake back in Nellie's native Ireland would be more enjoyable than this woeful ball at Hardgrave Estate, being held to celebrate the engagement of Dominic Lockhart to Lady Cecily Hardgrave.

From her discreet vantage point behind a large potted palm on the minstrels' balcony overlooking the ballroom, she watched the supposedly happy couple waltz round the parquet dance floor. They were barely touching each other. There was no smiling, no laughter, not even an exchange of pleasantries. It was as if dancing together was a duty, not a pleasure.

No, Nellie would never understand the upper classes. Their formality, stiffness and lack of passion.

It was as if they were a separate species from the rest of humanity.

She shook her head again. If this engagement party was taking place among people of her own class, there would be laughing, singing, hugging and kissing. People would be drinking to the health of the engaged couple, who would be brimming with love and happiness.

But this couple looked as if love and happiness were foreign concepts they had never heard of. She gave a quiet laugh. And even if they *had* heard of love and happiness, she suspected they would consider such things far too common for the likes of them.

Although Mr Lockhart certainly did look handsome—Nellie would give him that at least. Tall—slightly over six foot, she estimated—with coal-black hair, olive skin, and a strong, clean-shaven jawline that at this late hour bore a hint of dark stubble. Yes, he was quite something. And his black swallow-tailed evening suit certainly gave him a manly quality that was undeniably attractive. Especially as it showed off his broad shoulders—something Nellie had to admit she was a tad partial to. And that white-silk waistcoat, high stiff collar and white tie showed off his dark good looks to perfection.

As she watched him glide his partner across the dance floor and around the elegant ballroom, she also had to admit that Mr Lockhart was a superb mover. You'd think a woman would be pleased to be in the arms of such a commanding, graceful man, but Lady Cecily's tight face suggested it was all too much for her to have to endure.

Nellie drew in her lips, flared her nostrils and put her nose in the air in imitation of Lady Cecily's pinched expression. *All this touching and what not…it's simply not done.* She laughed quietly to herself.

The engaged couple did another circuit of the floor and Nellie's gaze was drawn to Mr Lockhart's dark brown eyes, eyes as dark as a moonless winter sky, and just as cold. She slowly shook her head, sighing deeply. Why did he have to look so miserable? This was his engagement party after all. He might be handsome, but all those good looks and that manly countenance were a bit of a waste really if there was no passion to go with it. No, Nellie would never understand the upper classes and nor would she ever want to.

She looked around the room and saw the Duchess of Somerfeld dancing with her husband. They seemed to be the only people at this dismal event who were actually enjoying themselves. Perhaps it was because the Duchess was American that she was able to relax and have a good time. She hadn't been infected by that unfortunate condition which affected so many members of the English upper class, the stiff upper lip.

The Duke and Duchess whirled round the floor, causing Nellie to smile. Unlike the engaged couple, there was no doubting their love for each other—it could be seen in every glance, every touch, every smile.

The Duchess was the only reason Nellie was present at this sombre engagement party. She had worked for the Duchess before her marriage, when she was still Arabella van Haven, and had accompanied her from America to England. The Duchess had always treated her with respect and they were as much friends as servant and mistress. The Duchess now had a new lady's maid, but for special occasions such as this society event she still liked Nellie to attend her. Although her days as a servant were over, Nellie was happy to oblige the Duchess. After all, the Duchess had done so much for Nellie, she had even financed her in her own business.

But Nellie planned to pay her back every penny and would add on a healthy amount of interest as well. The Duchess had said it was a gift, not a loan, but Nellie was determined never to be beholden to anyone.

She smiled with satisfaction over the direction her life was taking. At the end of the weekend she would return to her own London establishment, the Venus Hair and Beauty Parlour, proprietress Eleanor Regan. The hairdressing parlour catered to a growing number of middle-class women who wanted to look as if they had their own lady's maid, but couldn't afford the expense of another servant.

Oh, yes, she had come a long way from when she'd left Ireland for America ten years ago at the age of thirteen following the death of her parents and had found work as a scullery maid in the van Haven household.

She closed her eyes briefly and drew in a slow breath as the memory of her loving parents flooded her mind. Opening her eyes, she blinked away her unshed tears and forced away all sadness. There was nothing to be sad about. She had been lucky to find employment with the van Havens. It had been a much better fate than was suffered by many Irish immigrants trying to make a new life in New York.

She had been very lucky indeed and there was nothing to feel sad about, especially now. She flicked another glance in the direction of Dominic Lockhart and his fiancée. No, her life was exactly the way she wanted it and she wouldn't change a thing. Unlike people of their class, Nellie had worked hard for everything she had and that had been a good thing. It made her resilient and appreciate what she had, while those born to wealth had everything handed to them on a silver platter.

Or, more to the point, handed to them on a silver platter by their servants, who worked endlessly behind the scenes to make their lives run smoothly and ensure their every need was catered for before they even had to ask.

The ruling class might have a life of ease, but that didn't seem to be making them happy. Mr Lockhart and Lady Cecily were proof of that. The pinched expression on Lady Cecily's face gave the impression that dancing with her fiancé was something to be endured rather than enjoyed and Mr Lockhart's granite-hard face suggested he was performing a duty expected of him by society, rather than holding the woman he loved in his arms.

These people seemed incapable of letting go and truly enjoying themselves. They didn't seem to realise just how lucky they were to have so much wealth and privilege.

And no wonder. They had no challenges, no obstacles to overcome. Their only challenge was how to fill their endless spare time and spend their huge fortunes. That was a fate Nellie knew she could never endure. Being busy made her happy. She liked to know she was making something of her life through her own hard work. And she especially loved doing a job which she knew she was good at.

She scanned the room again and released a loud, disappointed sigh. She wasn't hiding out on the balcony to spy on Mr Lockhart and his fiancée, even if that is what she had ended up doing. Her only reason for lurking behind this large potted palm was so that she could observe the ladies' hairstyles. But she need not have bothered. Not one of the guests was wearing the latest French fashions or the more modern and daring styles coming through from America. None, that is, except for the Duchess of Somerfeld and that was due to Nellie keeping up with the latest trends. She certainly had no competition from any of the other guests' lady's maids.

Now that she had got what she came for, there was no reason to remain up on the balcony watching the ball below. Her gaze moved once again to Dominic Lockhart. No reason at all. And there was certainly no reason to keep staring at the guest of honour, a man who, even if he wasn't way out of her class, she wouldn't be interested in anyway.

Just by looking at him she could tell what sort of man he was. He was certain to be arrogant—that superior tilt of his head and the way he held himself so erect proved that. He probably knew just how handsome he was as well—after all, it was certainly something Nellie had noticed right away. But a handsome face and aristocratic bearing doesn't make a man attractive, not in Nellie's eyes anyway. How could a man be attractive when there's no laughter, no enjoyment of life?

No, Mr Lockhart was certainly not her type.

She looked over to where the footmen were standing, lined up like a row of soldiers in uniforms of red and gold livery. Those men were more her type. They were having to act all proper and formal while they were working, but she was sure that, when they were off duty, they'd know how to have a good time. And one footman in particular interested her. He wasn't quite as handsome as Mr Dominic Lockhart, but he came a close second. The footman wouldn't be finished his duties until well after the last guests had left, but hopefully he'd be up for a bit of flirting to round off the evening. And looking down at the doleful event, she suspected the footman would be free from his duties very soon. Most guests had the look of people wanting to make their escape and only a few couples were still dancing. Nellie swayed gently as the band played 'The Blue Danube' while she watched the remaining dancers shuffle round the floor, their noses firmly in the air, their bodies rigid.

Unlike the footman and the other servants, Nellie knew her services would not be needed again this evening. While most lady's maids were required to help their mistress undress, the Duchess preferred to leave that task to the Duke.

No, there was nothing keeping her here. She sent

one last gaze in the direction of Mr Lockhart, then headed towards the back stairs that would take her to the servants' area. As a lady's maid she was entitled to spend her non-working time in the housekeeper's comfortable sitting room with the other higher-ranked servants, but that would be as much fun as the engagement party. The upper servants aped the manners of their employers and seemed to see laughing and enjoying themselves as something far beneath people of their exalted station. Instead she would spend the rest of the evening in the kitchen, with the jolly cook and the giggling scullery maid while she waited for the handsome footman to come off duty.

Dominic Lockhart took his fiancée's gloved hand and escorted her off the dance floor and back to her parents, the Duke and Duchess of Ashmore. The party was a triumph for both families. His engagement to Lady Cecily would restore his family to its rightful place in society, a place that should never have been denied them. And Lady Cecily was assured the comfortable life a woman of her status expected. A life that her increasingly impoverished family was struggling to provide.

He nodded to the Duke of Ashmore, his future father-in-law, and bowed to the Duchess, both of whom smiled at him with satisfaction. They, too, could see the advantage of this marriage. While Hardgrave Estate was a magnificent country home, set in many acres of lush farmland, one didn't have to look too hard to see that it was in dire need of extensive repairs, something the Hardgrave family could ill afford.

Even this once-elegant ballroom was displaying signs of neglect. If one looked closely enough you could see the patches where gold leaf had flaked off the ornately carved ceiling. The large crystal chandeliers had candles in only every second candle holder and some of them were tallow rather than wax. This gave the room an unfortunate acrid smell that couldn't be entirely disguised by the large bouquets of scented flowers adorning every corner. And a discerning eye could tell that some of the paintings lining the walls had been replaced with cheap reproductions, not to mention the occasional square of faded wallpaper, showing where the family had had to sell off art works to pay their mounting debts.

He had met Lady Cecily a few times over the years, as, like himself, the family had a home in the Kent countryside, but had never considered her a prospect for marriage. He had been somewhat surprised when her father had suggested this arrangement, but it was an eminently satisfactory one. At twenty-seven he knew it was time he settled down and got married. He had been in the process of taking an inventory of the available young women with the required status who would make a suitable match, but the Duke of Ashmore had cut short this process by suggesting his daughter Cecily as a suitable bride.

A family with such a long and distinguished lineage as the Hardgraves' might once have been reluctant to align themselves with a man who came from such a dubious background as himself, but now their reduced circumstances meant they were more than happy with their daughter's intended.

And it wasn't just a perfect match because it would be so advantageous to the Lockhart and the Hardgrave families. He and Lady Cecily were so well matched in temperament as well. She was serious and demure and would make any man an ideal wife. Perhaps they were a little cool towards each other, but surely that was all for the best. Look where great passion had led his parents, on a downwards trajectory until they were completely shunned by society.

He smiled at Cecily and received a pinched smile in return. One could only hope that in time she would start to relax and they could have a more cordial relationship. After all, her father had told him she had agreed to the engagement readily enough when he had suggested it to her and she had repeatedly told Dominic she was pleased with the arrangement.

But they would have plenty of time to get to know each other better before their marriage. It had been one short week since the Duke had approached him and suggested the arrangement, so it was not surprising they were still ill at ease with each other. The Duke had been insistent that he wanted to announce the engagement immediately, presumably so he could reassure his bankers that money to settle his debts would soon be available through a sizeable cash injection from his future son-in-law.

Dominic had agreed, as had Lady Cecily. No one

could see the point in putting off what was such a suitable match.

And even if this reserve between himself and Cecily never ceased, it would still be a suitable marriage. After all, a sensible marriage where the couple was well matched in temperament and the position of both families was advanced was certainly better than one where people let their emotions rule their heart, causing them to make unwise choices.

Dominic suppressed as sigh and he tried to focus on what the Duke was saying and forget about his parents' marriage and the problems it had caused.

How his otherwise sensible mother had let her passions get the better of her and marry so far beneath herself he would never understand. She had been the daughter of a baron and had thrown that all away to marry a former stable boy, of all people, and had been snubbed and ridiculed by society as a result, as had their children.

He looked over at his sister, as usual sitting on the side of the dance floor, ignored by the gentlemen present. His marriage would put a stop to that. His sister would have her choice of beaus once their family became linked to one with such a long and distinguished lineage as the Hardgraves'. She would no longer feel ashamed of her family's lowly status, but would be able to hold her head high in polite society.

And shame was something Dominic himself was familiar with. Hadn't he endured enough taunts at school about being the son of a stable boy, even if that former stable boy had risen to become an extremely wealthy man, a level of wealth that Dominic had further increased when he inherited his father's estate.

Yes, this was a perfect engagement. He had every right to feel satisfied and he was sure they would have a successful marriage. After all, they both came from excellent stock, at least he did on his mother's side. His mother could trace her ancestry back to the Norman conquest, but that counted for nothing when your father started life as a lowly servant.

But that was all now in the past, where it belonged.

Lady Cecily excused herself, muttering something about needing to see to the servants. The tension in Dominic's shoulders released as she departed. Making polite conversation with his future bride did tend to be hard work. She seemed reluctant to even try to establish any sort of rapport between them. If she was having regrets about the coming marriage, she had certainly never said and he had given her ample opportunity to do so.

'Let me introduce you to the Duke of Stonebridge,' his future father-in-law said, breaking in on his thoughts and drawing his gaze from the departing Lady Cecily. The Duke took him by the arm and led him across the ballroom floor. 'He's definitely a man of influence and worth knowing.'

That was exactly what Dominic was hoping for. His marriage would lead to countless connections that would be so good for his business and the advancement of the Lockhart family. The Season was almost at an end and his sister hadn't had one expression of interest yet. Next year his younger sister Violet would come out, then in eight years his youngest sister Emmaline would have her debut. If he was to find suitable husbands for them, then the more connections he had with men like the Duke of Stonebridge the better.

He had become so engrossed in talking to the Duke and the other notable guests who had attended the engagement ball that he had failed to notice his fiancée had not returned. When she finally did join him, it was near the end of the evening and there was only one more dance left on the card.

He escorted her round the floor for the final waltz, unable to ignore how rigid her body was, how impassive her face. Not for the first time Dominic fought to quieten that small voice at the back of his mind that was telling him this engagement was a big mistake.

He danced past his sister, sitting alone on the edge of the dance floor, and guilt drove out any sense of disquiet over his engagement. Dominic had been remiss. He should have danced with Amanda, instead of talking business all night. But his sister's days of sitting on the edge of the dance floor during a ball would soon come to an end. His marriage to Lady Cecily would elevate the family's position to the very peak of society and make Amanda a desirable catch for many an aristocratic man. She would have both money and position. And the marriage prospects would be even better for his younger sisters. Lady Cecily had been presented at court for her own debut, so the Hardgraves would be able to arrange for the Lockhart girls to be presented when they came out. Once that happened, they would be able to attend court balls and the chances of making an eminently suitable match would be greatly increased.

The final dance over, Lady Cecily immediately excused herself, providing Dominic with the opportunity to speak to Amanda. As he crossed the ballroom, he said goodnight to several well-wishers, most of whom would have not given a man of his lowly status the time of day before his engagement had been announced. They had all been happy to deal with him when it came to business, but never previously would have deemed him worthy of their society. Prior to this engagement he had been dismissed as a member of the plutocracy, someone with money but no breeding, all because of his parents' unfortunate marriage.

He smiled at his sister and received what was possibly the first genuine smile of the evening. 'I'm so sorry, Amanda, I should have asked you to dance instead of leaving you sitting all alone.'

'Oh, I don't mind.' She patted the empty seat at her side and he sat down. 'I didn't want to dance anyway, well, not with anyone here.' She gave a small moue of disapproval. 'But I've enjoyed myself. I got to meet the Duchess of Somerfeld. Her husband is friends with Lady Cecily's brother.' Amanda gripped his arm in excitement. 'Did you know that she's the famous actress Arabella Huntsbury? She married the Duke of Somerfeld, but she still acts on the stage. She's in rehearsals at the moment for a Gilbert and Sullivan production. She's so beautiful. And did you see the way she was wearing her hair? So much more stylish than anyone else here tonight.'

Dominic had no idea who she was talking about. He didn't read the society papers so knew nothing of actresses. And all the women's hair looked the same to him, rather ornate and decidedly fussy, but he smiled indulgently at his younger sister. 'I'm pleased you've enjoyed yourself. And I promise I won't neglect you when we host our own ball at Lockhart Estate.'

The moue of disapproval returned to his sister's lips. 'I suppose you'll be inviting the same old bunch of snobs that attended this party. They're all so dull, Dominic, and I really don't fit in.'

Dominic swallowed an annoyed sigh. 'They're not dull. These people are among the most powerful and prestigious in the land. And you will fit in soon, Amanda, I promise.'

Amanda raised her eyebrows in disbelief.

'And if no one else is sensible enough to ask you to dance, then I will dance with you all night.'

Amanda's eyebrows raised further up her forehead. 'Dancing with my brother, what fun.' Her look of disapproval turned into a mischievous smile, telling him that she was up to something. 'The Duchess of Somerfeld told me that she has her hair done by her former lady's maid, Nellie Regan, who now has her own hairdressing parlour in London.' Her smile became coquettish and he knew he was about to be asked for a favour. 'If you could arrange for her to attend me and do my hair before our ball, then I'm sure I wouldn't be left sitting on the edge of the dance floor all by myself. Then you wouldn't have to worry about me and you could spend all night dancing with your fiancée.' She smiled at him expectantly.

Dominic shrugged. It was an odd request, but if it would make his sister happy, he would indulge her. 'So, who is this lady's maid and where would I find her?'

Amanda's face lit up with pleasure. 'She's staying here, at the estate. You might be able to find her in the servants' hall. Then you can organise for her to attend me at our ball and even show my own lady's maid how to do hair in the latest styles.' She leaned towards him, batting her eyelashes. 'Please, Dominic, please, please, please.'

Dominic shook his head but knew he could refuse his sister nothing. 'Oh, very well. I'll ask my valet to have a word with her.'

Amanda's smile faded and she shook her head. 'No, Dominic. You're going to have to speak to her yourself. Please, don't send a servant.' She grasped Dominic's arm as if this was a life-or-death situation. 'I asked the Duchess of Somerfeld about this and she said Miss Regan doesn't usually style hair for anyone outside her London parlour. She's also a bit, um, sensitive about being treated like a servant. If the man hosting the ball makes a special appeal to her, and if he's really polite, then she might just make an exception for me.' She clasped his arm even tighter. 'Please, Dominic, please get her to agree before she leaves.'

So much fuss for a silly hairstyle. Dominic doubted he would ever really understand women. 'All right, all right. I'll ask her myself and do everything I can to get her to agree to do your hair for you.'

Amanda released his arm and smiled. 'Thank you so much.'

With that he kissed his smiling sister's cheek and headed downstairs toward the servants' hall. It seemed such a trivial matter, but if it would make his sister happy to have her hair styled like a famous actress, then he would end his evening in pursuit of an ex-lady's maid.

Chapter Two

Nellie was in her element. She had the attention of all the laughing servants as she regaled them with entertaining descriptions of the stiff formality she had just witnessed in the ballroom. Their laughter was becoming almost raucous as she put on what she considered to be a convincing impersonation of Lady Cecily and Mr Lockhart.

After a long, hard-working day that had started at six in the morning, the servants were tired, but still ready to enjoy themselves and have fun, despite the late hour.

She danced another circuit of the kitchen, adopting an exaggeratedly rigid posture, her nose in the air, a supercilious look on her face, to the accompaniment of cheers of encouragement from her captivated audience.

The servants' area was a stark contrast to the lavish ballroom Nellie had just left and not just because the occupants down in the basement knew how to laugh. While the ballroom had been brightly illuminated, a few smoking oil lamps struggled to light the grim downstairs area. Instead of plush furniture covered in red and gold brocade on which the guests could lounge, the servants' hall contained a few threadbare, faded armchairs, a scrubbed pine table and some straight-backed wooden chairs. Furniture which provided little comfort for the weary servants when they grabbed a few minutes' rest during their infrequent breaks.

The aroma of the delicious ten-course banquet the cook had prepared for the guests upstairs still lingered in the air. As did the heat generated by the coal stove, which still burned at a low temperature. It was waiting for the scullery maid to stoke it up again in the early hours of the morning so she and the cook could prepare a lavish breakfast buffet, while those upstairs still lingered in their beds.

Nellie halted her dance and looked at her appreciative audience. 'And if they danced together like that at their engagement party, can you imagine what their wedding night is going to be like?' She lifted her nose higher in the air and puffed out her chest, in imitation of Mr Lockhart's manly countenance. 'I suppose we better get to it, Lady Cecily. After all, we do have a future generation of toffs to sire,' she said in a deep voice.

The plump cook laughed louder and wiped away her tears with the bottom of her apron, while several footmen smirked their approval at Nellie's risqué performance. Nellie knew Mr Lockhart's straight posture was not so rigid and comical, but her exaggerated stance got a good laugh from the servants, so who cared if it was accurate or not? The servants were obviously enjoying seeing *them upstairs* being ridiculed.

Adopting a look of disgust, Nellie continued in a high, squeaky voice, 'Yes, I suppose we must. It's just unfortunate we have to touch each other while we do it. All that horrible kissing and such like, it's so common, don't you think?' She shuddered and pursed her lips in disgust.

The laughter increased in volume, spurring Nellie on. The cook had stopped wiping away her tears of laughter and was letting them course down her round, apple-red cheeks. The tiny scullery maid was gripping her sides, bent double with laughter, and the footmen's smirks had turned to ribald laughter. Only the handsome footman Nellie had earlier spotted in the ballroom wasn't joining in. His was the one disapproving face among the laughing servants. It looked as if he was a far too serious type of man for Nellie and flirting with him was now off the cards. Oh, well, too bad, but she was determined to enjoy herself anyway.

She deepened her voice and flared her nostrils as if she could smell something unpleasant. 'Yes, it is unfortunate that breeding is the one job we can't leave to the servants, but I'm afraid we have no choice.' She waved her arms around as if she was removing her clothing, looked down, frowned theatrically, then looked up at her appreciative audience. 'Oh, I am sorry, my dear. It looks like I will have to leave this task to a servant after all. It seems the only thing that's stiff tonight is my upper lip.'

The cook screeched with laughter, then her laughter died. Her eyes bulged. Her face turned red.

'Oh, Nellie, Nellie, no,' the scullery maid gasped, before covering her mouth, turning around and randomly rearranging the copper pots on the shelves beside the stove. The room had become deathly silent. As one the other servants turned their backs on Nellie and busied themselves with imaginary tasks in the neat and spotlessly clean kitchen.

Slowly, Nellie looked over her shoulder. An indrawn breath caught in her throat. Mirroring the scullery maid, her hand shot up to cover her mouth. He was standing behind her. The man she had just been ridiculing. He was staring straight at her. And there was no trace of laughter in those coal black eyes.

Heat flooded to her cheeks. He continued to glare at her, not saying a word.

Her heart pounded loud and fast. She was finding it impossible to breathe. A nervous fluttering erupted in her stomach. And this impossible situation wasn't helped by the fact that up close Mr Lockhart was even more handsome than he had been when she had looked down at him from her hiding place above the ballroom. An aura of masculine strength surrounded him that she hadn't previously noticed. It wasn't just his height, or the breadth of his shoulders. It was some intangible quality that was pure, raw manhood. She seriously doubted such a powerful, vital man would ever have any performance problems and, looking up at his stunningly handsome face and his strong, vigorous body, she couldn't imagine any woman objecting to having him in her bed.

But that only made her own performance more embarrassing.

She gulped down her discomfort and felt herself grow smaller as his dark eyes continued to bore into her. And small is what she wanted to become. So small she could disappear through a crack in the floor and not have to deal with this mortifying situation or the wrath of this powerful man.

As she waited for him to admonish her, her gaze was drawn to his mouth. Watching him from up on the balcony, she had been too far away to see those full lips, lips that gave his stern face a sensual look that was a stark contrast to those hard eyes, although right now those lips were clamped tight together in disapproval. Her gaze moved back up to his eyes and she braced herself for the expected tirade of anger.

Her behaviour was appalling. How could she be so rude, so disrespectful to one of her superiors?

One of her superiors?

What was she thinking? And why was she letting this man make her feel small? He was not superior to her. He had more money than her, yes, but that was all. Money didn't make you superior, it just made you richer. She was not his, or anyone else's, inferior. She didn't care who he was or how much money he had, she would not let him, or anyone else from his class, ever belittle her again. As she straightened up, anger made Nellie feel taller, stronger, more defiant.

Ignoring her rapidly beating heart and strangled

breath, she lowered her hand from her mouth, turned to face him fully, squared her shoulders and tilted up her chin. She would not be cowered by him or anyone else ever again. Why should she care what Mr Dominic Lockhart thought of her? He meant nothing to her. Why should she care how much of her performance he had heard? Why should she care if he was angry with her? He was not her employer. He had no power over her. She was a free woman. She would not let this commanding man frighten her. Let him do his worst. No matter what he said to her she would give him back as good as she got and let him know that neither his wealth nor his position meant a thing to her.

Dominic looked down at the feisty young woman glaring up at him. Her eyes were narrowed, her chin lifted high and her hands placed firmly on her hips. The scullery maid had called this impertinent miss Nellie. With a sinking heart Dominic realised this must be Nellie Regan, the lady's maid he was expected to charm so she'd agree to style his sister's hair.

She was staring him straight in the eye, something servants never did. In fact, no woman of any class had ever looked at him with such defiance and few men had the tenacity to adopt such a confrontational stance as this little vixen. The firebrand was glaring at him as if she was getting ready to launch into a round of fisticuffs.

Despite his irritation at her lack of respect for her betters, he suppressed a smile. If that was her intention, she was certainly the prettiest pugilist he had ever seen.

As she barely came up to his shoulder, he doubted she could do much damage to anyone. Certainly not in the boxing ring anyway. But with those sparkling green eyes, luxurious wavy red hair, and skin so smooth it looked as if it was made of silk, he suspected she did a lot of damage to men in other ways.

His own reaction was testament to that. No woman had ever affected him as powerfully as this lady's maid had. Despite his outrage at her disrespectful behaviour, when she had turned to look at him, for a moment he had forgotten everything else. Forgotten why he was here, what he wanted to say, and forgotten how he had just been insulted. All he could see was those stunning green eyes, sparkling like cut emeralds, or crisp green grass on a dewy spring morning. All he could think of was those full, soft, decidedly kissable red lips. All he could imagine was running his tongue along the seam where red lips met soft white skin, of pushing his tongue between her lips, forcing them apart, entering her mouth.

Dominic coughed to clear away such inappropriate thoughts and forced himself to stand up straighter.

Where on earth had that thought come from? Wherever it had, it had better go back there, immediately. It was highly inappropriate and certainly not the sort of thing he usually thought about when he first met a woman, even one as beautiful as the one standing in front of him. And there was no denying that she was a beauty. There was also no denying she was quite the comic actress.

While her performance had been rude, disrespectful and insulting, it did have its funny side and, dare he admit it, an element of truth when it came to the formality that still existed between him and Lady Cecily. He could see why she had been able to make the servants laugh with such gusto.

But it was still inexcusable, as was her present behaviour. Her impertinence seemed to know no bounds. She had insulted him, mocked him for the sport of the other servants and, instead of looking suitably shame-faced, she was glaring back at him as if *he* had done something wrong. Well, he had done nothing wrong. All he had done was interrupt her somewhat coarse performance. He was well within his rights to repri-mand her. It was he who should be angry with her. He should be the one standing with his hands on his hips, ready to severely reprimand her for disrespecting him in front of the servants of his future in-laws.

But from that defiant look on her face he suspected harsh words would serve no purpose. He doubted if the strictest reprimand would have any effect on this ill-mannered young lady. Plus, he had made a promise to his sister and was unlikely to secure this upstart's services as a hair stylist if he gave vent to his fury.

Dominic dragged in a deep breath and exhaled slowly, remembering the real reason why he was standing in the servants' hall. He was not here to reprimand an impertinent servant. He was here at the behest of his sister. This was going to require some diplomacy, a level of juggling between letting her know her behaviour was unacceptable, while at the same time securing her hairdressing services.

'You're Nellie, I presume,' he asked, fighting to keep his voice as neutral as possible.

'No, my name is Miss Regan and I'll thank you to address me as such.'

Dominic's jaw tightened and he exhaled loudly. 'Miss Regan, then, I presume,' he said through clenched teeth.

'That's right. I am. Who wants to know?' He caught a hint of a lilting Irish accent in her stern reply and the tension in his jaw released. It was such a lovely, soft voice. One that matched her beauty, with a sing-song quality that was quite enchanting. She'd hidden her accent when she'd been making fun of him and adopted a comically exaggerated upper-class English accent, to the obvious delight of the servants.

But now was not the time to think of that. 'May I have a word with you in private, Miss Regan?' He made sure his face revealed nothing of his reaction to her charming accent, nor her surprising beauty, and in doing so his words took on a harsher tone than he intended.

He gestured towards the small room off the kitchen where the housekeeper did her bookkeeping and stood back so she could enter.

Instead of following as she should, she continued to glare up at him, her hands still firmly on her hips, as if she was rooted to the spot. She glanced over at the door, looked at his arm directing her to enter, then back up at his face. She raised her chin even higher and shook her head. 'No. I'm afraid it's rather late and it's been a long day. I'm planning to retire. I don't have time to talk to you.'

Dominic's arm dropped to his side. Had he heard her correctly? Had she really refused a request that was extremely reasonable under the circumstances? He had not admonished her in front of the servants as most men in his position would have done. He had merely requested a private word with her. And this was how she responded? Unbelievable. Who on earth did this woman, who was little more than a lady's maid, think she was? He stared down at her, waiting for her to explain herself.

No explanation came. Dominic dragged in an irritated breath and slowly exhaled as she continued her defiant glare. 'This will only take a minute of your time, Miss Regan.' Was he really having to beg a lady's maid? It seemed, for his sister's sake, that was exactly what he was going to have to do.

'I don't care how long it's going to take. If you have anything to say to me, then it will have to wait until morning. I don't have time to talk to you, or anyone else, right now.'

'No, Miss Regan, this will not wait until tomorrow,' Dominic said, losing the battle to keep annoyance out of his voice. 'I said I want to talk to you. Now.' His voice became louder, more impatient with every word. He gestured once again to the housekeeper's room.

She shook her head, drawing his eyes to that glorious mane of red curls. 'And I said no.'

Like two immobile statues they continued to glare at each other. This was unheard of. No servant ever spoke to him like this. In fact, no one ever spoke to him in such a disrespectful manner. He looked her up and down, unable to believe that he was in a stand-off with a servant, of all people. His gaze took in her unadorned white blouse and simple grey skirt. It was strange how a woman in such plain clothing could look more stunning than the ornately dressed women who attended society balls. But then few other women had the voluptuous figure of this young miss, with her full breasts, cinched-in waist and rounded hips.

He coughed and his gaze shot back to those dis-approving green eyes. He should never have allowed himself to look at her that way. It was disrespectful to her and unsettling for him.

She glared back at him and for the first time since he had entered the kitchen, she had a right to disapprove of him. Although the pink flush on her cheeks, the part-ing of her full lips and the way she was now leaning towards him, suggested she didn't entirely object to having him look at her in such an appreciative manner.

But he could not think of that now. Should not be thinking of that now, or ever.

Dominic swallowed down his confusion over his unexpected reaction to this irritating woman. All he should be thinking about was securing her services for his sister.

He breathed in deeply to steady his thoughts and bring his mind back to the task at hand. 'I am sure you can spare a few minutes of your time, Miss Regan. That is if you're not too busy.'

Too busy being rude to me.

'Busy—' her voice rose in indignation '—yes, I am busy, very busy. Unlike some people I have to work for a living. Now, if you'll excuse me.' She lifted her head even higher in the air, brushed past him and, with her hips swaying, she walked out of the kitchen.

Dominic turned and watched her leave, too stunned to speak. Was she really walking away and refusing to speak to him? Unbelievable. Who did she think she was? Was she trying to be insulting? If she was, then she had certainly succeeded. He had never met such a rude, irritating woman of any class and certainly not one from the servant class.

He forced his hands to unclench, drew in a deep, strained breath and turned his attention from the door through which Nellie Regan had swept and back to the servants. They had all stopped what they were doing and were staring in his direction with matching looks of wide-eyed astonishment. Then they quickly adopted the requisite impassive look of all servants and busied themselves with non-existent kitchen work. It was obvious they had not missed a word of the exchange between himself and Miss Nellie Regan. And it was likely to be the topic of conversation below stairs for many weeks to come.

Dominic stormed out of the kitchen, muttering under his breath. This was an intolerable situation. He had been made a fool of by a woman who was little more than a servant and that was something he would not soon forget. But even worse than that, he still hadn't fulfilled his promise to his sister. If he was to do so, he would be forced to see that vexatious woman again.

Chapter Three

Perhaps she had gone too far. It wouldn't be the first time and Nellie suspected it wouldn't be the last. But making fun of Mr Lockhart for the entertainment of the servants was perhaps a wee bit too disrespectful, even for her. Perhaps she shouldn't have walked away from him in such a brazen manner. And just maybe she shouldn't have been so snappy with him when she did it.

Nellie brushed out the Duchess's long hair, ready to style it into a suitable daytime look, one that would be attractive but also more practical than last night's intricate styling.

Although her decision to walk away hadn't just been to avoid him telling her off. She was sure she had seen desire sparking in his dark eyes when he had looked at her and that had set off a whirlwind of responses within her she had been unsure how to deal with. He was certainly a desirable man, if you liked that sort of thing. He wasn't her type, though, of that she was certain. He was far too authoritative. Just because he was rich, handsome, tall and manly, he thought he was, oh, so special. Not her type at all. She could never be attracted to a man who thought himself so superior.

Not that it mattered. It was also highly unlikely that such a man would really be attracted to her.

In the cool light of day, it was obvious that she had imagined that spark of desire in his eyes. She must have simply misinterpreted his anger. But unfortunately, one thing she hadn't imagined was her own reaction to his gaze. That had been decidedly unsettling and confusing. When his gaze had moved up and down her body, presumably in disdain, every inch of her skin had come alive. It was as if he was gently caressing her with his eyes. It was ridiculous. She was ridiculous.

She realised she had come to a halt, her brush poised above the Duchess's head. She continued brushing, forcing herself to focus on what she was doing and not be distracted by that hoity-toity, stuck-up man. How dare he think that he could tell her off? How dare he think he could treat her like an underling in need of being pulled into line?

Yes, focus on that and not on how he made you feel when he looked at you.

She clipped a line of curls into place, determined to regain that satisfying sense of indignation towards that infuriating man. And she had every right to be indignant. After all, she had done nothing wrong when she walked away from him. He deserved to be put in his place, thinking he could tell her off when she was not even one of his servants. Walking away from him *was* the right thing to do. Hopefully it would have made him see that he couldn't push everyone around, just because he had lots of money.

And, what did he expect her to do when he came barging into the kitchen all full of self-righteous indignation? Did he expect her to just stand there like some contrite child and let him tell her off? Well, if he had got his wish, if she had stayed in the kitchen while he told her off, he would have been in for more of a surprise than the one he got when she walked away. If he had tried to give her a dressing down, it would have been unlikely that she would have been able to keep her temper in check. If she had remained in the kitchen and listened to what he had to say, she probably would have made things even worse by giving him the sharp edge of her tongue.

Nellie smiled to herself. Haughty Mr Dominic Lockhart would not have liked that. He would not have liked it one little bit if she had let him know just what she thought of men of his class who thought they could lord it over everyone else.

She used the pointed end of her comb to tease out a few strands of hair, giving a soft appearance around the Duchess's face. Smiling to herself, she remembered the servants' reactions to her when she had joined them for breakfast. All conversation had died when she entered the kitchen. They had all looked at her with a sense of amazement and the scullery maid had served her breakfast in such a reverential manner, as if she were a conquering hero returning from battle.

Everyone seemed to be in awe of her. Everyone,

that was, except the butler and housekeeper. They had looked down their noses, as if she was something unpleasant the cat had dragged in. But as they had no authority over her there was nothing they could do or say. She could tell they were just itching to give her what for, but they had no choice but to keep any reprimands to themselves.

Nellie inserted the tortoiseshell combs that would keep the Duchess's hair in place and released a small sigh. The encounter with Mr Lockhart had been disturbing, to say the least, and a reminder of why she was pleased not to be in service any more.

Helping the Duchess dress today would be the last task she would perform before she left this house and returned to London. And it wouldn't be a minute too soon. She was more than happy to get away from the rigid hierarchy of a country estate and not just the hierarchy between those who lived upstairs and downstairs, but between the servants as well. A hierarchy that put the poor scullery maid at the bottom of the heap, having to be a servant to the servants, as well as spending all day scrubbing pots in a fiercely hot kitchen. It was a life Nellie knew well. It was one she had endured when she had first gone into service. But those days were all now behind her.

She stood back to observe the Duchess's hair and smiled with satisfaction at a job well done.

'You're unusually quiet this morning, Nellie,' the Duchess said, looking up at Nellie's reflection in the mirror. 'Has something upset you?'

Nellie shook her head. 'No, I think it's the other way around. I've upset the household.'

The Duchess gave a small laugh, swivelled round on the tapestry-covered bench in front of the dressing table and smiled up at Nellie. 'What have you done now? Flirted with the wrong man? Said the wrong thing to the butler? Insulted the housekeeper?'

Nellie removed the Duchess's morning outfit from the wardrobe, folded it over her arm and sent the Duchess a contrite look. 'Um, no. Worse than that, I'm afraid. I was rude to Mr Lockhart. Very rude. He caught me doing a rather insulting impersonation of him and Lady Cecily for the entertainment of the servants.'

The Duchess bit her lip to suppress a smile. 'Really, Nellie? It looks like you've outdone yourself this time. Was he very angry?'

Nellie smiled conspiratorially. 'Mmm, yes, very.'

She helped the Duchess into her skirt and jacket, and, while the Duchess buttoned up her jacket, Nellie hooked closed the buttons on her ankle boots. 'He was so angry that I think it might be a good idea if I returned to London as soon as possible, before I see Mr Lockhart again.' She paused in her work and looked up at the Duchess. 'Would that be all right? Or will you be needing my services again today?'

'Don't worry about that. I can get one of the house servants to assist me. And thank you so much for coming with me this weekend.'

Nellie shrugged and went back to buttoning up the boots. There was no need for the Duchess to thank her. Nellie owed her so much that there was nothing she wouldn't do for the Duchess. She'd been thirteen when she joined the van Haven family ten years ago, fresh off the boat from Ireland and lost in the big city of New York. Arabella van Haven, as the Duchess was then called, was only a year older than her. Along with Mr van Haven's ward, Rosie Smith, the three girls had grown up together and Nellie had always been treated kindly. The two girls were now duchesses, with Rosie having married the Duke of Knightsbrook and Miss van Haven now the Duchess of Somerfeld.

And despite being elevated to the top of English society, they still treated her respectfully. The Duchess of Somerfeld had financed Nellie's hairdressing parlour and, along with the Duchess of Knightsbrook, they did everything they could to promote her business. They had even endorsed her services in the advertisements she had placed in various journals read by middle-class women. That had all but guaranteed the success of her business. As soon as the advertisements were published she had been swamped by clients wanting to have their hair styled by the woman recommended by the Duchesses of Somerfeld and Knightsbrook.

'You don't have to thank me, I'm happy to do it,' Nellie said. 'I just hope I haven't caused any problems for you and your husband by my bad behaviour.'

Arabella laughed. 'No, not at all. Oliver always loves it when someone misbehaves and I know he'll laugh when I tell him what you've done. Dominic Lockhart and Cecily Hardgrave are lovely people, but they can be a bit formal and serious at times. As Oliver would say, it never hurts to shake things up a bit.'

Nellie smiled. The Duke of Somerfeld had quite a reputation himself for misbehaving and shaking things up. Nellie had always liked him and was pleased her former mistress had married him, even if it had originally been against the Duchess's wishes.

'Well, I'm glad you're not annoyed. But I still think it would be best if I leave as soon as possible.'

'Certainly, Nellie.' The Duchess stood in front of the full-length mirror as Nellie brushed down her skirt and jacket. 'I'll ask Oliver to arrange for his carriage to take you to the station.'

The Duchess smiled at her reflection. 'Perfect, as always.' She turned her head from side to side to observe the hairstyle from different angles. 'Last night, just about every woman at the ball commented on my hair and I made sure I told them all about your hairdressing parlour. I think a few lady's maids might be sent in your direction for some extra training.'

Nellie smiled at her former mistress. 'Thank you. And I'm happy to attend you any time, you know that. I owe you so much.'

The Duchess waved her hand in dismissal and headed towards the door. 'Not at all. But for now, I think we'd better organise your escape.'

Dominic sipped his morning coffee and looked out of his third-floor bedroom window. Luggage was being loaded on to a carriage bearing the Duke of Somerfeld's crest and Nellie Regan was supervising. Although she seemed to be doing a lot more chatting than supervising, much to the pleasure of the footman and coachman.

The Duke and Duchess were presumably leaving after breakfast, so Dominic would have to find time to talk to the Duchess's former lady's maid before they left. He took another sip of his coffee. Sparring with her last night had been irritating, yet unexpectedly invigorating, and, despite himself, he was anticipating talking to her again with some pleasure.

Watching her, unobserved from his hidden vantage point, was certainly a pleasure to be savoured. The morning sunlight was sparking off her red hair, making the lighter, blonde strands shine with reflected light. It was so appropriate, her hair was like fire, just like the woman herself.

The coachman buckled a portmanteau on to the back of the coach and laughed at something Miss Regan had said. Breaking with protocol, the footman joined in their laughter and said something that made all three laugh even more. The two men were obviously quite taken with Miss Regan, but there was no surprise there.

What man wouldn't be taken by such a feisty, not to mention stunningly attractive, young woman? She had certainly captured his attention last night and not just because of the somewhat unconventional nature of their encounter. She was unlike any woman he had ever met, so spirited, so vivacious, so full of life.

Despite their differences in class he, too, had found himself somewhat fascinated by the young lady. More than somewhat, if he was being completely honest. It wasn't just her beauty, although there was no denying that she was strikingly attractive. It was her energy and vitality that were particularly captivating. And despite his best efforts he hadn't been able to stop thinking about those green eyes all night, their striking jade intensity invading his dreams.

The coachman continued to cast glances in her direction as he went about his work, although there seemed to be more laughter and chatter than work taking place. Dominic even suspected the coachman was drawing out his task so he could continue to talk to Nellie Regan. They were fortunate it was such an early hour and most occupants of the house would either be still in bed or dining in the breakfast room. Dominic was sure such public revelry among the servants would be frowned upon by the Duke and Duchess of Ashmore and most of their guests. But at this hour the only people about were the household servants and the troop of gardeners, who were busy trimming the topiaries in the formal gardens that surrounded the house.

Miss Regan clapped her hands together and laughed louder at something the footman had said, the musical tinkling of her laughter reaching Dominic high up in his hidden eyrie. As she laughed, she placed her hand on the footman's arm and the man smiled down at her, as pleased as Punch that his joke had elicited such a reaction.

Burning bile ripped up Dominic's throat as if the coffee were too bitter. What could the man have said that had caused her so much delight? What was there between them that meant she could be so familiar as to touch him? Was she involved with the footman? Was he her beau?

She released her hand and said something to the coachman. Standing up on the carriage, he grinned down at Miss Regan, his face flushed with pleasure. It seemed the footman was not someone special in her life. The little minx was flirting with both men and both men were thoroughly enjoying it.

Dominic scowled at the coffee cup and placed it on the side table beside the window. It hit the saucer with an angry clink. Was the coachman the sort of man who could capture Miss Regan's heart? Or would she prefer the footman? Whoever did have that honour would be a lucky man. She really was a rare beauty that any man would be proud to call his wife.

Although he would have his work cut out for him. A demure, subservient woman Miss Regan most definitely was not. He could hardly imagine her becoming someone's obedient wife.

The contrast between Nellie Regan and Lady Cecily couldn't be more striking and he didn't just mean in terms of the class into which they'd been born. Miss Regan was chatting and laughing with these two men as if she had known them all her life. Even though he and Lady Cecily were now engaged to be married, there was still not that easy familiarity that Miss Regan had already established with these two men. Cecily had never looked at him with laughter in her eyes or touched his arm affectionately as they shared a joke. In fact, conversation between them still remained the polite, strained exchanges of people who barely knew each other and had little common ground.

He looked away from Nellie Regan and the laughing servants, out at the horizon, over the rolling parklands of Hardgrave Estate to the distant horizon, where the summer sun was shining in a clear blue sky.

He should not be thinking like that. He was engaged to Lady Cecily and she deserved his respect. She did not deserve to be compared to other women. In fact, he should not even be thinking about any other woman and certainly not someone who was only one step above a servant. If his parents had taught him anything, it was the devastating outcomes that eventuated when people of different classes mixed.

Not that he had any interest in Miss Regan. None whatsoever. He wished the coachman luck, or the footman, or whoever. If Miss Regan was involved with the coachman, the footman, or any other servant, it would be entirely appropriate. Just as his engagement to Cecily Hardgrave was entirely appropriate. The classes mixing only caused heartache.

He looked back down at the scene taking place before him. The coachman had finally finished his work and was now sitting on top of the carriage, the reins in his hands. Presumably he was going to park the carriage and wait for his passengers. The Somerfelds had a surprisingly small amount of luggage. Only one case was strapped to the back of the carriage.

Still chatting and laughing, the footman held out his hand and Miss Regan climbed into the carriage. The coachman flicked the reins and with a snort of compliance the two black horses trotted off down the drive, the wheels crunching on the gravel.

What was happening? Was Nellie Regan leaving? All by herself in the Duke's private carriage? She couldn't be. He still hadn't had the opportunity to talk to her. He couldn't disappoint his sister. Grabbing his jacket, Dominic rushed towards the bedroom door. Pulling it on, he raced down the long corridor, sped down the three flights of stairs, out through the entrance hall and down the outside stairs.

The footman looked at him in surprise and then stood to attention.

The carriage was now at the end of the long, tree-lined drive and about to turn on to the country road that led away from the estate. He had missed her.

'Miss Regan, I must speak to you.' His loud shout broke the silence of the quiet morning air, causing a nearby peacock to squawk and the gardeners to look up from their work.

The carriage turned the corner and she looked back at the house. He had caught her attention. Thank goodness. She would now return so he could arrange for her to attend to his sister. She leant out the window. From this distance it looked as if she was laughing. When her gloved hand emerged from the window and she gave a little wave goodbye he was certain. She was driving away from him, but not without having a last laugh at his expense.

Chapter Four

Nellie stood outside her shop and hairdressing parlour and looked up at the sign etched out in cursive script above the door: *Venus Hair and Beauty Parlour, Eleanor Regan Proprietress*. She'd been open now for six months, but every time she saw that sign it filled her with a sense of immense pride. And never more than today. After that disconcerting encounter with Mr Lockhart at the weekend she couldn't be more pleased to be able to return to the sanctuary of her own business, a place where she was in charge and no one was able to push her around. She exhaled a sigh of impatience at the memory of that infuriating man.

Who did he think he was, chasing after her like that all because she had been a bit rude to him? Well, extremely rude. But still.

Anyway, that was all over now. She was now back in her own world, away from men who thought they were better than others just because they were born wealthy.

She pulled open the door and the bell rang out a

friendly greeting. All was just as she had left it on Friday evening. She looked around the shop with satisfaction. Along with providing hairdressing services the business sold an array of beauty products that an aristocratic woman would expect her lady's maid to provide. Bottles of rosewater skin fresheners, lavender skin lotions, hand salves and an array of colognes made from essential oils were displayed on satin cloths. A selection of bejewelled hair clips and other hair decorations adorned the counter, along with ostrich, emu and peacock feathers, artificial flowers, ribbons and lace of all colours to decorate hats.

Nellie also sold a range of cosmetics, including tinted lip salves, rouge and face powders, but told her clients they were purely for therapeutic use and were most definitely not make up. That way they could feel that using a bit of help to enhance their appearance was still socially acceptable.

The scent from the muslin-wrapped lavender bath salts and rose petal pot-pourri filled the air, making the store a lovely feminine retreat. She breathed in, enjoying the sweet fragrance, pleased to be home.

She greeted her two assistants, Harriet and Matilda, who were anxious to hear all about Nellie's weekend. Under the circumstances Nellie felt it best to leave out details of her encounter with Mr Lockhart. Instead she entertained the girls with descriptions of how beautiful the ballroom looked, what fashions the women were wearing and the grandeur of the Ashmores' estate. Once the girls had finished recounting their own escapades over the weekend it was down to business.

As usual, the appointment diary was booked solid for the day and the first customer arrived on the dot at nine o'clock. Nellie greeted her and escorted her through to the private hairdressing parlour at the back of the premises.

As happened every morning, when Nellie entered her parlour pleasure washed over her. It was as if she was seeing it for the first time. She had decorated it herself in a style that resembled a fashionable dressing room of an aristocratic lady. She knew that being attended to in such surroundings was an important part of the experience for her middle-class customers. They wanted to feel as if they were having their hair dressed by their own lady's maid in their own luxurious room. Her customers weren't to know that the antiques and paintings were all sourced from flea markets and many of them were cheap but good reproductions. It was the illusion that they wanted and that was what Nellie gave them.

Her customer seated herself on the delicately embroidered bench in front of the dressing table and looked at her reflection in the gilt-edged mirror. A mirror that Nellie knew was decorated with gold-coloured paint rather than gilt, but no one knew the difference and it provided the necessary impression of opulence.

The woman patted her hair. 'I'm off to the theatre tonight and I've decided I want something different from my usual style.' She reached into her beaded purse, pulled out a newspaper cutting and handed it to Nellie. 'I want to look like that.'

Nellie looked at the clipping from the *Illustrated*

London News, with its pen-and-ink drawing of the famous actress Arabella Huntsbury. Nellie smiled as she saw her own hair styling, with the elaborate tresses piled up high on Arabella's head, exposing her swan-like neck, and the feminine curls cascading over her slim shoulders. Few people outside Arabella's immediate circle knew that the famous actress was also the Duchess of Somerfeld, Nellie's former mistress.

'Make me look like that, please, Nellie.' The customer tapped her finger on the drawing, then turned back to the mirror, smiling with satisfaction and expectation.

Nellie looked from the drawing of the young, elegant and beautiful Duchess to her customer, a portly middle-aged woman with several double chins. She knew it was the woman's dream to look twenty again, but this hairstyle would not do it. It would have the opposite effect and make it even more apparent that the customer's youth was far behind her.

Nodding her agreement, Nellie began styling her hair in a way that, although unlike the one in the drawing, would flatter her client and draw attention to her still attractive eyes and smooth skin.

Sharing gossip was an integral part of the experience of being attended to by a lady's maid, so she asked her customer whether she had been to any interesting social events lately.

'Oh, yes, we dined at the Savoy last night. And that was quite an experience, I can tell you.'

Nellie brushed out the woman's greying hair and began backcombing it to give the thinning locks more volume. 'That must have been fun. It's rather grand and luxurious, isn't it?'

The woman huffed her disapproval. 'Luxurious, is that what you call it? Well, I don't. They've put that horrid electricity all through the dining room. It's outrageous. It shows up every line, every blemish. Candlelight is so much more flattering to a woman's complexion.' She frowned at her reflection. 'I admit, electricity is good for street lighting, but it should never be installed inside. No woman in her right mind would have it in her home. Mark my words, it will never catch on. Not when candlelight is so much more flattering.'

'Hmm,' Nellie said non-committally as she smoothed the woman's tresses over a roll of false hair which would give it a fuller look. She chose not to point out that for the woman's maid it would be so much easier to just flick a switch rather than lighting countless candles, trimming all those wicks, scraping spilled wax off table cloths and furniture, and extinguishing all those flames at the end of a long working day.

'But I did see that Daisy Brook, the Countess of Warwick, when I was there,' the woman continued, puffing herself up with self-importance. 'They say she's the Prince of Wales's latest mistress.' She pursed her lips in excited disapproval. 'I don't know what this world is coming to, men in his position having mistresses. I pity England when the old Queen dies and that reprobate becomes King.'

Nellie teased out a few curls around the woman's face and stood back to assess the effect. 'Well, Queen Vic has lived this long, maybe she'll outlive her son.'

'Yes, we can only hope. With Bertie's eldest son, Eddie, dying so tragically the second son will be King eventually. We can only hope the good Queen does outlive that philandering Bertie and George becomes our next ruler. Then we won't have to put up with these endless scandals.' The woman nodded once, as if that was the final word on the matter. Then she smiled at her reflection. 'Oh, yes, Nellie, you've captured that look perfectly.' She moved her head from side to side.

Nellie returned her smile. 'I'm pleased you like it. It's very flattering on you.'

'Oh, yes, it's perfect. We're off to see that new play tonight, *The Shop Girl*, at the Gaiety Theatre. Have you seen it yet?'

'Yes, I treated my assistants to it a few weeks ago.'

'I've heard it's rather good, even if the plot is a bit silly. I mean, a shop girl marrying her wealthy suiter would hardly happen in real life, but it makes for an entertaining musical comedy.'

On this point, Nellie had to agree with her client.

Harriet parted the gold shot silk curtains that separated the parlour from the shop and quietly informed Nellie that a gentleman wanted to talk to her. 'He said he needed to see you immediately.'

Nellie teased out one more cascading curl, excused herself and went through the curtained divide. Her smile of greeting died. She froze to the spot, gripping the silky curtain tightly as if she was in danger of falling. It couldn't be. But it was. It was him. Mr Lockhart. He had followed her to London. This was getting ridiculous.

What on earth was wrong with the man? Didn't he have anything better to do with his time? Apparently not.

Harriet and Matilda were smiling at her and raising their eyebrows up and down in admiration. They obviously thought there was nothing wrong with Mr Lockhart. But they could only see a sublimely handsome gentleman, his masculine presence somewhat out of place among all the feminine bits and bobs. They didn't know that he was also a pompous, authoritarian ass and he was here to give Nellie a telling off.

While Mr Lockhart continued to look disapprovingly at a display of artificial flowers and coloured ostrich feathers, Nellie took a moment to compose herself. She released her hand from its grip on the silk curtain, smoothed down her apron and wished she was wearing something a bit more attractive than the simple brown skirt and jacket she wore to work.

Now, who was the one being ridiculous? Who cared what she looked like? Did she need to be dressed up and looking her best just so Mr Lockhart could reprimand her? No, she did not.

She coughed lightly to clear her dry, constricted throat and walked up to the counter. He replaced the hair comb decorated with peonies and forget-me-nots back on the display and turned to face her.

'Miss Regan. You left before I had a chance to talk to you.'

Nellie drew in an agitated breath and breathed out slowly. That had been the whole point of yesterday's early-morning departure, so he wouldn't have a chance to berate her. Yet here he was, still wanting to get his revenge, just because he'd been the subject of a small joke.

It seemed he was more than just a pompous ass. He was an insufferable pig who deserved his come-uppance and Nellie would really like to be the one to give it to him. But now was neither the time nor the place for her to let him know just what she thought of him and his high-and-mighty behaviour, or which animal, pig or ass his behaviour most resembled.

He continued staring at her, waiting impatiently for her answer. She refused to be affected by those dark eyes boring into her. She refused to be cowed by his handsome countenance, his perfectly symmetrical face, strong jawline and high cheekbones that looked as if they'd been carved out of granite. She would not be overawed by his full, sensual lips. And she most certainly would not be undermined by his height, his wide shoulders, or the way his masculine presence seemed to fill the room.

She tilted up her chin and stared back at him. Nothing about this man would affect her or cause her to defer to him in the way he obviously expected. 'Well, I am far too busy to speak to you at this moment. I'm with a client—' she gestured over her shoulder towards the curtains that separated the parlour from the shop '—and it would be rude to keep her waiting.'

She could see him stifling a sigh of irritation that she was once again claiming to be too busy for him. When she had left him standing in the Ashmores' kitchen, nothing had been preventing her from staying and listening to what he had to say. Nothing, that was, except her own refusal to be treated like an insolent servant. But this time it was true. She did have a customer waiting and she would never be rude to a customer. But that didn't mean she couldn't be rude to this self-important oaf.

After all, wasn't he being rude to her? Thinking he could come into her shop and reprimand her in her own premises, in front of her own staff and customer. That was what Nellie would call rude.

'I assure you, Miss Regan, this won't take more than a minute of your time.'

Nellie shook her head and stared unflinchingly into those dark brown eyes. She would not look away, even though her body was starting to burn under his gaze and she was forgetting how to breathe properly.

'I'm afraid I can't even spare you one minute.' Nellie released her held breath, pleased that her voice had come out with sufficient self-assurance.

Time was not really the issue. It never had been. She simply would not let this impertinent man reprimand her. She wasn't going to let him do it at Hardgrave Estate and she certainly wasn't going to let him do it here.

And that wasn't just because he had no right to do so. It was also because she couldn't guarantee she wouldn't lose her temper and she certainly didn't want to do that with her staff and customer listening in. 'I don't have even one single second to spare you. Now if you'll excuse me.' She took a step towards the curtains, then paused as a wicked thought occurred to her.

She turned to face him. 'The parlour closes at six

o'clock. If you want to talk to me, it will have to wait till then. Harriet, Matilda and I are going for a drink after work at The Hanged Man public house. If you've got something to say to me, you can say it there and I'll have all the time in the world to listen to what you have to say.'

She smiled in the direction of Harriet and Matilda, who were looking at her with stunned surprise. Nellie knew exactly what they were thinking. A gentleman like Mr Lockhart wouldn't be seen dead in a common place like The Hanged Man, a tavern frequented by shop girls, local workers and other people he would consider far beneath him.

'Harriet will give you directions. So, until then, goodbye, Mr Lockhart.' Smiling to herself, she disappeared behind the curtains.

Dominic stood outside the doors of The Hanged Man and forced himself not to get angry. Nothing would be gained by losing his temper, but it was hard not to. That little Irish madam was still giving him the run around and all he wanted to do was offer her work. But letting her irritating behaviour get under his skin would do no one any good and wouldn't help his sister.

He pushed open the door and was met with a fug of tobacco smoke, a cacophony of loud voices and a sea of men in cloth caps. The tavern was packed wall to wall and, as he looked at the attire of the patrons, many had come straight from work. The men were mostly dressed in stained overalls or rough trousers and coats, and some were without jackets, their shirt sleeves rolled up over weather-beaten tattooed arms. He could also see shop girls in their uniform of plain black skirts and white blouses, and a few patrons who looked as if they worked as day servants in the local houses.

He pushed his way through the jostling crowd and spotted Miss Regan and her assistants sitting at a small round table in front of the window, tankards of ale in front of them, chatting and laughing together.

How was he supposed to have a sensible conversation with her in this raucous environment? But he suspected that was exactly Miss Regan's intention, to make things as difficult for him as possible. The woman truly was insufferable. He drew in a deep, irritable breath and edged his way through the jostling crowd.

When he reached her table, she looked up at him. Her big green eyes grew even wider and he was sure a gasp of surprise escaped her lips, although he couldn't hear a thing above the racket of a room full of people all talking at once. He would have taken pleasure in her discomposure, but right now it was hard to feel anything except annoyance.

'Miss Regan,' he shouted down at her, trying to be heard above the noise. 'Hopefully, now that you have finished work for the day, you finally have time to talk to me.'

She gestured to a spare chair. 'Get yourself a drink and join us,' she called back to him, sending a small smile in the direction of her assistants. She'd obviously thought he wouldn't want to drink in an establishment such as this. Well, she didn't know him very well, did she? He had visited rougher drinking dens than this with his father and was not fazed by either the clientele or the surroundings. Despite his father's change in circumstances and fortune, he still liked to socialise with people he considered the salt of the earth and many a time had taken his young son along with him.

But that did not mean he had any intention of staying any longer than was entirely necessary to talk to Miss Regan, even if that was proving to be a near impossibility. As soon as he had engaged her services for his sister he would be leaving.

He pushed his way back through the crowd to the bar, ordered an ale and another round of drinks for Miss Regan and her staff. The man poured four drinks into pewter tankards and Dominic carefully elbowed his way back through the crowd, angling himself around the heaving mass so he would not spill a drop.

'Now, Miss Regan, I would appreciate it if I could talk to you,' he called out to her as he seated himself at the table and handed tankards to the two smiling assistants.

She put her hand to her ear, feigning an inability to hear.

Dominic bit down his irritation. 'I said I would appreciate it if I could talk to you now,' he repeated, raising his voice. And he would also appreciate it if they could leave this infernal place and go somewhere where he didn't have to shout so loud it was straining his throat.

'All right. What do you want to say to me?' she called back to him, leaning over the small table.

'Can we go somewhere quieter where we can talk?'

He looked around to see if there was a less crowded area in the packed bar where they could retire to, but the tavern seemed to consist of just this one small, low-ceilinged room. This was hopeless. And to make matters worse, he saw a man approach the small upright piano and raise the cover.

The moment he started playing the entire room erupted into loud, boisterous singing. Dominic's jaw clenched tightly. This was an absurd situation. Surely even Miss Regan could see that she had gone far enough now. She had made her point, whatever her point might be, and she should now do the decent thing and leave with him so they could have a proper conversation.

He turned back to face her, and to his intense irritation saw that she, too, was singing along, while waving her tankard happily in the air. And what was worse, she had what could only be described as a triumphant smile on her face, suggesting she felt she had won a decisive victory over him, even though he had no idea what they were fighting about.

Chapter Five

Nellie smiled with satisfaction. She had made him feel uncomfortable and out of place. Good. It was as if she had won a small victory over every toff who had ever looked down his nose at her, her family or her friends. He appeared so out of place she wanted to laugh out loud. Dressed in his expensive grey suit, with a dark grey waistcoat embroidered with black thread and maroon silk cravat, he couldn't look more different from the working men who frequented this bar if he had tried.

Although Nellie suspected Mr Lockhart would stand out wherever he went and however he was dressed, and not just because of his superior mannerisms and his haughty demeanour. He was so manly it was breathtaking and when Nellie had first seen him enter the public house it had literally taken her breath away. She hadn't been the only woman in the room who had been unable to stop staring at him, drawn to his aura of virile masculinity. Some of the women might have been interested in his obvious wealth, but she was sure many more were drawn to that elusive quality of manliness that was undeniably attractive.

Not that such things had any effect on her, not really. He might be extremely handsome, but he was still a wealthy man here to throw his weight around and put her in her place. And that was a goal she would do everything in her power to stop him from reaching.

She continued singing, louder and with more enthusiasm, causing his dark eyebrows to draw deeper together, his jaw to clench tighter, much to Nellie's immense pleasure.

She had been certain he would not turn up. Or, if he did, that he would take one look inside The Hanged Man and turn tail, back to the richer, more genteel side of London. She would never have expected a man of his class to enter an establishment such as this, or to remain for as long as he had. He was persistent, she would give him that. Either that, or he was so determined to confront her over her unflattering impersonation of him that he would even endure an evening singing and drinking with people he wouldn't normally give the time of day.

He tried to say something to her. She sung even louder, spurred on by the look of frustration on his face.

She smiled as he raked an impatient hand through his glossy black hair, causing his carefully groomed appearance to become disordered. Nellie was tempted to lean over the table, to run her hands along his head and smooth his thick black hair back into place. That must be the hairdresser in her. She could see no other reason why her fingers were itching to touch him, to run themselves through that tousled hair.

The song came to an end and the noise in the room settled down from raucous to simply loud. He tried again to shout something at her.

'Please, Miss Regan. I must talk to you. My sis…'

Whatever he was trying to say it was drowned out when Patrick Kelly staggered over to their table. 'Nellie, m'darling, are you going to honour us with a tune?' he slurred, weaving on the spot and showing he was slightly the worse for drink.

Nellie rarely consented to playing the piano in public, it brought back too many painful memories, but the chance to further annoy Mr Lockhart was too good an opportunity to miss.

She excused herself and smiled when she saw the look on his face move from frustrated to exasperated. It wouldn't be long now. He would soon reach the limit of his endurance and would depart, completely defeated. Although that would put an end to Nellie's fun, which she had to admit would be a shame. There was so much fun to be gained by tormenting Mr Dominic Lockhart.

With Patrick's help she pushed her way through the crowd and over to the piano. Nellie had been taught to play by her mother when she was a young girl, but she was a bit out of practice. Although it hardly mattered. The crowd was so boisterous she doubted anyone would notice the occasional missed note. She began playing her mam's favourite Irish ballad. As the rest of the room burst into song, tears sprang to Nellie's eyes. It was the sound of her home, of the fire warming the small front parlour. Of Nellie playing the piano while her mam sang in her sweet voice, her da looking on with love in his eyes.

Her parents had both lost their own parents in the Irish potato famine. They'd been driven off their land by the wealthy landowner because the crop failures meant they had been unable to pay their rent. When her mother's parents had died in poverty, Nellie's mother had been placed in a workhouse, where she remained until she was old enough to go into service as a maid for the same landowner who had driven her family off their land. That's where she had met Nellie's father. He had also returned to the same land and worked as a tenant farmer. Her parents had been happy together, but childhoods spent in poverty and the resulting ill health had shortened their lives, leaving Nellie an orphan at a young age.

Through her tears she looked around the room. Everyone was singing and waving their tankards of beer in the air. She wasn't the only one who was remembering their home back in Ireland, their family and a time before poverty and misfortune had made them leave their homeland.

Her gaze moved to Dominic Lockhart. He was the only one not singing. Instead he was looking round the room and scowling. Nellie played the wrong note and her voice quivered. How dare he scowl at her people. Yes, they were poor and, yes, they had perhaps drowned their sorrows in a bit too much drink, but a wealthy, privileged man like him had no right to disapprove of them.

It was time to put an end to this charade. It was time to tell him to sling his hook and take his disapproval, his snobbery and his reprimands with him.

Nellie finished the song early, slammed shut the piano lid and pushed her way back through the crowd. This game she was playing with Dominic Lockhart had lost all appeal. She wanted him and his disapproving scowl gone and out of her life. Despite the noise of the crowd, despite the fact that her assistants would hear her, Nellie would let him know in no uncertain terms to leave this public house and never bother her again.

'Nellie, m'dear, that was wonderful as always. You're a talented wee thing, that you are.' Patrick Kelly grabbed her around the waist and pulled her towards him.

Nellie gritted her teeth in annoyance. Dealing with the antics of a drunken man was the last thing she needed right now. 'For goodness sake, man, let me go, or you'll be feeling my knee so hard between your legs you won't be able to walk for a week.'

Patrick laughed and tightened his grip on her waist. 'Come on, girl, give us a little kiss.' His rough, unshaven face came towards her, his wet lips parting, his breath smelling of beer and pipe smoke.

Nellie put her hands on his shoulders and pushed him away. He flew back, crashing against a nearby table, and fell in a drunken heap on the floor, overturning several tankards on the way down, much to the patrons' disgust. It seemed Nellie was stronger than she thought. She'd only given the man a small shove to let him know he was wasting his time.

She looked up from the startled Patrick Kelly to see Dominic Lockhart, glowering down at the prone man, his fists clenched tightly, his face rigid, his feet planted wide apart as if he was ready for a fight.

He had jumped to her defence. Who would have thought it? After a lifetime of fighting her own battles Nellie was unsure what to make of this apparent gallantry. All she knew was her heart seemed to be swelling in her chest and warmth had flooded her body. He looked so manly standing over the prone Patrick. This strong, red-blooded man was acting as her champion, ready to defend her honour. Nellie had to admit it was rather nice and decidedly flattering.

Behind him she saw a row of angry faces, faces that did not think Mr Lockhart's defence of Nellie was anything to be impressed by. 'There weren't no need for that,' one angry voice said.

This was not good. Not good at all. Patrick might be a bit of a lecher who had trouble keeping his hands to himself, but he was well liked by the other men in the bar and Dominic Lockhart was an obvious stranger. A wealthy, well-dressed stranger who certainly did not belong here. His gallant behaviour had put him in imminent danger.

Conversation had died and everyone in the now silent bar had turned to face them.

'You had better leave. Now,' Nellie whispered.

'Not until this man apologises for treating a lady in such a disrespectful manner.' Mr Lockhart's voice sounded loud in the suddenly quiet room as he continued to glare down at Patrick.

She took hold of his arm. 'No, the best thing you can do is leave.'

He stood his ground.

'Come on.' She pulled at his arm. Several men helped Patrick to his feet, then, as one, they turned towards Dominic, their faces belligerent, their bodies tense as if itching for a fight.

Nellie tried to laugh it off. 'No harm done, lads. It was just a bit of fun between me and Patrick.' She turned to Mr Lockhart and lowered her voice to a whisper again. 'We need to leave. Right now.'

He didn't budge.

'If it's people not respecting me that you're worried about, then you'll respect my wishes and leave with me, now. I don't want any more trouble here. These are my neighbours, people I have to live with.'

He looked down at her, looked over at Patrick and, to Nellie's immense relief, nodded his agreement. They crossed the crowded public house, watched by a roomful of silent, angry men.

Nellie breathed a sigh of relief as the door swung shut behind them and they walked out into the night air. The street was dark and cool, and the cobblestones glistened from recent rain that had fallen unheard while they were inside. It was a stark contrast to the noise and heat of the busy public house.

Mr Lockhart looked down at her, a grim smile on his face. 'If nothing else, that altercation got you out of that noisy tavern to somewhere quieter where we can talk.'

Nellie's relief was short-lived. Oh, that. She'd momentarily forgotten that he was here to tell her off.

She gestured towards the door behind them. 'I could have looked after myself, you know. I've been dealing with men like Patrick Kelly all my life. I know how to handle myself.' She did not want him to think she was beholden to him in any way, or that his behaviour gave him the right to admonish her further.

'Perhaps, but you shouldn't have to.'

Nellie shrugged. She couldn't argue with him there. But that was the way of the world. Women like Nellie had to be able to defend themselves. They weren't like Lady Cecily who lived in a protected world, a world where they could always behave in a demure and ladylike manner. Nellie had grown up knowing she had to be tough to survive.

'Anyway, allow me to escort you home. It will finally enable me to talk to you.'

Nellie bristled. She did not want him to think that just because he had defended her so-called honour that it gave him the right to tell her off. But they did need to get away from the public house and those enraged men.

They walked along the narrow footpath, bordered by closed shops and rows of brick terraced houses. The neighbourhood changed at night, after the well-heeled shoppers departed and only the people who lived and worked in the area remained.

It wasn't far to Nellie's business premises, where she had rooms above the shop. Thankfully, with only a few yards to travel he wouldn't have much time to give her a telling off. She'd just have to endure a quick reprimand, try not to prolong it by arguing with him, then she could escape back to her sanctuary.

'Miss Regan,' he said and Nellie braced herself. 'I want to ask you if you would be kind enough to do my sister's hair for a ball I'm hosting at Lockhart Estate next month. She was very taken with the style worn by the Duchess of Somerfeld and wondered if you could do her hair in a similar style.'

Nellie nearly stumbled over the cobblestones and stopped mid-step. She looked up at him. There was no anger in his expression. He was merely waiting politely for her answer.

She covered her mouth with both hands, but she couldn't stop a small giggle from escaping.

He furrowed his brow and frowned slightly. 'You find that funny?'

'No, no, not at all,' Nellie said, still laughing as she lowered her hands. 'Was that what you wanted to ask me when you came down to the servants' hall at the Ashmores' home?'

'Yes.'

'And that was the reason why you came down to London, came to my shop and followed me to The Hanged Man?'

He nodded.

Nellie laughed again. 'I thought you wanted to tell me off for...well, you know, that act I put on in the servants' hall.'

The furrows on his forehead grew deeper. 'You thought I pursued you to London, followed you to that drinking establishment, all because I wanted to tell you off?'

'Well, yes.'

He continued to stare down at her as if she was a curiosity and a burning blush exploded on her cheeks. Whether that was because she was embarrassed at her foolish behaviour or because looking up into those midnight-dark eyes had such an unsettling effect, she couldn't say. All she knew was her heart was performing a strange fluttering motion in her chest and the cool night air seemed to have suddenly become very warm.

'You must think I'm very vindictive, or I have nothing better to do with my time,' he said.

Nellie shrugged and began walking again. That was exactly what she had thought of him. That was what she thought of most men from his class. But it seemed, in his case, she had misjudged him.

They rounded the corner and their progress was halted by Patrick Kelly and a group of his friends. They were panting loudly, either with rage or, more likely, because they had taken the back streets and run ahead so they could cut them off. But there was no doubting the fury they still harboured over what had happened in the public house. Each man had adopted a fighter's stance, his fists clenched, his body taut and face rigid.

'Patrick, there's no need for this. No harm was done,' Nellie struggled to say, her throat so constricted her voice came out as a squeak. She took hold of Dominic's arm, pulling him backwards, hoping he'd have the sense to make a run for it. But his stance was just as belligerent as his assailants, his lips a thin hard line, his cold black eyes fierce and implacable.

Patrick Kelly stepped forward, his jaw jutting high in the air. 'No harm's been done yet, but this posh nob is about to come to some frightful harm. Isn't he, boys?'

It happened so fast Nellie had no time to do a thing. One moment she felt Mr Lockhart's hands on her shoulders, pushing her firmly behind him. Then all she heard was the sound of men grunting, of fists smacking skin, of boots connecting with bone.

She heard a woman's loud, piercing scream, then realised she was the one crying out for the men to stop.

As quickly as it began it was over. Patrick and his friends limped off, blood on their faces, bruising and swelling already starting to appear.

But they had got off easy compared to Mr Lockhart. He was lying immobile on the ground, his face bloodied and bruised, his lip split, his clothes torn.

The ground seemed to move under Nellie's feet and she collapsed down beside him. This was all her fault. Unlike herself, Mr Lockhart had done nothing wrong. All he had done was try to engage her services for his sister, then defend her from the unwanted attentions of a drunken fool. And the poor man had paid a terrible price for that gallantry.

Chapter Six

'Are you all right?' Nellie asked, clambering to her feet.

He looked up at her, one eye already starting to swell shut, as if to say of course he wasn't all right, far from it.

'Here, let me help you up. We need to get you off the street.' She reached down and put her hands under his arms to haul him to his feet. He was now vulnerable. A man as wealthy as him, in his condition, would be easy prey for those who wanted to make some quick money by robbing a defenceless person.

'Leave me. I am all right,' he murmured as he pushed her hands away. He tried to stand by himself and fell back, his face contorted with agony.

'No, you're not and you'll be in an even worse condition if I don't get you off the street.' Nellie looked around. Thankfully the street was deserted. They were safe for now. 'Some of the people who live in this neighbourhood are right scavengers. They can smell blood and they'll be in for the kill, after anything they can get their hands on to pawn for a few shillings, even the clothes off your back.'

She crouched down lower, edged her shoulder under his arm and levered him to his feet. He emitted a low groan, causing Nellie to wince, but there was nothing she could do to ease his pain now. She had to concentrate on getting him off the street as quickly as possible.

'Just don't pass out on me, will you?' She started to move forward, slowly. 'I can't carry you, that's for sure.'

'I won't,' he said, but his staggering gait suggested he was close to doing just that.

Straining under his weight, Nellie made her clumsy, stumbling way down the road. Her progress wasn't helped by the disconcerting experience of having him so close. With his arm heavy on her shoulder, his warm body pressed against her, it was impossible to ignore the strength of the man, the powerful muscles in his shoulders and arms, and the hard wall that was his chest. Through the metallic smell of blood, she could still detect the clean, fresh scent of sandalwood from his cologne and a deeper, underlying musky scent that was all male.

Was it that scent, or his body warm against her, or the weight of him on her shoulder that was making Nellie weak? Whatever it was, she'd do well to get over it immediately and keep moving. She had to get him to safety and quickly.

She stumbled a few more steps, then paused to catch her breath, her hand braced against the brick wall as she tried to balance herself. She could not let him fall.

She doubted she had the strength to get him to his feet one more time. Taking another deep breath, she forced herself to continue. As they turned the corner, pleasure surged through her at the sight of her home, although for once it wasn't pride that filled her heart, but the knowledge that they would soon be safe.

The sight of the shop sign giving her renewed strength, she stumbled the last few paces down the street. Wedging him against the wall, she unlocked the door, then foisted him back on to her shoulder and entered the building, locking the door behind her. At the bottom of the stairs she paused and looked up. They stretched out before her like a formidable mountain. They had never looked so high nor so steep. But she had no choice, she had to get him up to her room where he could lie down, even if she broke her back in the process.

'I can do this,' he murmured and gripped the banister. His bloodied hand slid off. He staggered back a step, righted himself and paused to drag in a series of strained breaths.

'No, you can't. Now do as you're told and put your weight on me.'

'I can do this. Just give me some time,' he mumbled, grabbing the banister again.

She glared back at him, her hands on her hips. 'If you don't do as you're told, you'll fall and I won't be able to move you. Now stop being a fool and put your weight back on me.'

He drew in a deep breath, coughed and winced with pain.

'Well? Are you going to do as you're told?'

He nodded and put his arm around her shoulder. 'You're very bossy, you know,' he mumbled.

Despite their predicament Nellie smiled. Bossy, he'd called her. He didn't know the half of it. In fits and jerks, they made their way slowly upwards, their feet scuffing on the bare wooden stairs. Nellie was forced to pause at each step to get her breath and, after what felt like an interminable amount of time, they made it to the landing. Now they were on a flat area it felt slightly easier, but his weight was still pressed down on her, causing her to crouch lower and lower. Stumbling the last few steps, they made it to the bed. She lowered him on to the edge, certain that she was incapable of taking one more step.

'Right, now let's get you settled.' She helped him lie down, then, still puffing from her exertions, undid his leather boots and with a thump dropped them to the wooden floor. She rushed to light the oil lamp and closed the curtains, shutting out the pale white moonlight that had streamed across the room.

They had made it. He was safe. Now she could relax. Her hands on the small of her back, she arched it to try to bring some relief from the strain. Closing her eyes, she rolled her aching shoulders and released a small moan of fatigue.

Her moans were drowned out by a loud groan of agony from the bed. Her eyes flew open and she rushed to his side. He was obviously in a great deal of pain. Her own sore back and shoulders were nothing compared to the injuries this poor man had suffered, all because she wanted to play a trick on him and make him feel like a fool. She was a terrible, terrible woman.

His hands gripping the edge of the bed, he attempted to sit up, but Nellie was not having that. He needed to rest. He needed to recover. She leant over the bed, put her hands on his shoulders and as gently as possible pushed him back down, her hands lingering for a moment more than necessary. He looked up at her through bloodshot eyes and she quickly stood up and brushed down the front of her already straight skirt.

'Now, do as you're told and stay where you are,' she said. 'Patrick Kelly and his gang have given you a fair old beating and you don't know how bad your injuries are. Best if you stay where you are while I fetch the doctor.'

He tried to say something through his swollen lips, then gave up and closed his eyes.

'And don't fall asleep until the doctor's had a chance to look at you. I'll be back soon.' Nellie bit her lower lip. She was reluctant to leave him. Should a man injured as badly as he be left alone? What if he fell asleep and never woke up? But she had no choice. He needed to be seen by a doctor.

She rushed out of the room, ran down the stairs and out on to the street.

Doctor Larkin lived in one room above the corner shop. Everyone in the neighbourhood still called him doctor, but, due to drink and indulging too much in other substances, he had lost his medical licence many years ago. However, he was a godsend for the local people who could never afford the services of a regular doctor.

She pounded on his door and he instantly appeared,

looking as dishevelled as she expected, but thankfully he wasn't yet the worse for drink, not completely. She told him her plight and promised him the price of a bottle of gin if he would come immediately.

They rushed back to her rooms and hurried up the stairs, only to find Mr Lockhart collapsed in a heap on the floor, his breathing laboured, his face contorted with pain, as he clutched at the side of his chest. The foolish man had obviously tried to leave while she was away. It was a blessing in disguise that he had only made it across the room—who knew what might have happened to him if he had gone out on to the street in this condition?

With the doctor's help they returned him to Nellie's bed.

'You've been in the wars, haven't you, my son?' the doctor said as he opened Mr Lockhart's jacket and shirt and pressed his palms on his chest and stomach.

'I'm all right, I just need to—' Mr Lockhart's words were cut short. He grimaced as the doctor pressed his hand down on his ribs. Nellie winced along with him as she looked at his poor chest, covered in bruises, although that didn't stop her eyes from running over the sculptured muscles, the firm stomach and his wide strong shoulders. Nellie swallowed and put her hand over her mouth. What a terrible lass she was. The man was in pain. He was bruised and battered, had taken a terrible beating. How could she possibly be thinking about how magnificent he'd look without his shirt on? How could she be looking at those dark hairs on his chest, or that line of hairs that ran down his stomach like an arrow and disappeared into his trousers? She was shameless, just shameless.

'There doesn't seem to be too much damage, although you might have broken a rib,' the doctor said, still palpitating Dominic's firm stomach.

Nellie flicked her gaze away from Mr Lockhart's muscular body and looked at the doctor.

'Unfortunately, there's no way to see inside the human body, so we'll just have to wait to find out what the damage is,' the doctor said. He fixed his rheumy gaze on Nellie. 'Don't let him move for a day or so. If there's a broken rib, there's always the danger it could pierce a lung, then he'll be in real trouble. If there's no broken ribs, you should know after a few days, once he starts to mend. If there is a broken rib, he'll have to stay where he is for four or five weeks.'

Four or five weeks.

Mr Lockhart opened his swollen eyes and stared at Nellie, no doubt thinking the same thing. He couldn't possibly stay here for four or five weeks. But that was a problem for another day.

Nellie looked back at the doctor. 'But can you do something for him, Doctor? Anything, so that he can—'

'Not much you can do,' the doctor interrupted. 'Not if it's a broken rib.' He looked back down at his patient. 'I'll bind up your chest, but you're not to move for a few days until we know for sure.'

He turned back to Nellie. 'You make sure he stays perfectly still. Hopefully he'll be right as rain soon. He's young, healthy and strong. If it's just bruising, he'll heal up quickly. You might want to get him some laudanum for the pain, though.' The doctor looked over at his black medical bag sitting open on the bedside table and frowned. 'I don't have any on me at the moment, but you can get some at the pharmacy when it opens in the morning.'

Nellie wasn't surprised. Any laudanum the doctor might have possessed would be used for his own private consumption and was unlikely to ever be dispensed to a patient.

'But for now, Nellie, help me remove his clothes so I can get these bandages on.'

Nellie rushed forward and slowly and carefully the two of them eased Mr Lockhart out of his jacket and shirt. The bruises were just as bad on his back. It seemed there was no part of his torso that had avoided a pounding from boots and fists.

The doctor wrapped his chest in bandages, then they gently lowered him back to the bed.

'Just let him rest, that's the best you can do for him,' the doctor said. 'And you might want to clean him up a bit.' He looked back at the patient. 'We should be grateful his assailants just used their fists and no knives. The cuts don't look too deep, so I don't think he'll need sutures. The cuts will heal on their own, just keep them clean. Bacteria, you see.' He looked over at Nellie and thrust out his chest. 'Do you know about bacteria? They cause disease, you know. Have to keep things clean. Didn't do that when I was a young doctor, but that's what we do now. In my day it was a badge of honour to have a bloodstained apron, showed how hard you worked, but these days it's all cleanliness. They can actually see bacteria down a microscope, you know. Do you know about microscopes?'

'Yes, good, right, thank you, Doctor. I can take if from here.' Nellie pulled up her patchwork quilt and tucked it in, as much to cover Mr Lockhart's chest from her gaze as to make him more comfortable.

The doctor remained standing in the middle of the room, smiling at Nellie. She thought he was going to continue his talk on the wonders of modern medicine, then realised her mistake.

'Oh, yes, I'll be right back.' She rushed through to her small kitchen area, took some money out of the jar she kept at the back of the cupboard and removed enough for a bottle of gin.

'There you go, Doctor. And thank you for coming so quickly.'

He counted out the coins in his hand. Nellie knew exactly what he would do now. He would head straight from her rooms to the nearest gin palace and drink away whatever it was he was trying to forget, and he wouldn't be much use to anyone else for the next few days.

She followed him out, taking with her a wooden pail so she could fetch some water from the nearby pump. When she returned, she lit the stove and put some water on to boil, then went through to her bedroom while she waited for the water to get warm enough to tend to his wounds.

Once again guilt coursed through her. This was all her fault. She had wanted to teach him a lesson and she had certainly done that, but he had done nothing wrong. He was wanting to offer her work, for goodness sake, and now he was beaten and bloody.

'I'm so sorry about this,' she murmured.

He shook his head, then grimaced. 'No need,' he muttered through his swollen lips, his eyes still closed. 'Not your fault.'

Nellie also grimaced, but not from physical pain. He was wrong. It was all her fault. Everything that had happened tonight was her fault and she had to make amends as best she could.

She returned to the kitchen, filled a large china bowl with warm water, carried it through to the bedroom and placed it on the bedside table. Sitting as carefully as she could on the edge of the bed and using a piece of soft flannel, she wiped his face.

'I'll try to be as gentle as I can,' she said, wincing every time he flinched. 'If the pain is too much to bear, I'll get some laudanum as soon as the pharmacy opens tomorrow.'

He shook his head. 'No, it's not too bad and I'd rather not take that drug, I've seen the damage it can do.'

Nellie nodded her agreement. Laudanum certainly put an immediate end to all pain, both physical and emotional, but it created a dream-like state that became intoxicating. She'd seen many a person come to enjoy that state too much, until they were no longer interested in reality and preferred to live in their own befuddled world.

As slowly and gently as possible she cleared away

the dried blood, turning the water a deeper shade of red with each rinsing. She leant down to remove the stubborn blood beside his lips and felt his warm breath on her cheek. A shiver ran through her body. She paused in her work. Her gaze moved upwards to look into his eyes. Despite the pain he was in, or because of it, he was staring at her with a disturbing intensity. Nellie couldn't look away. Her face was so close to his they could be about to kiss. She looked back down at his lips and realised the ridiculousness of her thought. His bottom lip was split. His face was swollen and he was in pain. The last thing he would be thinking about was kissing anyone and she shouldn't be thinking that way either.

She sat up straight, tightly wrung out the flannel, then gently ran it one more time over his face. It looked slightly better now that the blood had been removed and she was pleased to see that the doctor was right, none of the gashes was deep enough to require stitches. Her home remedy kit contained a suitable needle and thread, and she'd had to suture wounds before, but she was loath to do it, particularly on his lovely face.

'Right, you look as good as you're going to get tonight.' She stood up and brushed down her skirt.

'Thank you, you are very kind.'

Kind—that was the last thing Nellie was. He shouldn't be thanking her. He was completely within his rights to give her the reprimand she had been expecting and, now, after all that she had put him through, she would accept it. She thoroughly deserved his chastisement.

Wincing, he tried to pull himself to a seated position. 'Now, if you could send someone to summon my valet, he'll arrange for a carriage to take me home. I don't want to put you to any more trouble than I already have.'

Nellie shook her head. The doctor had said he shouldn't move. It seemed he wasn't going to listen to the doctor's instructions and he cared little for the pain that moving was so obviously causing him. For his own sake, Nellie needed to take a different approach.

'I'm sorry, I can't do that. There's no one else here that I can send and I'm reluctant to go out at this hour all by myself.' She did her best impression of a helpless woman. Nellie had walked home by herself on many a night. She knew how to avoid trouble and keep herself safe. After all, she'd been doing that since she was thirteen. It was just a shame she had been unable to keep Mr Lockhart safe tonight.

'In that case…' he made to climb off her bed, causing Nellie's patchwork quilt to fall towards the floor and once again exposing his naked chest to her gaze '… I'll find my own way home.'

Nellie put a restraining hand on his shoulder and fought not to react to the touch of his naked skin or his rippling muscles under her fingers. 'You're in no fit state to make your own way home. You can stay here tonight and then, if you still insist on leaving, I'll fetch your valet tomorrow.'

'I can't spend the night here.' He winced with pain, closed his eyes and gripped the side of his chest. He took in a deep breath, opened his one good eye and looked at her, his brows drawn together, his swollen lips frowning. 'Your reputation. People will know you've had a man in your room all night.'

Nellie couldn't help but laugh. Oh, this man really was so gallant, even if it was misdirected. 'I don't think anyone in this neighbourhood would notice and, if they did, they'd not care. I'm not Lady Cecily. My value on the marriage market isn't going to go down because my reputation has got a bit sullied.' She pointed towards his bandaged chest. 'Anyway, with the condition you're in at the moment, I think my virtue is pretty safe.'

He exhaled and looked around the room. 'I can't stay here. I can't take your bed. Where will you sleep?' He attempted to rise from the bed and once again Nellie put a restraining hand on his shoulder and gently pushed him back towards the pillows.

'I'll be fine. I can sleep anywhere.'

He made to rise again. 'You can't. I can't take your bed. It would be unforgivable.'

'Oh, for goodness sake. You're injured and the doctor says you can't be moved in case you've broken a rib. Now do as you're told and lie down.'

'But I won't ruin a woman's reputation.'

'You don't have to concern yourself on my account,' she said, her voice rising. 'I can take care of myself. Now do as you're told and lie down.'

He looked at her for a few moments then dropped back down on to the pillows. 'You are very kind to put yourself out like this.'

'And stop saying I'm kind. If I hadn't told you to come to The Hanged Man you wouldn't be in this state.

I'm not kind at all and certainly not to you. I've insulted you, played tricks on you and now I've caused you to get beaten up. I'm most definitely not kind and the least I can do is let you stay here the night while you recover.'

'All right, I'll stay the one night. Thank you for that, you're very kind…' He smiled, then winced as the split on his lip opened further. 'You're very beautiful,' he said and closed his eyes.

Nellie watched as he drifted off to sleep. *Beautiful.* He had called her beautiful. The man was clearly in a great deal of pain and becoming delusional.

Chapter Seven

Mr Lockhart slipped into sleep and Nellie lowered herself into her one armchair. Her back still ached from the exertion of heaving him up the stairs. She still had a painful crick in her neck and her shoulders were knotted with tension.

A long soak in a hot scented bath would do wonders for her aching body, but that would not be happening tonight. She certainly didn't have the energy to drag out the tin bath and heat up enough water to fill it. And even if she did, she wasn't about to strip off in front of Mr Lockhart. Nellie smiled to herself and looked at the man sleeping in her bed. Well, stripping off in front of Mr Lockhart wasn't an entirely unpleasant thought, although it was obviously not something she would do, or should even be thinking about.

She continued to stare at his sleeping face. He was so gallant, jumping to her defence, then worrying about her reputation. Sweet, really. But what she had said to him was true. She was capable of looking after herself, had been doing so successfully for the last ten years. And as she wasn't from the same class as Lady Cecily he did not need to concern himself with her reputation. Lady Cecily belonged to a class where a woman's value on the marriage market could be irredeemably tarnished if there was any suggestion that she had lost her virginity before her wedding night. For Lady Cecily this meant she had to be chaperoned at all times so no one could call her chaste condition into question.

While Lady Cecily would never have been alone in the company of a man, such conditions would be impossible for a woman of Nellie's class. How would a maid perform her duties if she always had to be watched to ensure she was never in the company of a man? How would the shop girls get to work if they all required a chaperon to accompany them when they walked the streets?

Nellie had had to look after herself, but she wouldn't have it any other way. Unlike Lady Cecily, she was free to flirt, laugh and have fun with anyone she wanted to. Her gaze moved slowly over Mr Lockhart's sleeping face, down to his broad shoulders exposed above the sheets. She drew in a shaky breath and placed her hand on her chest to still her suddenly thumping heart. She could even take a man to her bed if she wanted to.

She quickly looked away. Not that she would be taking a man to her bed any time soon. She would not risk getting pregnant and suffering the dreadful fate of an unwed mother, and she certainly had no plans to marry. If she did, her business would automatically become her husband's property and she had worked too hard to build up her business to surrender it just to get a ring on her finger.

She looked back at the man sleeping in her bed. She would never risk what she had for any man, but some men were certainly more tempting than others. He rolled over, exposing more of his shoulders to her gaze. It was strange to think she had seen more of Mr Lockhart's body than his fiancée probably had. She closed her eyes and remembered his muscular, naked chest, the feeling of his arm heavy around her shoulder, that heady scent of him, all sandalwood and musk. Mmm, lovely.

As pleasant as that memory was, she should not really be thinking about such things. Particularly as he was a respectable man, an engaged man, one who she had caused to get beaten up, all because he was trying to protect her from the unwanted attentions of Patrick Kelly. She needed to remember that, nothing else, and stop thinking about his chest, his arms, or any other part of his body.

She picked up her copy of Arthur Conan Doyle's latest book from her bedside table and flicked it open. Reading Sherlock Holmes until sleep came was a much more sensible idea than dwelling on Mr Lockhart's muscles, his scent or any other part of him.

Several pages later, it became obvious that sleep was not going to come easily to her tonight. Her body was too tense, her mind too active. Even the excitement of Holmes and Dr Watson pursuing villains around London wasn't enough to distract her mind from her aching body, or the whirling thoughts of everything that had happened since she first saw Mr Lockhart dancing around the ballroom at Hardgrave Estate. She wriggled down in the chair to try to get comfortable and moved the cushion to behind her tired shoulders.

It made no difference. How was she ever going to put in a full day's work tomorrow if she didn't get a good night's sleep? She looked over at the sleeping man. She didn't begrudge him her bed. How could she, considering it was her fault that he was having to sleep the night in her rooms rather than his own comfortable bed, but it *would* be nice to stretch out and get some sleep.

She looked at the empty space beside Mr Lockhart. It wouldn't disturb him if she quietly climbed into the bed and slept on the other side, would it? He was sleeping so deeply he would never know. And after many years in service she was still in the habit of waking very early. She would be awake well before him, up and dressed before he even stirred. He'd be none the wiser that he had slept the night alongside her.

No harm would be done and she'd get a good night's sleep. She continued to stare at the empty side of the bed. It was a sensible idea after all.

The thought of a comfortable night's sleep was already having a beneficial effect and the tension had started to leave her shoulders. And if she was really going to be comfortable, she needed to get out of her dress and her corset.

As quietly as possible, she returned her book to the bedside table and began undressing. Keeping a watchful eye on Mr Lockhart, she undid her ankle boots and placed them in the cupboard. She unrolled her stockings and removed her skirt, jacket and petticoat. Trying not to make any noise she unlaced her corset and pulled off the restricting garment. Then, moving as quickly as she could, in case he opened his eyes, she removed her chemise, pulled on her nightdress and wriggled out of her drawers.

On tippy toes she crept across the room, slowly pulled back the quilt and carefully climbed into the bed and under the covers.

Mr Lockhart emitted a gentle snore. Good, he was still sound asleep. He was getting some much-needed rest and was oblivious to the fact that a woman had just stripped off before him and that he was now sharing the bed with her.

Nellie smiled to herself and snuggled down under the covers. With his warm body beside her it was easy to imagine what it would be like if she really was sharing her bed, her life, with a man like Mr Lockhart. He was so strong, so brave, so gallant, a woman would feel safe and protected with a man like him in her life. It would almost be worth the legal sacrifices a woman had to make when she married and became effectively a man's possession. Almost, but not quite.

She gently rolled over and gazed at his sleeping face. Despite the swelling and his bruises, he really did have the loveliest of faces. In repose that worried furrow that often creased between his dark eyebrows had disappeared, that stern countenance had softened. Yes, it certainly was a beautiful face. And those lips, so soft, so inviting. If they weren't swollen and if they didn't bear a cut where some man's fist had connected with his face, his lips would be oh, so kissable.

In some ways his injuries were a good thing. Otherwise she might be tempted to lean over and do a little test, just to see if the touch of his lips on hers would be as wonderful as she imagined.

But such a liberty would be so wrong, particularly under the circumstances, and would be too bold, even for her. It was quite a cheek to even think of such a thing.

She gently hoisted herself up on to one elbow and gazed down at the handsome sleeping face, better to just observe those tempting lips.

She leant down slightly. No, she couldn't do it. Could she?

She looked around the room as if there was an invisible audience disapproving of what she was thinking. The room was empty. Obviously. No one would know. Not even Mr Lockhart. After all, he was sound asleep.

But even so, it really would be so wrong. She looked back down at him. Slowly she leant forward, until her face was so close she could feel his soft breath on her cheek. She moved a fraction closer. Her lips lightly touched his. She was right. Soft, sensual, delicious. And oh, that lovely masculine scent of his. Nellie drew in a deep breath and closed her eyes. She moved her tongue gently along his bottom lip.

He stirred slightly in his sleep.

Her eyes flew open. She sat up straight, her body rigid, her heart pounding. She looked around the room as if the invisible audience had suddenly appeared and were tut-tutting at what she had just done.

No one was objecting, not even Mr Lockhart. He had stopped moving and had remained fast asleep. Nellie exhaled her held breath. She should never have kissed him. It was a shocking thing to do. She should be utterly ashamed of herself.

She ran her tongue along her bottom lip. Yes, utterly ashamed. But she wasn't. Smiling, she extinguished the oil lamp and snuggled back down in the bed, luxuriating in the warmth of the man beside her. It had been a terrible thing to do, but she had no regrets, and any shame she might have felt was buried deep beneath the pleasure of having discovered what it felt like to have his delicious lips on hers.

Chapter Eight

Dominic woke and looked around the unfamiliar room. Where was he? What had happened? He tried to sit up and a searing pain ripped through his chest. Memories of last night came flooding back as he registered the pain in every part of his body: the noisy public house, that ruffian manhandling Nellie Regan, the brawl in the street, then being helped through the streets by Miss Regan, back to her rooms.

Another image entered his mind, of kissing Miss Regan, of holding her while she slept, of feeling her warm, soft body up against his. He lay back down and closed his eyes. That had to be a dream and one he most certainly should not have had. She had kindly given up her bed to him, despite his protestations, but he could not expect her to sleep in that uncomfortable armchair another night. He would have to make arrangements to return to his town house today.

The sound of soft footsteps made him open his eyes and he saw Nellie Regan enter the room, still in her nightdress, carrying a jug and bowl. She turned in his direction and he quickly closed his eyes, guilt searing through him at the mere thought that he had dreamt of kissing her.

A door squeaked open. He opened his eyes a fraction and saw her remove some clothing from the cupboard. With her back to him, she stood at the washstand and began her morning toilette. Dominic knew he should close his eyes, look away from this intimate scene, or warn her that he was awake. But despite what his mind was commanding, he couldn't do it. He was transfixed. She looked too beautiful for him to deny himself the pleasure of watching her. She was like a woman in one of the pre-Raphaelite paintings he had recently seen at an art exhibition. Her long red hair was flowing down her back in gentle curls and, with the morning light coming through the thin curtains at the window, he could see the outline of her curvaceous body under the muslin of her nightgown.

His gaze moved slowly over her body, taking in every beautiful inch of it: the tiny waist, the round hips and the curve of her buttocks. He imagined encircling that small waist with his arms as he inhaled the scent of her hair, running his hands over those enticing curves, across her hips, taking those round buttocks in his hands. A stirring in his groin alerted him that one of his body parts had apparently not been affected by last night's altercation.

She really was a beautiful woman, with a sensual, feminine body, and she had the most beguiling face he had ever seen. He was wrong. She wasn't like a woman in a pre-Raphaelite painting. She was even more beautiful. But what he was doing was certainly wrong. He should not be watching her. He should close his eyes, turn his back on her. It would be the gentlemanly thing to do. But right now, he had no interest in being a gentleman. What he wanted to do with this woman was much more primal than that. And if he could actually move, he would have a hard job stopping himself from acting on his base instincts.

She turned and looked over her shoulder at him. Now he most definitely should look away. But how could he? With her body side on to him, the sunlight was exposing the outline of her breasts to his gaze. Full, round, firm breasts, just waiting for a man's hands to caress them. The stirring in his groin grew more intense. He must look away. He must. Slowly, reluctantly, his eyes left those beautiful breasts and he looked up at her face. She was staring at him. For one intense moment she held his gaze. Like a prisoner, trapped by his desire, Dominic continued to stare back at her. The very room seemed to hold its breath as he waited for her to react. She had every right to be outraged by his libertine behaviour. If she threw him out of her rooms right now and on to the street it would be no less than he deserved.

Her gaze moved down to where the shape of the bed-clothes revealed the powerful effect she was having on him. She bit her lip and a delicate blush appeared on her cheeks. 'Well, you seem to be on the mend,' she said with a small, embarrassed laugh. 'But I think it might be an idea if I dressed in the other room.' With that, she picked up her clothes and disappeared into the adjoining room.

It was Dominic who should be embarrassed, not her. This young woman had tended his wounds, had given up her bed for him, and he repaid her by spying on her, by lusting after her. He tried once more to rise from the bed and a searing pain shot through his chest and back, the ripping agony of his injuries completely removing the shameful evidence of his reaction to seeing Miss Regan in her nightgown.

Despite his pain, Dominic could not stay in these rooms a second longer. He had imposed on this young woman long enough and now he had embarrassed her by his lustful behaviour. He placed his hand on the iron bedstead. Slowly he eased himself up to a sitting position. Inch by inch he manoeuvred his legs across the bed and over the side. Taking a few deep, slow breaths so he could bear the pain, he stood up. Burning agony shot through his body, causing him to double over, and fall back on to the bed as an animal cry escaped his mouth.

Miss Regan's hands caught him before he slipped to the floor. In his agony he hadn't heard her enter the room and he was incapable of resisting as she gently eased him back on to the bed. Her lovely face was contorted with concern. In her haste to help him she had left her blouse unbuttoned. Through his pain he registered the soft round mounds of her décolletage. The creamy skin was so inviting, so tempting. He released another moan, but this time for an entirely different reason.

'Do not try to get out of bed again,' she admonished him while pulling her blouse together, hiding that beautiful sight from his inappropriate gaze. 'The doctor said you might have broken a rib and it could pierce your lung.'

'I can't stay here. I've imposed too long.' *And despite my injuries I'm finding it increasingly difficult to behave like a gentleman.* Broken rib, pierced lung or not, it was time Dominic left.

'You're being ridiculous. If you die on me, that will be an even bigger imposition. Now promise me, you will not try to get out of bed again.'

She waited, staring at him, her eyes blazing.

'I said promise. You are not to try to get out of that bed.'

'I should go. I shouldn't be here.'

'Well, you are here. And unless you promise me you're not going to move I'm going to tie you to the bed. So, do as you're told and don't move.'

He smiled despite his pain. Those green eyes were flashing in anger, just as they had when he'd first seen her standing in the servants' hall at Hardgrave Estate, her hands on her hips, her chin lifted in defiance. This little slip of a girl really did have a streak of iron in her.

'All right. All right. I promise.'

She nodded in satisfaction.

'But, please, can you send someone to fetch my valet? He'll be able to arrange for me to be transported back to my own home.'

She leant over him and pulled up the quilt. He tried desperately to ignore the temptation to look down at her soft breasts. He fought not to inhale her delicate scent of roses, so soft and feminine. He needed to think of other things if he was to avoid once again revealing to her just how much of a cad he was. He should not be thinking such lustful thoughts while she was doing all she could to help him.

She left the room again and a few minutes later returned with a tray containing a teapot, two cups and a plate of toast and jam.

'I'm sure it's not quite as grand as what you usually have for breakfast,' she said, pouring the tea. 'But I'm afraid this will have to do.'

He thanked her as he took the cup and saucer from her outstretched hand. 'You are very kind to put yourself to all this trouble.'

'Oh, stop saying that. You kept saying that last night and I told you to stop. It's my fault you're in this condition. You should be reprimanding me, not thanking me.'

Dominic laughed, a laugh that was cut short by pain searing through his side. 'Would you actually listen to anyone who reprimanded you?'

She smiled and shrugged one shoulder. 'Probably not.'

He took a sip of the hot drink, avoiding the cut on the edge of his bottom lip, and looked around the small room. It was quite humble accommodation, but she had made it attractive and feminine, with patchwork quilts, embroidered cushions and an array of knick-knacks. He settled back into the pillows. It was a comfortable room and he imagined it provided her with a welcoming retreat at the end of her working day.

He took another sip of his tea. He should make conversation. Discuss anything other than his inappropriate behaviour, anything other than how he had shamefully embarrassed this lovely young woman. 'You must be very enterprising to open your own business. What made you decide to leave the security of a job in service to take such a risk?'

Yes, her work...that was a much safer topic.

She shrugged. 'It didn't feel like a risk and I've always wanted to work for myself. When I worked for the Duchess of Somerfeld, when she was still Arabella van Haven, back in New York, I had so many society ladies asking me if I'd work for them that I knew people wanted my services. Not that any of them deemed to ask me directly.' She pulled a face of disapproval and Dominic smiled. That was the disapproving little madam he had seen in the kitchen at Hardgrave House.

'They always got a member of their staff to do that. Too high and mighty to talk to me themselves.' She sniffed. 'And it was the same when I came to London. Then I noticed that a lot of middle-class women only had a few servants, or even just one maid of all works. Not many had their own lady's maid. They're all trying desperately to copy the aristocracy, but they haven't got the staff to achieve the look. So, I thought a hair and beauty parlour would be a good business. And it has been. I've only been in business for six months and already I'm completely booked out most days.'

'Yes, very enterprising.' He took another sip. 'Although I'm surprised you're booked out.'

He suppressed a smile as she glared at him through narrowed eyes. 'Why would you say that? My work is greatly admired.'

'I'm sure it is, but you don't exactly make it easy for people to hire your services. Last night was the third time I tried to ask you if you'd be willing to do my sister's hair.'

'Oh, yes, about that...' She laughed to try to cover up her embarrassment. 'Sorry, but you know, I got that one a bit wrong.'

'You thought I wanted to tell you off for impersonating me?'

She bit her bottom lip and blushed slightly. 'Well, I was pretty rude.'

'Yes, you were. But it hardly matters.' He smiled at the memory of her strutting round in front of the servants mocking him and Cecily Hardgrave. His smiled faded. He wasn't the only one she had mocked.

'You can make fun of me as much as you like, but Lady Cecily doesn't deserve to be laughed at.'

'Yes, I'm sorry about that.' She pulled a small frown that didn't look particularly sorry to him.

Dominic looked down at the cup in his hand. He hadn't thought of his fiancée since he had left the Hardgrave Estate. That *was* unforgivable. In fact, just about everything he had done and thought since he'd met this pretty former lady's maid had been unforgivable.

And as rude as she had been, she had, unfortunately, not been far from the truth. He had never looked at

Cecily the way he had looked at Miss Regan this morning. He had never had thoughts of ripping off Cecily's clothing and feasting his eyes on her body, had never felt that primal, lustful urge to take her and make her his own, but that was exactly what he wanted to do with Nellie Regan.

He moved uncomfortably in the bed. He had to get his thoughts under control. It was an insult to Miss Regan, not to mention highly inappropriate for a recently engaged man.

He coughed to clear his throat. 'So, you lived in America for a while,' he asked, once again trying to move the conversation on to safer ground. 'But that gentle brogue is Irish more than American.'

'Mmm, I was born in Ireland, but moved to America when I was still a young lass. I came to London last year, when Arabella—I mean the Duchess of Somerfeld's father sent her over to England to find a husband with a title. He's a right social climber, that one.' Her hand shot to her mouth and a soft blush tinged her cheeks.

Was that how she saw him, as a *right social climber*? Is that why she thought he was marrying Cecily? Dominic released a long sigh. Well, she would be right. But his social advancement was not for himself, but for his sisters. Wasn't it? Dominic was starting to wonder why he had ever thought marrying Cecily Hardgrave was a good idea. He shook his head and pushed that thought away. Of course it was a good idea. How could he think otherwise?

'Perhaps advancing his daughter's position in society was the kindest thing her father could do for her.'

She rolled her eyes. 'I think letting his daughter live her life in a way that made her happy would have been kinder.'

It was his turn to roll his eyes. 'Being secure, having a place in society are what's important, not some wishy-washy idea of happiness. And anyway, the Duchess of Somerfeld looked happy enough to me.'

'Well, she is, but that's because she's in love, but that wasn't anything to do with her father.'

'Love,' he snorted. 'Love and happiness, how many lives have been ruined because people have chased those illusive concepts?'

'You don't think it's important to love the person you're married to?' She blushed slightly. 'Sorry, that's none of my business.'

She was right. It was none of her business, but he felt compelled to make her see how wrong she was. 'I believe there are many important things to consider before deciding who to marry and love is not one of them. A couple should be well matched socially and temperamentally. The decision should be made based on reason, not some illusive concepts like love and the desire to be constantly happy.'

She bit her lip and her drew her eyebrows together as if trying to understand a difficult concept. 'So, how long have you known Lady Cecily?'

Dominic tried to think back to when he had first met her. She had always lived in the same county and they had attended many social functions together so he must have known her for quite some time, but he couldn't actually recall when they first met. In fact, until her father had suggested they marry he had never paid her much attention. Since then they had taken several long walks together around their estates, under the watchful eye of Cecily's chaperon, but their engagement party was the first public event they had attended as a couple. 'We've known each other for many years,' he finally replied.

'So, when did you decide that she was the one you wanted to marry?'

'It was quite simple. Her father suggested it. I realised it was a highly suitable match. I proposed to Lady Cecily and she agreed.'

She raised her eyebrows. 'So, what are you saying? You don't love Lady Cecily, but you're engaged to her because it's a highly suitable match?' she asked quietly. 'Does Lady Cecily love you?'

He shook his head impatiently. 'That hardly matters, does it? We're well suited and I'm sure as time passes we will become much closer and grow to have a shared affection for each other.' And that will be much better than love and passion, he wanted to add. His parents had married for love and all that had done was cause damage to the family and their position in society, damage that his marriage to Cecily would finally undo. But he couldn't expect an ex-servant to ever understand that.

'Well, it looks like your marriage to Lady Cecily will be a great success then if your expectations are so low. If you don't expect love, and you don't even expect happiness, nothing can go wrong.' Her voice had grown terse, as if he had offended her in some way.

She stared at him for a moment, then shook her head. 'I'm sorry. Sometimes I speak my mind before I have time to think. That was rude of me. I'm sorry, I keep being rude to you. Your relationship with Lady Cecily has nothing to do with me and I'm sure you'll both be very happy.'

She gave a little laugh, which sounded more annoyed than amused. 'Well, maybe not happy, you don't want to be happy, do you? But I'm sure it will be very successful and it will be great for both families, socially and what not.'

Dominic released an exasperated sigh. 'Sometimes it's important to sacrifice your own happiness for the benefit of others. My marriage will be good for my sisters. You might scoff at people marrying to advance their position in society, but my marriage will mean my sisters will move in society's highest echelons. It will mean they will have much better opportunities for making suitable matches and maybe even meeting your criteria and finding so-called love and happiness.'

Dominic was unsure why he felt the need to explain himself. He did not need to justify his marriage to anyone, but for some reason it was important to him that she did not see him as some grasping man desperate to align himself with the aristocracy at any cost. He didn't want her to despise him, didn't want her to be annoyed with him. He wanted to see that laughing Nellie Regan once more.

'Yes, it will be important to sire another generation

of toffs,' he said, making sure his voice sounded completely serious. 'But believe me, that is something I'll be more than capable of doing myself and it's one task I won't have to pass over to a servant.'

She looked at him with wide, surprised eyes, then laughed out loud. It was such a delightful sound and he smiled back at her.

'Yes, I'm sorry about that as well,' she said, trying to stifle her laughter. 'That impersonation I did of your wedding night was very rude, even for me.'

'Well, the servants seemed to enjoy it.'

'Yes, but still, I did go a bit far, didn't I? Sorry.'

She took a sip of her tea. Hopefully, now that he had made her laugh, she would stop grilling him about his relationship with Cecily Hardgrave and his attitudes to love and marriage.

'Although heaven knows what Lady Cecily will have to say when she finds out you spent the night in another woman's bed,' she said, still smiling.

It seemed she wasn't going to drop the subject after all. 'I very much doubt if she will be concerned.' It was Dominic's turn to regret what he had said. Just as Nellie Regan professed to do, he had spoken without thinking, otherwise he would never have revealed such a personal detail about his relationship with Cecily Hardgrave. It seemed Miss Regan was having a bad effect on him.

She stared at him, her gaze long and considered, her head inclined slightly to one side, her eyebrows raised in curiosity. 'Really? She won't? Why not? Even if she's not jealous that you spent the night in another woman's bed…' Her cheeks exploded with colour. 'Just sleeping that is, nothing else, won't she be concerned about you? Won't she be worried?'

Dominic wondered whether she would be. Cecily seemed to be completely unconcerned about everything to do with him and their forthcoming marriage. Not for the first time he wondered why a young woman would be so keen to marry and yet be so uninterested in her future husband.

A silence stretched out between them and she continued to stare at him in expectation, her cheeks still that delightful shade of pink. Once again he was being drawn into a conversation he did not want to have. And despite those green eyes staring at him with curiosity, he would not be answering any more questions about himself and Cecily Hardgrave.

'I have no desire to discuss Lady Cecily's feelings with you,' he said in a voice that sounded bombastic even to his own ears. 'I thank you for helping me last night but, as I've asked you already, would you be so kind as to contact my valet so he can arrange for my transportation home.' He could hear his voice becoming more pompous with every word, but he had to stop this young woman from asking any more awkward questions, had to put an end to a discussion that was causing him to examine his decisions and forget his responsibilities and his commitments.

Chapter Nine

The real Dominic Lockhart had returned. The man she had briefly seen, the one who could laugh, who could relax, even talk about how he felt, had once again become hidden behind that wall of superiority and reserve.

Well, so be it. She might have harboured ridiculous fantasies last night when they were side by side in bed, but that's all it could possibly be. A ridiculous fantasy. To think otherwise would be foolhardy. Nellie knew she had many faults, but foolhardiness was not one of them.

The way he had spoken about love and marriage showed just what sort of man he was: a passionless, social climber. If he saw marriage as a way to advance his position, then Lady Cecily was welcome to him. And what did it matter to Nellie anyway? Why had she been so interested in his relationship with Lady Cecily and his reasons for wanting to marry her? It had nothing to do with her.

'Right, well, I for one have work to do today,' she said, standing quickly. 'The hairdressing parlour doesn't open until nine o'clock, so I'll go around to see your valet before then. I'm sure he won't still be in bed. After all, you probably don't know it, but servants start work at six o'clock, while the rest of the household is still sound asleep.'

'I'm well aware of the long hours that servants work.'

She stared at him for a moment, wanting to give him a lecture on the working conditions of most servants, but once again registered the bruising on his face, now turning various shades of green, blue and yellow. He did not need lectures from her. She'd accused him of being haughty, but if she hadn't been so haughty when they first met, if she hadn't been so determined to make him feel uncomfortable, he'd now be lying in his own bed, his face unscathed by the fists and boots of Patrick Kelly and his friends.

'Right, I'll be back soon.' She poured him another cup of tea as consolation for her outburst and handed it to him. 'And try to eat something while I'm away. She indicated the toast and jam left untouched on the tray.

He took the cup from her outstretched hand and she was pleased their fingers did not make contact. She didn't need her composure upset any further by the touch of his skin on hers.

'And don't move, while I'm gone.' She pointed an admonishing finger at him. 'After all, you did promise me.'

'I won't move. I promise. But before you go, you still haven't answered my question.'

She shook her head. 'Question, what question?' She had been the one asking the questions, not him.

'Last night you didn't respond when I asked you if you'd do my sister's hair for the ball next month at Lockhart Estate.'

'Oh, that. Yes, of course I will. After all, it's the least I can do for you.'

He smiled at her. 'Thank you, that will make Amanda very happy.' And what a smile. It lit up his face and brought warmth to those usually cold dark eyes. He should smile more often. Just as quickly as it had appeared it disappeared. He winced slightly and put his hand to the split in his lip.

Nellie cringed with guilt. Thanks to her this poor man couldn't even smile properly. Not that smiling was something he did a lot of, but still.

Meeting her had caused him so much harm. He was right. He should return to his own world as soon as possible. Away from the damage that her actions had inflicted on him. Away from her nosy questions and her bad behaviour.

At least he didn't know just how bad her behaviour was. He didn't know that she had kissed him last night. Nellie blushed at the memory and pretended she was looking for her purse to cover her embarrassment.

'I do appreciate it,' he continued. 'You will have to travel to my estate in Kent to do Amanda's hair, but you will be well rewarded for all the hours you are away from your business. Plus, I will ensure that all travel arrangements are made to your convenience and you will be provided with suitable accommodation rather than staying in the servants' quarters.'

Nellie nodded her thanks. He was being very generous. More than she deserved. Her days of being a servant were now behind her and the Duchess of Somerfeld was the only person whose hair she styled away from her London parlour, but for his sister she would make an exception. After all, she owed Mr Lockhart so much. He didn't need to go to so much trouble to make it worth her while, but she appreciated that she would not be treated as a servant but as a professional providing a specialised service.

She tucked in his quilt as he told her the address of his town house, asked him one more time if he needed anything, to which she received a definite no, and headed out on to the bustling street.

It was already busy at this early hour with shop girls heading to work, clerks in bowler hats walking briskly to their offices and heavily laden delivery carts bringing in the daily goods to the nearby shops. The noise of the vibrant city always invigorated Nellie. She loved the sound of the horses' hooves clipping on the cobblestones, the carriages whirring past and the cheerful sounds of people calling out greetings. Even the shouts of annoyed drivers cursing those who got in their way was a pleasure to hear. It was the sound of busy people going about their productive daily lives.

She caught the first horse-drawn omnibus that passed, paid the conductor and climbed up the outside circular stairway to sit on the cramped benches, crowded with people going to work. Fortunately, despite the cool breeze, it was a pleasant summer's day and Nellie enjoyed the feeling of sun on her face as she travelled through the jostling streets.

She changed buses several times before arriving at his Belgravia address. The affluent street was so calm and tranquil after the noise and commotion of the rest of the city. Nellie looked around at the well-tended homes and the almost empty street. Unlike the rest of London, the roads in Belgravia weren't jam-packed with traffic. She could actually hear the sound of birds tweeting in the trees. It was such a stark contrast to the rest of the city, where such quiet sounds would be drowned by the hubbub of a multitude of people and vehicles.

But here, life was lived at a more genteel pace. No one had to rush to get to work on time, no one had to jostle through the crowded markets to do their daily shopping.

It was a different world for a different class of people. She looked up at the impressive three-storeyed white façade of his town house and its black wrought-iron balconies. Then she looked down at the two buttons beside the gate. One for servants, one for visitors, clearly demarking the two worlds of the people who occupied his house.

She firmly pressed the one for visitors, pushed her way through the gate, marched up the outside stairs and stood defiantly at the front door. She was here at Mr Lockhart's behest. She wasn't doing the work of a servant so she would be treated with the respect she deserved.

The door opened and the footman looked her up and down. She wasn't dressed as a servant, but nor was she dressed as a member of the gentry or aristocracy. Nellie could almost see the footman's mind working, trying to place her into the correct classification so he would know how to treat her.

'There's no need to look at me like that,' she said. 'I'm not a servant and, no, I'm not a visitor either. But you may have noticed Mr Lockhart didn't return home last night. So, if you want to know where he is, you're going to have to let me in and tell his valet I need to talk to him.'

The footman's eyebrows momentarily rose, then he stepped back to allow her entry. He walked quickly through the house and Nellie had little time to take in the grand entranceway, with its black-and-white-tiled floor and sparkling chandelier suspended from the ceiling, three storeys above them. They rushed up the richly carpeted curved staircase with its polished brass banister and into the upper servants' sitting room. The footman asked her to wait, then departed.

Nellie was impressed. The upper servants' sitting room was a cut above most she'd seen. It was spacious. The furniture was new and comfortable. And it had large windows with a view over the street. It seemed she had to give Mr Lockhart credit for something. He treated his servants well.

The valet rushed in, his stern expression exactly

what she'd expect from a senior servant. 'Where is he? What's happened? Tell me now!'

Nellie shook her head. It never failed to amaze her how the upper servants adopted that terse manner when addressing anyone they considered their inferior. It was as if they forgot that they, too, were servants.

'Presumably you're Mr Lockhart's valet. It seems you forgot to introduce yourself. I'm Nellie Regan.'

The man gaped at her, then collected himself. 'I'm Mr Burgess and, yes, I'm Mr Lockhart's valet. So, Nellie, where is he and what has happened?'

That was better, although he had assumed he had the right to call her by her first name, something that he would never do with someone he considered his equal. But Nellie decided to let that go for now. 'Mr Lockhart was set upon last night.'

The valet gasped and Nellie held up her hands to reassure him. 'He's not badly injured. Well, he's badly bruised, but he'll live. He stayed at my rooms overnight as the doctor said he shouldn't be moved in case he's got a broken rib. Mr Lockhart asked me to come and tell you what has happened.'

'Right. You wait here. I'll organise everything.' He rushed out, leaving Nellie alone in the sitting room. She wandered out into the hallway and looked over the banister down at the grand entranceway, then up to the high ceiling and the elegant chandelier. The doors were shut so she couldn't see into any rooms and Nellie wasn't quite rude enough to go exploring. But what she could see was magnificent. The hallways were laid with rich, deep red carpets, and Nellie was tempted to take off her boots to feel the thick wool under her stockinged feet. The walls were lined with large oil paintings, an array of marble sculptures and other artworks. Nellie doubted any of *them* had been sourced from flea markets. What Mr Lockhart had made of her rooms above her shop she couldn't imagine, but she doubted he would have been impressed.

But what of it? Her rooms and her business were all hers and she was proud of what she had achieved. She didn't need anyone looking down their nose at her because they were born into the sort of wealth that allowed them to have a three-storey town house in a wealthier part of London.

The valet rushed back up the stairs. He sent Nellie a disapproving look for not remaining where she had been told and signalled for her to follow. They raced back down the stairs and out the front door into the waiting carriage.

'Give your address to the coach driver,' the valet ordered as he climbed into the carriage.

Nellie did as he asked, then joined him in the carriage. The valet said nothing as they crossed London, either because he was worried about Mr Lockhart or because he deemed Nellie too lowly to converse with. Instead Nellie watched the city go past. It was certainly easier, more comfortable and a lot faster to travel by carriage than omnibus and the coach driver manoeuvred his way through the busy traffic with the skill of a professional.

When they arrived at her shop the valet rushed through the door and up the stairs, not waiting for an invitation and ignoring the greetings from Matilda and Harriet.

Nellie said hello to her curious assistants and told them she'd be back soon to explain everything, then followed the valet up the stairs. The valet was standing beside Mr Lockhart's bed, ringing his hands. He sent Nellie an accusatory glare, as if she had personally caused the bruises and cuts over Mr Lockhart's body. An accusation Nellie could only agree with.

'I'll arrange for you to be transported home immediately, sir,' the valet said.

'Thank you, Burgess.' Mr Lockhart carefully pulled himself into a seated position.

'Not if you want to risk killing him,' Nellie said, for which she received another accusatory glare from the valet. 'The doctor said he might have a broken rib and it's best if he stays still for a few days. Then if the pain reduces it will mean he's all right to move. But if it is a broken rib and he does move he might pierce his lung.'

The valet's glare turned from accusatory to worried.

'This is most improper,' he mumbled, looking from Nellie to Mr Lockhart. 'Perhaps I could organise someone to look after you, sir. A trained nurse, perhaps.' He sent another disapproving look in Nellie's direction. 'Someone who can make you comfortable and care for you.'

Nellie could feel her hackles starting to rise at the man's superior manner. She was perfectly capable of caring for an injured man. 'No, you won't. This is my home and no one gets admittance without my permission.'

'You have been very kind, Miss Regan, but Burgess

is right. It's too much to ask of you. Perhaps I could pay for you to stay in a hotel while I recuperate and Burgess can organise for a nurse to attend me.'

'No.' Nellie shook her head and glared back at the valet. 'As I said, no one comes into my home uninvited and I have no intention of being thrown out of my own home, even if it is to a fancy hotel.' Nellie was unsure why she was being so stubborn. She just knew she did not want to leave and did not want anyone else nursing Mr Lockhart. She had caused his injuries and she would be the one to tend him and make him better.

'In that case I'll have another bed sent over, so you'll have somewhere to sleep rather than in that armchair,' Mr Lockhart said.

Heat rushed to Nellie's cheeks. Little did he know that she had slept perfectly comfortably last night beside him in her own bed. Thank goodness he didn't know about that kiss. To cover her discomfort Nellie bustled forward and picked up the tray containing the uneaten toast, then put it back down again.

Mr Lockhart watched her pointless activity, then turned back to his valet. 'Can you please arrange for a bed to be delivered, Burgess?'

The valet nodded. 'Yes, right away, sir.' He lifted his head and looked down his nose at Nellie. 'And I'll make sure the Duke of Ashmore is informed. I'm sure his Grace and your fiancée will be most anxious to know about what has happened and that you are safe.'

Nellie was sure she heard an emphasis on the word fiancée. What did this man think she was doing, trying to kidnap Mr Lockhart, lure him away from his intended? The heat on Nellie's cheeks intensified. That was such a ridiculous idea it was laughable. She picked up the tray again and took it through to the kitchen.

'And is there anything else I can get you?' the valet was saying when she returned. 'Perhaps I could bring back some shaving gear, a change of clothes…' he looked around the room and scowled '…and other items to make your stay here as comfortable as possible.'

Nellie shook her head. The valet really was a disapproving snob, but that was no more than she would have expected.

'Well, gentlemen, I'll leave you to organise everything you need. I have a business to run.'

'Thank you, Miss Regan. You're very…' He smiled. Nellie smiled back. He was obviously going to tell her she was very kind, then realised she had already told him to stop saying that. 'Thank you, Miss Regan, for everything you've done.'

She paused for a second, as if reluctant to leave him in anyone else's care, then gave herself a little shake. The valet was more than capable of looking after him and, from the pinched expression on his face, was impatient for Nellie to leave.

She headed down the stairs and was greeted by the wide-eyed curiosity of Harriet and Matilda, who were anxiously waiting to find out what all the commotion was.

When the flurry of questions had died down, Nellie recounted everything that had happened since they had left The Hanged Man last night, although she chose to leave out any reference to her surreptitious kiss and

Mr Lockhart's equally surreptitious observation of her washing this morning.

The memory of how he had looked at her was something Nellie doubted she would ever forget. Despite the state of his bloodshot, swollen eyes, she could see the smouldering of desire in his gaze. It was as if he wanted to devour her. She also doubted she would forget her own reaction. She had loved the way he had looked at her. She should have covered herself up immediately. Instead she'd wanted to reveal more of herself to him, had wanted him to continue looking at her, admiring her, desiring her.

She shook her head to drive out that memory and dragged in a few, quick breaths. Now was most definitely not the time to remember this morning's encounter. She had work to do.

Once again, they were fully booked all day with women wanting their hair styled and Matilda and Harriet were kept busy with customers dropping in to purchase ornamentations for their hair and hats, and discreet beauty products. While Nellie chatted to her clients and curled and clipped their hair, it was hard to not let her thoughts stray to Mr Lockhart and all that had happened. Something she knew she should not be doing. Yes, they had shared an intimate moment this morning and, yes, he had obviously been attracted to her. But then what man wouldn't react when he saw a woman in her nightdress? It didn't mean anything more than he was a normal man with normal reactions. He was an engaged man from a different world from the one Nellie inhabited and she needed to remember that at all times.

After all, she was not some silly shop girl fantasising about a rich gentleman. She was a businesswoman with much more important things to concern herself with. And she was sure Mr Lockhart would not be thinking of her or getting all giddy and ridiculous.

The valet left and at mid-morning he returned, laden down with goods and followed by two foot-men carrying a small bed, hamper baskets, suitcases and heavens knew what else. You'd think Mr Lock-hart was going on a long sea voyage, not recuperat-ing from his injuries on the other side of the same city from where he lived.

He was also accompanied by a man in a black suit, carrying a black doctor's bag, who rushed up-stairs without greeting Nellie, then a few minutes later walked back downstairs and left, again without ex-changing a word with anyone in the shop.

The valet poked his head into the parlour before he left. He gave Nellie strict instructions on what meals she was to serve and when and informed her he would return the next day to shave Mr Lockhart again and ensure he was comfortable. He also informed her that Mr Lockhart's private physician had said that Mr Lock-hart should not be moved until they were certain he had no internal injuries. He made this statement as if it was something Nellie had been unaware of. Then, with one last disapproving look, he departed.

* * *

Nellie's day was typically busy, but between each customer she rushed upstairs to check on the now shaven Mr Lockhart, cleanly dressed in his nightshirt, but each time he either said he was fine and needed nothing or he was asleep.

At lunch time she served him a selection of delicacies packed in the hamper by his valet, although he seemed reluctant to eat more than a morsel. She left the food within easy reach and, after an admonition to eat something, returned to her parlour.

Smiling to herself she re-entered the shop. A sudden pain hit her hard in the chest, as if she'd been punched. Her throat closed up, her body froze. She drew in a deep breath, slowly exhaled and forced herself to smile in greeting.

'Hello,' Lady Cecily said. 'You must be Nellie Regan. I'm Lady Cecily and this is my father, the Duke of Ashmore.'

'Your Grace…my lady,' Nellie said, giving a small curtsy and adopting her most respectful manner. 'Mr Lockhart is upstairs. I'll show you where he is.'

'No need, my dear,' the Duke said. 'I'm sure we can find our way. You get on with whatever it is you girls do down here.' He waved his arm around the room as if what happened in such a shop was a mystery known only to women.

Nellie nodded and pointed the way to the stairs as she fought to control the guilt surging through her. But whether she felt guilty for the harm that had come to Mr Lockhart, or because of the thoughts she had had about this young woman's fiancé, or even worse, that illicit kiss and that intimate moment they had shared when she was dressing, Nellie couldn't say. Nor could she say what that other emotion was that was possessing her, although the bile burning up her throat felt uncomfortably like jealousy. An emotion she had absolutely no right to feel.

The two disappeared up the stairs.

Nellie took a step towards the door, curious to know what was being discussed. She was tempted to find an excuse to go up to her rooms, but her next client arrived and she had no option but to escort her through to the parlour.

As she styled her customer's hair, she couldn't stop her eyes from straying up to the ceiling, nor her mind from speculating about the conversation that was taking place.

She showed her customer out and was surprised to find Lady Cecily standing in the shop, looking at a display of ostrich feathers. She looked up at Nellie, not smiling, causing Nellie's mouth to go dry.

'While I'm here, Miss Regan, would you have time to style my hair? I greatly admired what you had done with the Duchess of Somerfeld's hair. And it will give us a chance to talk.'

Nellie swallowed down her objections and nodded her agreement. What on earth could Lady Cecily want to talk to her about? Whatever it was, Nellie was sure it was something she did not want to hear.

Chapter Ten

What choice did she have? Nellie had another customer booked in for this time, but she could hardly say no to Lady Cecily. Not when she had caused her fiancé to be injured. Not after she had made fun of Lady Cecily in front of her own servants. And certainly not when she had admired her fiancé's naked chest, slept snuggled up beside him, and had even stolen a sneaky kiss. She would style Lady Cecily's hair and for once she would act like the obedient and deferential servant she normally refused to be.

She quickly whispered to Harriet to tell the next customer that the daughter of the Duke of Ashmore was having her hair styled and there would be a delay. Nellie knew her customer would be so thrilled that she was in the same establishment as a high-ranking member of the aristocracy that she would be more than happy to wait.

Lady Cecily swept through to the parlour, her skirt rustling as she sat down in front of the mirror. Nellie was suddenly conscious of how she looked in the plain brown skirt and jacket. It was such a contrast to Lady Cecily, dressed in an elegant mauve-and-white-striped gown with an intricate lace collar. When Mr Lockhart saw his fiancée in all her finery, he must have thought how dowdy Nellie looked in comparison. Although his reaction this morning showed he hadn't thought her dowdy then. Nellie blushed slightly. This morning's encounter was something that should never have happened and the very reason why Lady Cecily had every right to object to her fiancé sleeping in another woman's bed.

Nellie unclipped Lady Cecily's hair and brushed out the long brown strands. 'I'm sure Mr Lockhart was pleased to see you,' she said and braced herself for an uncomfortable conversation that was no more than she deserved.

'Mmm, yes. It's very good of you to take care of him. Father has quite a lot he wants to discuss so I thought I might as well make good use of the time and get my hair done. Feel free to do it in any style you think suits me, Miss Regan. After all, you're the expert.'

Nellie nodded her agreement.

She had observed Lady Cecily at the ball and already knew exactly what sort of style would suit her. 'I'm sure Mr Lockhart will be much better soon and will be able to return home, but the doctor said he shouldn't move for a few days, so unfortunately, he's going to have to remain where he is.' She sent Lady Cecily's reflection a small reassuring smile.

'Hmm, yes, that is unfortunate,' she said, her voice flat as if discussing something of no real importance.

'But the doctor also said if there are no internal injuries he should heal really quickly as he's so young, strong and healthy.' Nellie blushed slightly, remembering his naked chest and just how healthy and strong he was.

'That's good.'

Nellie paused in the process of dividing Lady Cecily's hair into sections and took another quick look at her reflection. Did she not want to hear all about Mr Lockhart's condition, how it had happened, what the doctor had said, how long he needed to recuperate? If it was Nellie's fiancé lying beaten and bruised, she would want to know every single detail. And was she not concerned that her fiancé was lying in another woman's bed? Nellie would be very curious about that as well. More than curious. She would not stand for it. Would be insisting that she took over his care herself. But then perhaps Lady Cecily saw Nellie as just a servant, someone who could tend to her fiancé, but could never be competition for his affections. Something Nellie had to admit was true. Mr Lockhart might have said he wasn't actually in love with Lady Cecily, but she was the woman he wanted to marry, the woman he wanted to share his life with. The woman he considered suitable to be his bride.

'I have to say, the Duchess of Somerfeld did look so elegant at my engagement party,' Lady Cecily continued. 'You really are very talented. I feel quite lucky to be able to have my hair styled by the same person who did the Duchess's hair.'

'Thank you, my lady.' It seemed that all talk of Mr Lockhart had come to an end. Nellie didn't know if she was relieved that she had dodged a potentially uncomfortable conversation or shocked at Her Ladyship's lack of interest. How could she be thinking about her hair at a time like this? Once again Nellie was confounded by the behaviour of the British upper classes.

'Did you work for the Duchess in America?' Lady Cecily asked.

Nellie clipped a curl in place and began rolling up another long tress. 'Yes, I worked for the Duchess in New York when she was still Arabella van Haven. I came with her to England a year or so ago.'

Lady Cecily sighed. 'I'd love to go to America. I've heard society is much less rigid over there.'

Nellie paused in what she was doing and looked at Lady Cecily's reflection again in the mirror. She had such a wistful, dreamy look on her face. 'Yes, I suppose it is.'

Lady Cecily looked up at Nellie's reflection. 'I'd love to hear all about America. I believe people can completely reinvent themselves there, become the people they would like to be.'

Nellie nodded and teased out a series of curls. 'Well, yes, I suppose that's true. The Duchess of Somerfeld's father, Mr van Haven, was born into poverty. His father was a miner, but now he's at the very top of New York society, attends all the leading social events, is a member of all the best clubs. I don't imagine that would happen in England.'

Lady Cecily shook her head, her eyes glowing with interest. 'No, indeed not. Imagine that. The grand-daughter of a miner is now the Duchess of Somer-feld and she's also an actress. It sounds like a country where you can do whatever you want, become who-ever you want.'

'Hmm.' Nellie decided there was little point inform-ing Lady Cecily that not everyone in America became a millionaire. Many of the Irish immigrants who had travelled to America on the same ship as Nellie ended up living in the overcrowded, crime-ridden and dis-ease-infested Five Points area of New York. They were not much better off than they would have been if they'd remained in Ireland. But that was not the sort of polite conversation one made with a member of the aristoc-racy when you were styling their hair, so Nellie kept quiet on that unfortunate detail.

'And it's such a big country, isn't it?'

On that subject Nellie could be completely honest. 'Oh, yes, it's definitely a big country. Lots of wide, open spaces, that's for sure.'

'I would imagine in a big country like that a person could lose themselves, become whoever they want to and no one would be any the wiser.' She looked up at Nellie's reflection again, her eyebrows raised in ex-pectation.

'Yes, I suppose so.'

'I'm surprised the Duchess of Somerfeld left such a wonderful place where she had so much freedom.'

'Hmm.' Nellie was not sure how much of the Duchess's private life she should reveal. She wouldn't be telling Lady Cecily that the Duchess was forced to come to England by her father. Nor would she be saying that the Duchess was tricked into marrying the Duke of Somerfeld. 'Well, the Duchess is happy to be in England now. She's married to a man she loves and working as an actress, which she also loves.'

'Love.' Lady Cecily nodded. 'Yes, love changes everything, doesn't it?' She looked up at Nellie for confirmation. Nellie chose to give a non-committal smile. She had discussed love with Mr Lockhart that morning. That had been an uncomfortable conversation which she should never have had. She wasn't about to repeat her mistake by discussing love with his fiancée. Not when the mere mention of that word had set off a burning deep within her, a burning that had risen up her throat and was making her feel decidedly uncomfortable.

'It changes how you see your surroundings, the decisions you make, the actions you take,' Lady Cecily continued, oblivious to Nellie's fumbling. 'It makes you question everything. Sometimes I think we're all just slaves to that wonderful, devastating emotion.'

Nellie paused, a lock of hair in her hand, and looked at Lady Cecily's reflection. Her expression had changed from expectant when she had been talking about America to a more melancholy demeanour. She really was the most enigmatic of women. She professed to being in love, to being a slave to that emotion, yet she'd rather have her hair done than spend time with the man she loved, a man who had suffered a terrible beating and was at this very moment lying upstairs in pain.

Lady Cecily looked up, her face still wistful. 'Have you ever been in love, Miss Regan?'

The question caused fire to explode on to Nellie's cheeks. She dropped the lock of hair she was holding, then with fumbling fingers re-rolled the tress.

'Me, no, no, never.' Why Nellie should be embarrassed she had no idea. She had answered honestly. She had never been truly in love. She'd had flings that she'd enjoyed, but there'd never been anyone who she could say she loved. She'd certainly never met anyone who caused her to question everything, the decisions she made, the actions she took, or made her see her surroundings differently, as Lady Cecily claimed love made you do.

Lady Cecily inclined her head and raised her eyebrows. 'That blush makes me think there is someone special in your life. You're very lucky and I hope he loves you back.'

'No, no, there's no one, honestly.' Why did Mr Lockhart's handsome face enter her mind when she made that denial? Nellie shook her head slightly to drive out that unwanted image. She was most emphatically not falling in love with Mr Lockhart. The mere thought of it was ludicrous. And she should not even be having such a thought, particularly in the presence of his fiancée.

She put down the hairclip she was clasping, which had somehow become bent out of shape, and picked up another one.

But if she was having these ludicrous thoughts about Mr Lockhart, perhaps she *should* find a nurse to tend to him, if his presence in her bed was causing her to become so disorientated and to act so strangely, especially in front of his fiancée.

She looked at the new hairclip, which had also strangely become bent out of shape.

'No, I am not in love,' Nellie stated emphatically. She met eyes with Lady Cecily in the mirror and was itching to ask her if she was in love with Mr Lockhart. If she was, why had she danced with him as if she had no desire to even touch him? Why was she sitting down here, having her hair done, instead of upstairs with the man she was engaged to be married to? But they were questions she could not possibly ask and ones she suspected she wouldn't want to hear the answers to.

Instead she put the finishing touches to Lady Cecily's hair in silence. When she had finished, she stood back to assess her work. Despite her fumbling fingers she was pleased with the result and looked at Lady Cecily to see if she liked it.

She patted the voluminous rolls on her head and nodded her approval. 'Oh, Miss Regan, that's wonderful. I'm so pleased.' She stood up, admired her reflection one more time, then walked out to the shop front.

'Thank you so much and I did so enjoy our little chat about America. It sounds like a wonderful country.' She gave a little laugh, which sounded forced. 'Perhaps we should all emigrate there and improve our position in life.'

Nellie responded with a small, polite smile. For a

woman who was the daughter of a duke and about to marry a man who was fabulously wealthy Lady Cecily hardly needed to emigrate to America to improve her position in society—she already was as high as she could possibly go.

Nellie expected her to go upstairs and show off her new look to Mr Lockhart, but she seemed content to examine the beauty products and accessories on display while she waited for her father.

Nellie's next customer also seemed more interested in observing Lady Cecily than moving through to the parlour, so Nellie just let her be.

Before long a man's boots sounded on the wooden stairs and the Duke of Ashmore appeared in the shop, causing the awestruck client to simper and smile with delight.

'Looks like you're doing a fine job looking after that young man,' the Duke said. 'He couldn't be in better hands, could he, my dear?' The Duke approached Harriet with the intention of paying for his daughter's hair styling, but Nellie waved her hand to let him know there was no charge.

'Right kind of you, my dear, but I suppose the cost is already being covered.' The Duke gave a curious laugh and sent Nellie a quick wink.

Lady Cecily put back the combs she had been observing and turned to the Duke. 'If you're finished, Father, shall we depart? I want to do some shopping before we leave London.'

It seemed this was to be their only visit to Mr Lockhart. Nellie would have expected Lady Cecily to want to stay in town, visit him every day, even keep vigil by his bed until he was better. Wasn't that what you should do for the man you intend to marry? It would appear not.

The Duke of Ashmore opened the door for his daughter and Nellie accompanied them out of the shop. Lady Cecily took the footman's hand and entered the waiting carriage. Once she was inside the Duke turned to Nellie.

'I just want to let you know I have no objection to Dominic keeping a mistress—after all, what man doesn't?' he whispered. 'And I thank you for your discretion in front of my daughter. But if my daughter ever finds out, then I'll ruin Dominic, and that won't be good for you either, so bear that in mind, my dear.' With that he walked off briskly to the carriage and drove off down the street, leaving a disorientated Nellie standing at the open door of her shop wondering whether she had heard correctly.

'Nellie, are you all right?' Harriet asked.

Nellie retreated into the shop and tried to make sense of what the Duke had just said. He thought she was Mr Lockhart's mistress. What's more, he didn't care, as long as his daughter didn't know. She looked at her two assistants and the smiling customer. It seemed no one had heard the Duke's outrageous words, but that didn't diminish Nellie's shock.

But she had to pull herself together, she still had work to do. She ushered her customer into the parlour and, as expected, the woman seem to take it as a personal compliment that she'd had to wait for someone as esteemed as the daughter of the Duke of Ashmore and that was all she wanted to talk about.

Nellie let her prattle on, while her mind tried to make sense of the Duke's shocking accusation. He didn't care if Dominic had a mistress. Did Lady Cecily care? Did Dominic? She had no idea. The only thing she knew for certain was it was something about which *she* cared very much.

Chapter Eleven

Nellie slowly climbed the stairs at the end of her busy working day. It wasn't weariness that was causing her to be so sluggish—she enjoyed her work and was energised by it. She was suddenly uncomfortable about having Mr Lockhart in her rooms. Perhaps she shouldn't have been so stubborn. She should have let the valet arrange for a nurse to attend to him while she stayed at a hotel. Then there would be no confusion. The Duke of Ashmore would realise she was merely someone who was helping Mr Lockhart in his time of need and was most definitely not his mistress. And she would also be clear in her own mind. Having him in her rooms, insisting that she alone would nurse him back to health, did suggest that she felt something for Mr Lockhart. *Did* she feel something for him, other than compassion because of his injuries and guilt because she was the cause of them?

She paused on the stairs. Her feelings might be confused, but one thing she knew for certain. The Duke was wrong. She did not want to be Mr Lockhart's mistress. She did not want to be any man's mistress. The Duke was right that men from his class often kept a woman of Nellie's class as their little bit on the side. But he was wrong about Nellie. She would never become involved in such an arrangement. She would never be some rich man's plaything.

She continued walking up the stairs. But who cared what the Duke of Ashmore thought? Not her, that was for sure. He meant nothing to her. So, she wasn't going to change her living arrangements just to prove the Duke wrong. She didn't want to stay in a hotel. Nor did she want some stranger in her rooms. And she certainly did not want that condescending valet thinking that he could order her around and tell her what to do in her own home. He might be able to boss around the rest of Mr Lockhart's servants, but he couldn't boss *her* around.

She reached the top of the stairs, puffed up with indignation at the very idea that the valet thought he could tell her what to do. Then she paused at the door, gripping the handle and took in a few breaths. Mr Lockhart did not need her self-righteous indignation, nor her offended pride. She would forget all about what the Duke had said, forget that look of disapproval from the valet and put aside her confused emotions. Instead, she would concentrate on the task at hand, making sure Mr Lockhart recovered from his injuries as quickly as possible so he could return home. Opening the door, she put on her sunniest smile.

'How are you feeling now?' she asked, her voice sounding overly jolly.

He smiled at her, then winced when given a painful reminder of his split lip. 'Much better, thank you. The pain is easing so I don't think I've got a broken rib or have any other internal damage. Both doctors said if the pain gets better it's a good sign.'

Nellie continued to smile, determined not to feel uncomfortable in his company, determined not to think about what the Duke had said. 'That's excellent news,' she trilled. 'Now, I dare say you're ready for something to eat. Shall we see what else your valet has sent you?'

Nellie went through to her small kitchen, where the table was piled with wicker baskets.

She opened one, peered in the top and saw an array of pies, cheeses, cartons of tea, bread, slices of cold meat, dried and fresh fruit, and jars of soup. *Impressive.* She warmed up some soup, poured it into two bowls, cut some slices of bread and carried one of the bowls through to the invalid.

'Here you go. Fresh vegetable soup, prepared by my own fair hands, or at least prepared by the fair hands of your cook, delivered by the fair hands of your valet and served by me.'

He smiled as she placed the tray on his lap. 'Are you having something to eat? You must be famished after your busy day.'

'Yes, your valet brought enough food to feed the entire street. We're certainly not going to go hungry.' Nellie went back to the kitchen and returned with her bowl of steaming soup on a tray. She tasted it and sighed with contented approval. How wonderful it must be to have someone on your staff who could create such delicious fare.

'It was nice of Lady Cecily and the Duke of Ashmore to visit,' Nellie asked as casually as possible. 'I hope Lady Cecily wasn't too upset when she saw the state of you.'

She certainly wasn't upset when she was having her hair styled, but perhaps that was just the impassive face she put on in front of the lower orders. Nor did she seem to share the concerns of her father. It seemed she saw Nellie as merely a servant performing her duties, and not as a real woman who could possibly pose a threat. Not that Nellie saw herself in those terms either. She blushed slightly and took another sip of her soup to cover her awkwardness.

'Hmm,' he said, revealing nothing to Nellie.

'And I hope the Duke didn't think it strange that you were recuperating here?' she probed, looking at him carefully to see his reaction.

His lips tightened slightly, but he made no other reaction. 'No, the Duke didn't think it strange.' It was another response that revealed little to Nellie.

She took another spoonful of soup. Had the Duke said anything to Mr Lockhart about Nellie being his mistress and, if he had, how had Mr Lockhart responded? They were questions Nellie was longing to ask, but couldn't. Usually she had no qualms about discussing anything with anyone. But this was different. Nellie didn't know why, but it was.

He lowered his spoon and stared at her. She braced

herself, determined that she would not be embarrassed by the conversation to come. If he was going to discuss the Duke's preposterous assumptions, she would respond sensibly and not be unnerved in the slightest. After all, she had nothing to feel embarrassed about.

'How did you know what Lady Cecily and I looked like when we were dancing together?'

'What?' Nellie shook her head, taken by surprise. It was not the question she was expecting from him.

'It's just occurred to me. You were making fun of me and Lady Cecily, but you had never met either of us before.'

'Oh, that.' Nellie laughed in relief. 'I'd been watching from up on the minstrels' gallery above the ballroom.'

He raised an eyebrow. 'Really? You were spying on us?' His slight smile told Nellie that he was not criticising her, merely teasing.

She shrugged her shoulders. 'Well, that wasn't really my intention. I wanted to observe the ladies at the ball, to see what fashions they were wearing and how their lady's maids had styled their hair.'

'Oh, I suppose I can forgive you then,' he said, still smiling.

Nellie smiled at him and took another sip of her soup. 'Are Lady Cecily and her father going to visit you again tomorrow?' Nellie was unsure why she had brought the conversation back to Lady Cecily's and the Duke's visit. Not when it made her so uncomfortable. It was like prodding a wound just to remind yourself how much it hurt.

'No, I've told them there is no need. I'm perfectly all right.' He looked up at her and smiled. 'And that I'm being well cared for.'

Nellie was pleased. She would not have to see the Duke again, but was still surprised that Lady Cecily didn't insist that she visit her fiancé. Perhaps she was waiting till he returned home. Perhaps she didn't like visiting Nellie's rooms, although she'd seemed perfectly comfortable in Nellie's hairdressing parlour.

'And I suppose your family will want to visit you as well,' Nellie asked.

He shook his head. 'I've given my valet instructions to not tell my sisters what happened. I don't want them worried. Instead he'll just send them a note to say I've been delayed in London for a while.'

Nellie nodded. 'And your parents?'

He shifted slightly in the bed. 'My parents are both dead.'

Nellie's spoon halted, halfway to her mouth. She lowered it to her bowl. 'Oh, I'm so sorry.'

He shook his head slightly. 'It was a while ago now.'

'But it still hurts, doesn't it?' Nellie was unsure whether she was speaking about the death of Mr Lockhart's parents or her own.

'Hmm.' Once again his response revealed nothing.

She looked over at him, her head inclined, waiting for him to explain further.

He sighed slightly. 'My mother died in childbirth when I was still at school and my father died not long after I finished my education. He had a recurrence of an illness he'd suffered from when he was a child and it affected his heart.'

He continued eating his soup as if that explained everything, but Nellie suspected that his curt response hid a wealth of pain.

'My parents also died when I was young,' she said quietly. 'It was scarlet fever and it took a lot of other people in my village as well.' Nellie rarely told people about her parents and was unsure why she was telling Mr Lockhart, but the words were out before she had time to consider her reasoning.

He stopped eating and looked at her, his brow furrowed. 'I'm so sorry, Nellie... Miss Regan. Did you have brothers, sisters, other family members?'

She shook her head. 'No, Mam was always poorly and I was her only child. They were both orphans.' She blinked a few times to brush away some pesky tears.

'I'm sorry. I was lucky, in that I had my sisters, Amanda, Violet and Emmaline. They're a responsibility and, as the eldest, I had to be strong when my parents died so I could care for them. Not that I begrudge that for one moment. I adore my sisters and will do anything for them.' He gave a small laugh. 'These bruises are proof of that. I'd even take a beating so my eldest sister can have her hair done by the famous Nellie Regan.'

She smiled at him, unshed tears still in her eyes.

'But it must have been hard for you, Nellie... Miss Regan, left all alone. What did you do? How did you cope?'

She blinked a few times and took in a deep breath.

'When they died, I knew I'd have to go into service, just as my mam had done before me. Then I heard you could get passage to America as there were wealthy people out there looking for servants. I decided if I was going to have to be someone else's skivvy I might as well make an adventure out of it, so I booked passage to New York.'

He was staring at her intently, still not eating. 'All by yourself? How old were you?'

'Thirteen.'

He shook his head slowly. 'Thirteen? That's so young. You are very brave.'

She shrugged off his compliment. 'Well, I've had to be, haven't I?' She picked up his bowl and piled it up on her tray, the bowls clashing together in her impatience. She wanted this conversation to end, even though she had started it.

He smiled at her, a sympathetic smile.

Nellie strode back into the kitchen. She did not need his sympathy, nor did she want his compliments. She had made her way in the world surviving however she could. It was no more than many other women in her situation had been forced to do and there was no point dwelling on misfortunes that were now in the past.

She looked into the hamper and with food like this on offer she did not feel unfortunate in the slightest. She put together a selection of cheeses, cold meats, fruit and slices of pie.

'I'll have to rescue men on a regular basis if I get to eat this well.' Nellie laughed as she carried through the tray and placed it on the bed. 'We can have a delicious picnic among the bedcovers.'

She looked over at his bruised face and stopped laughing. 'Sorry, that was cheeky. I didn't mean it and I'm sorry for what happened to you.'

He waved his hand in dismissal. 'Not your fault, but a picnic among the bedcovers is some compensation.' He smiled cautiously, trying to avoid further splitting his lip.

They chatted pleasantly throughout the meal, with Mr Lockhart asking her about her day, her business and her plans for the future.

When they'd finished eating Nellie returned their plates to the kitchen and boiled some water for the dishes. It almost felt like a comfortable domestic situation and Nellie found herself singing as she washed and dried the dishes and put away the plates.

She returned to the room and made up her bed for the evening. 'You must be getting a bit bored. Would you like some books to read?'

He pointed to his eyes. One was badly swollen, the other horribly bloodshot. 'Thank you, but it will be a bit hard to read with these eyes.'

Nellie nodded. 'Would you like me to read to you?'

'Yes, very much.'

Nellie picked up her collection of Sherlock Holmes stories and settled down to read 'A Scandal in Bohemia'. As he listened, Nellie smiled to herself. She could think of no better way to end her day than this cosy domestic scene, although it would be nicer if the man in her bed was there from choice and not because of Patrick Kelly's big fists.

Dominic lay back on the pillows and let her gentle Irish voice wash over him as she recounted the antics of the fictional consulting detective and his trusty companion, Dr Watson. He missed much of the story as he was too occupied looking at the reader. She was obviously enjoying reading to him. Her brow furrowed during the serious bits, a small smile alighted her lips during the humorous events, and every so often she looked up at him, so they could share a particularly interesting part.

It had been years since anyone had read to him. Not since his mother had died, ten years ago, giving birth to his youngest sister. Since then it had been his role to read to his sisters when they were young, a task that Amanda later took over from him.

If the Duke of Ashmore could see them now it would put paid to his assumption that he was having a torrid affair with Nellie Regan. The Duke had jumped to conclusions, although he had expressed no objections to the idea that Miss Regan was Dominic's mistress. The only time he'd shown any objections to anything during their visit was when Cecily had said she wanted to go downstairs and have her hair styled. The Duke had been adamant that she should remain in the room with them. It wasn't until Dominic assured him that it would be all right that the Duke had relented. He had assumed Dominic was informing him that Miss Regan knew how to be discreet, rather than letting him know that she was not his mistress.

And he'd been happy to see Cecily's departure. She had stood by his bed, looking uncomfortable, as if unsure what she was supposed to do or say. Visiting an injured fiancé was obviously not something she expected to be one of her duties as an engaged woman.

Once Cecily had left, the Duke had made it perfectly clear that he all but expected Dominic to have a mistress and that it would have no effect on his marriage to his daughter. The Duke had said he had no delusions about what the relationship between a husband and a wife was. It was an arrangement for the mutual benefit of both families. He'd even said he envied Dominic for having such an attractive mistress.

And that was one thing the Duke was right about. She certainly was attractive. Although he doubted Nellie Regan would consent to be any man's kept woman—she was too feisty and independent for that.

Although there was no denying it was a tempting proposition. Despite his injuries, spending time in her humble room, chatting to her, had been an enjoyable experience. The most pleasure he'd had for as long as he could remember. And their picnic among the bedclothes had been fun. It would have been even more fun if she really was his mistress and it had occurred after they had made love.

Visions of how she looked this morning, with the sun streaming through her nightgown, once again invaded his mind. He remembered her shapely body, her full breasts, her tiny waist, her rounded hips and the curve of her bottom, and groaned quietly.

She stopped reading and stood up, her face pinched with worry. 'Are you in pain? Your valet packed some laudanum. Do you need some?'

Dominic waved her away. Laudanum was not what he needed, being able to feel those luscious curves, to have her in his bed, writhing beneath him, that would relieve the ache that was consuming his body. But that was out of the question. 'I don't need laudanum. Please, just continue reading.' *And don't come so close to me that I can smell your tempting scent of fresh roses, so close I could reach out and caress those curves I so long to touch.*

What was *wrong* with him?

Nellie Regan was helping him. Without her he would have been left bleeding in the street, vulnerable to further attack. She had given up her bed for him and he was repaying that debt by lusting after her. That was something he had to get under control. Perhaps he should ask for some laudanum after all, to block out these wild, inappropriate thoughts.

He forced himself to concentrate on the story she was reading, only to realise it was the tale of an engaged man who had an affair with another woman, whom he was in love with but couldn't marry because she was of the wrong class. Of all the stories she could have picked, why on earth did she choose that one?

When it was finished Nellie looked up at him, a slight blush on her face. 'It's all a bit of nonsense really, but Arthur Conan Doyle definitely tells an exciting yarn.'

He nodded his agreement. Of course, it was a bit of nonsense. Falling in love with the wrong person, wasn't that exactly what his parents had done? They had let passions rule their lives and look where it had got them. Fortunately, Dominic was not like them. He had made a sensible arrangement with Cecily. He just had to remember that and stop these ludicrous images and thoughts from invading his mind.

She closed the book and put it on the bedside table. 'Well, you must be tired. I certainly am.' She looked over at the small bed.

'I'm sorry you had to sleep in your armchair last night and that I'm still taking your bed. I did ask Burgess to move me to the smaller bed but, most unlike him, he refused.'

For some reason her blushing cheeks turned a deeper shade of pink. 'I was perfectly comfortable last night. And your valet was quite right. Until we know for certain that you haven't broken a rib you mustn't move. Doctor's orders. That bed will be comfortable enough, I'm sure.'

She disappeared into the adjoining room and he was tormented by the sound of rustling fabric as she discarded her clothing. He tried hard not to listen. He tried not to think about her slowly peeling away the layers of clothing that kept her body from his appraising gaze. Fought not to remember what she looked like in her thin, near-translucent nightdress. He absolutely must not think of that. He tried to divert his mind with other thoughts—of those thugs and their rock-hard fists pummelling him, of the pain that was consuming every inch of his body, of his shocking, bruised face when the valet showed him his reflection in the shaving mirror— anything so he wouldn't think of that lovely woman and her even lovelier curves.

She emerged from behind the door. Was he relieved to see she was wearing a thick dressing gown or disappointed? Relieved, surely. But her hair was now released from its restricting clips and hung down her back in a long, thick plait. Why did women go to so much trouble over their hair when seeing it hanging free was so much more attractive?

'Well, I need to get some sleep, I've got another busy day tomorrow and I'm sure the more rest you get the quicker you'll heal.' With that she extinguished the lamp and plunged them into darkness. But that did not extinguish his thoughts or his senses. In the silence he heard the bedclothes being pulled back and the sound of her climbing into bed. She had said he needed rest, but with her lying so close, yet so far away, for him sleep seemed an impossible dream.

Chapter Twelve

Dominic woke the next day after an all-but-sleepless night. He had lain awake in agony for hours and it wasn't just due to his beaten body. Listening to Nellie's soft breathing as she slept had been pure torture. The darkness of the room prevented him from seeing her sleeping body, but he still couldn't shake the image of her lying in her bed, dressed only in her thin muslin nightgown. He was tormented by the memory of those luscious, tempting curves, that soft white skin, those shining green eyes, those full, sensual lips.

Lying awake, he came to a firm decision. He could not spend another day in this room and certainly not another night. It was more than any man should be expected to endure. Even if he did have a broken rib, even if it did pierce his lung or cause other life-threatening damage, he could not stay in this room. He could not endure another night of such torture. He had to leave.

A little later in the morning she rose from the bed and he had one fleeting vision of her in her nightgown before she covered up her body with her dressing gown. Quietly she took some clothes from the wardrobe and carried them through to the other room. It seemed she was sensibly not going to get ready for the day in the same room as him. Shame washed through him at the memory of how he had watched her at her toilette yesterday morning. And despite that shame he knew he would be incapable of not watching her again. Fortunately, she was taking the precaution of avoiding his predatory eye.

If he needed any more convincing that it was time he left, his despicable desire to watch this young woman who had offered her home to him, given up her bed for him and shown him such kindness, would provide it.

She emerged from behind the door, fully dressed and ready for her working day. A war of relief and disappointment raged within him. Relief that his self-control would not be tested once again, but disappointment that he was not to get one last look at her in her nightgown, her long red hair flowing freely down her back.

Despite fighting to keep those two reactions under control, he still couldn't help but notice how stunning she looked. Dressed in a plain brown outfit she was still a vision. She couldn't look more elegant, even if she was wearing an expensive gown and dripping with priceless gems.

She smiled at him, a smile as bright and welcome as the sun emerging from behind clouds. Her smile should have given him pleasure, but it only intensified his disappointment. This would be the last time he would be greeted in the morning by that glorious smile.

He sat up in the bed. Despite his injuries he forced his face to not register the pain that shot through him. 'I'm feeling much better this morning. It must have been because I had a good night's sleep.' *Liar.* 'There's no pain at all now.' *Liar, liar.* 'I believe it is time I returned home.'

Her smile quivered slightly, then returned just as bright, if perhaps a little forced. 'Oh, that is good news. I'm so pleased you're on the mend.' Her voice sounded strained. Was she also disappointed? Surely not. She must be looking forward to getting her life back and her rooms to herself.

'I'll make you some breakfast before you go.'

He shook his head. The sooner he left the better. Even sharing breakfast with this enchanting woman seemed a greater intimacy than he could bear. 'No, I don't wish to impose on you any longer.'

I don't want to impose my inappropriate desires on you.

'I'll eat when I get home.'

She looked towards the other room. 'It's no problem. Your valet brought plenty of food and it will only take me a few seconds to put something together.'

'Please, don't trouble yourself,' he said more harshly than he intended.

She looked back at him, her face registering her surprise at his tone.

'I'm sorry, but I've imposed on your hospitality long enough and I want to get home as soon as possible.'

He forced himself to smile, to show he was not being insulting. 'I've been away from home for far too long. My sisters must be starting to wonder about my absence. I don't want to worry them.' Finally, he was telling the truth.

'Oh, yes, right.' She bit her lip lightly. 'I'll go and fetch your valet so he can organise your carriage to take you home.'

'There's no need. I can get a cab.' Dominic wanted to end this torture as soon as possible and there was always the danger that between the two of them, Burgess and Miss Regan, they would decide what was best for his health and make him stay. Although if either could see into his mind both would be horrified and would insist that he leave these rooms immediately.

'It's no imposition. I'm happy to do it,' she said quietly.

He was being a cad. She was only trying to help and he was snapping at her, all because of this absurd attraction, this almost overwhelming desire for her. Regret at his harsh tone joined the war of emotions raging within him.

'Thank you, Miss Regan,' he said, keeping his voice as even as possible. 'But I'll just get dressed and then I'll hail a cab.'

She remained standing in the middle of the room, then her cheeks turned that delightful shade of pink. 'Oh, yes, right. I'll give you some privacy, shall I, so you can get dressed?' She turned and rushed out of the room.

Dominic slowly moved to the side of the bed and

swung his legs to the floor. He paused with his hands on the edge to take a few steadying breaths, than heaved himself into an upright position. Wincing with pain, he picked up the neatly folded clean shirt, the trousers and jacket his valet had left him. Slowly he pulled off his nightshirt, eased on his shirt over his battered body and pulled on his trousers and jacket. He clipped on his collar and tied his cravat around his neck and looked at himself in Nellie's small mirror.

The abomination he saw before him was a shock. His eyes were red and swollen, his face a range of colours, from black and blue to shades of green and yellow. He smiled ruefully at his reflection. He might have had to fight to resist the abundant charms of Miss Regan, but looking as he did he doubted it would have required any effort on her part to resist him. If anything, it was amazing she could bear to look at him.

Fully dressed, it was time for him to leave. He looked around the room as if committing every inch of it to his memory. He would never see this delightful room again. It was small, it was humble, but like Nellie Regan herself it was cheerful and welcoming. He looked back at the unmade bed, at the hand-stitched patchwork quilt that had covered him for the last two days. He ran his hand across the embroidered cushion on her armchair where she had kindly spent the first night while he had selfishly taken her bed. He stroked the fine lace cover on her washstand. Opening a bottle of perfume, he closed his eyes and inhaled the familiar scent of roses. It was Nellie's scent, a scent that was on the bedclothes, a scent that had tormented him as he had tried to sleep. He was tempted to slip the bottle into his pocket so he would have a lasting reminder of her.

Realising what he was doing, he quickly screwed the lid back on the bottle and replaced it on the washstand. The beating he had received had not only caused swelling and bruising, it had obviously caused some damage to his brain. It was making him behave in a foolish, sentimental manner. The sooner he left and returned to his real life the better.

Slowly he walked down the stairs, being careful not to cause any more damage to his battered body. As he neared the last few steps, he forced his pace to increase, dragged his body into an upright position and removed all expression from his face. He did not want to betray that he was still in pain. It was essential to look completely recovered so Miss Regan would not argue that he should stay. It was an argument that he was unsure he might not allow himself to lose.

He entered the shop and the gasps from Nellie's two assistants reminded him of just how terrible he looked. They continued to stare at him in wide-eyed shock as Miss Regan rushed over to him.

'Are you sure you're all right?' She placed her hand on his arm. 'You don't look too good. You've gone quite pale. Well, you're black and blue, but under that you're pale.'

He waved his hand in dismissal. 'I'm fine. I'm sure I look much worse than I feel. It's time I returned home.' His voice came out more clipped than he intended as he fought not to wince in reaction to the pain that was racking his body.

'Well, I'll walk with you to the end of the street where you should be able to hail a hansom cab.'

She held out her arm for him to take, as if he were an invalid, and smiled up at him. Dominic hesitated. The desire to touch this lovely young woman one last time was all but overwhelming. It was a desire that he should not be feeling for so many reasons. He was an engaged man. He was going to marry another woman. And until he had met Nellie Regan that was a situation that he was completely satisfied with. It was exactly what he wanted. But spending two nights and days with this lovely woman had made him question whether it was indeed what he wanted.

He drew in a deep breath. Another good reason why he had to leave, right now. Once he left this place he would once again see that he had exactly what he wanted. He would remember all the reasons why marrying Cecily Hardgrave was the right thing to do. The only reason he was questioning it now was because during the time he had spent with Nellie Regan in that small room an unexpected intimacy had developed between them, one that would never happen under usual circumstances. They were from different worlds and now he was returning to his real life and leaving her to her own world.

Her smile started to quiver as he continued to hesitate. He was being unforgivably rude. He took her arm. 'I can walk unaccompanied, you know, but thank you,' he said, his words once again clipped.

He opened the door for her and they walked down the street, arm in arm, to the busy intersection. The first cab he hailed stopped and once again that sense of disappointment descended on him.

'Thank you for everything you've done, Miss Regan,' he said as he opened the cab door. 'You've been most kind.'

And I've repaid your kindness by having inappropriate thoughts, unacceptable desires.

'You have nothing to thank me for. And I've already told you I'm not kind at all.' She smiled to show she was teasing.

Dominic remained staring down at her, his hand on the cab door, as if incapable of leaving.

'And will you still be available to style my sister's hair?'

She smiled and nodded. 'As I said, it's the least I can do after all that I've put you through.'

He declined to remind her once again that it hadn't been her fault that he had ended up black and blue. And the torment she had put him through was all of his own making. It certainly wasn't her fault that she was beautiful, charming and enticing.

He coughed lightly to drive out that thought. 'Thank you. And I know how much you resent being treated as a servant.'

'Well, I...'

He waved away her protests. 'You can be assured you will not be treated as a servant when you come to Lockhart Estate. You will be given the respect you deserve as a businesswoman. And everyone in the household will be made aware of that fact.'

'You don't need to go to that much trouble, really.'

'Yes, I do and it's not trouble. You will be well compensated for your time. I will arrange for first-class train tickets to be sent to you and for transport to and from the station. The coachman will be instructed to take you back to the station whenever you require. I hope that will be satisfactory.'

'More than satisfactory.'

He remained standing at the cab door. There was nothing more to say, except goodbye, but that simple word would not come.

The impatient horse snorted. 'Ready when you are, guvnor,' the driver said.

Dominic had no choice. It was time to leave. 'Goodbye, Miss Regan,' he said quietly.

'Goodbye, Mr Lockhart.' She sent him a surprisingly shy smile.

He climbed into the cab and shut the door. As he drove off through the busy London street a heaviness settled on him, as if he had lost something that he would never find again.

Chapter Thirteen

Lockhart Estate was even grander than Nellie had expected. Mr Lockhart's Belgravia town house had stated loud and clear that he was a man of wealth, but this magnificent three-storey mansion, surrounded by sweeping lawns adorned with fountains and statues, clearly showed that he was every bit as wealthy as the aristocracy he so blatantly wanted to join.

The carriage drove up the long, tree-lined drive, through the ornate gold and black wrought-iron gates and past the formal garden in front of the house. Nellie fought hard not to be overawed by the grandeur. But she was fighting a losing battle. How could she not be overawed by such splendid surroundings? How could she not wonder what he thought of her humble little rooms above her shop and parlour?

If Nellie still harboured any foolish illusions about herself and Mr Lockhart, this house had swept them all away. Even fantasising that a man who lived in such a place could ever mean anything to her was so ludicrous it was laughable. This was his world and it was as far removed from Nellie's small business and two-room living quarters as it was possible to get.

He had the wealth. Now all he needed was the position in society, and Lady Cecily would provide that. He might have shown a spark of interest in a former servant with a small but growing business, when he was recovering in her rooms, but that's all it ever would be, a tiny spark of interest that would never ignite into a bigger flame.

The carriage pulled up in front of the grand entrance. Nellie looked up at the imposing façade containing so many arched windows it seemed impossible to count them all. The house was big enough to accommodate all the families in her neighbourhood, with plenty of room to spare.

She lowered her head and remained frozen in her seat. She was going to stay in this home that was nothing short of a mansion. She had visited other stately homes when she was a lady's maid, but this time it was different. She was the one who had been invited, not her mistress. She wasn't going to be sleeping in the servants' quarters. She was almost, but not quite, a guest.

This was what she wanted. She had made it clear that she was not a servant and would not be treated like one. But perhaps she should have just accepted her place. Perhaps she shouldn't have tried to be grander, more important than she actually was. Nellie drew in a long, sustaining breath and exhaled slowly. It was too late to turn back now.

Oh, well, Nellie Regan, you've made your bed and

now you're going to have to lie in it. At least you'll be lying in a comfortable, feather bed with silk bedcovers.

She looked away from the splendid house and stared straight ahead. She could do this. She just had to re-member to behave herself, for once in her life.

Remember, you've already caused enough trouble for Mr Lockhart. So, no insults, no impersonations and no snide comments about the idle rich. You will be polite, courteous and a right little lady at all times.

The footman opened the door and helped her out of the carriage. Nellie forced herself to act as if arriving at the front door of such a stunning stately home was an everyday event for her.

The large, intricately carved wooden doors flew open and a smiling young woman raced down the stairs. 'Miss Regan?' she called out as she ran.

When Nellie nodded, the young woman's smile grew even bigger. 'I'm Amanda Lockhart. I'm so pleased you could come.' She clasped both of Nellie's hands. 'It's so good of you to agree to do my hair for tonight's ball. I couldn't believe it when Dominic told me, I was so thrilled.'

Still chatting excitedly, she led Nellie up the stairs and through the house. Nellie tried not to stare as they walked through the magnificent entrance hall, with its domed stained-glass roof, pink-marble tiled floors and columns, walls adorned with paintings, and statues, urns and antiques. Nellie gripped the carved wooden banister to steady herself as Miss Lockhart raced her up the marble stairs, then quickly followed her as she all but ran along the long corridor to her room.

She sat down at her dressing table and turned to smile at Nellie. 'Right, Nellie, shall we start on my hair now, then, if you'll be so kind, you can help me into my gown.'

Nellie's tense body relaxed. This was what she had come to Lockhart Estate for. Now she was in her element, doing what she knew she was good at. She brushed out Miss Lockhart's long hair and observed her face structure and appearance in the gilt-edged mirror to decide which style would best suit her.

'Now we're alone,' Miss Lockhart said, her voice lowered as if they weren't alone and she might be overheard, 'you must tell me all about what happened to Dominic. He's hardly said a thing, just that he had been set upon by some vagabonds when he was down in London and that you came to his rescue. So, what really did happen?'

Nellie recounted another edited version of the events that led up to Mr Lockhart being set upon by Patrick Kelly and his mates. She chose to downplay the part where Nellie had put Mr Lockhart in a compromising position by inviting him to The Hanged Man. And she thought it wise not to mention how she had been worried that he was going to tell her off because of her somewhat risqué impersonation following the engagement party. She most certainly did not mention how she had stolen an illicit kiss from him as he slept, or how his body had expressed its interest in her when he had caught her getting washed in the morning.

Miss Lockhart listened with wide-eyed interest as Nellie gave her vivid account of the attack and how, although he had been outnumbered, the men had shown him no mercy.

Miss Lockhart shook her head slowly and put her hand on Nellie's arm. 'That must have been terrifying for you, Miss Regan. I hope you weren't too scared.'

'No, I was more concerned for Mr Lockhart and I felt so guilty for causing him so much trouble.'

Miss Lockhart's brows knitted together. 'It wasn't your fault. You didn't attack him. And it's so like Dominic to forget about himself when he thinks someone else is being treated badly. I can just imagine him jumping in to defend a lady's honour, without a thought to his own safety.' She sighed and turned back to face the mirror. 'Although sometimes I wish he'd think of himself a bit more.'

Nellie began rolling up Miss Lockhart's long brown hair. 'Oh, what do you mean?' Nellie forced her voice to remain even, as if she were merely making polite conversation and not desperately curious to find out everything she could about Mr Lockhart.

'Well, take this engagement to Lady Cecily Hardgrave, for example. Dominic thinks it will be good for the family. He hasn't thought for a moment whether it will be good for him. He thinks we all live under the stigma of not being members of the aristocracy. We have no position in society, we're hardly even considered gentry, all because of our father's background.'

Nellie curled up a long lock of hair. 'Oh, and why is that?'

'Well, I don't know if you know, but our father started his working life as a stable boy.'

Nellie paused, a tress of hair suspended in mid-air. *A stable boy.* A position much lower in the social order than even a lady's maid. She clipped the hair in place. 'Oh, that's interesting,' she said as evenly as possible.

'But he advanced his position in the household until he was in charge of the stables and had responsibility for his employer's stud farm. He bred quite a few grand national champions, you know, and also winners at Royal Ascot. He became much sought after and he managed to secure a very good position with the Duke of Dalemont, managing his large stud farm.'

Miss Lockhart looked around as if about to impart a secret she wanted no one else to hear. Nellie leaned in, anxious to find out about the family scandal. 'My father put a few bets on his own horses and won a tidy sum. He used his winnings to set up his own horse-breeding and training business. It was very successful and grew rapidly. He also seemed to have a knack for making money, because he then increased his fortune substantially on the stock market. Making wise investments is a knack Dominic has inherited as well. That's why we've become so...' She waved her hand around. 'You know.'

Being a well-bred young lady, she knew better than to mention something as common as how much money they had, but that was what she meant. The Lockharts were now quite obviously a very wealthy family.

Nellie resumed her work. Miss Lockhart's confession wasn't quite as scandalous as she had expected or secretly hoped. Money was money. Who cared if her father had made it through horse breeding, gambling at the races and on the stock market, or had inherited it from a long line of ancestors?

'Your father sounds like a most impressive man.' Nellie suspected that the older Mr Lockhart would have been someone she would have admired, a man who had made it in the world on his own terms.

'Oh, he was. In many ways he was a lot like Dominic, hard-working, determined,' Miss Lockhart said, smiling brightly as she turned back to the mirror. 'I can see why Mother fell in love with him despite his background.'

Nellie began weaving strands of hair to create a final ornate effect. 'So, your parents married for love?' she probed, making sure her voice sounded as if she was still making idle chit-chat. But it was a question she was very curious about. If the parents did marry for love, it was one area in which the father differed from the son. Mr Lockhart junior did not see love as being a necessity for a successful marriage.

'Oh, yes.' Miss Lockhart nodded and sighed. 'And that's something Dominic was never able to forgive them for. My mother was a baron's daughter. She was expected to marry above her station, not below it. When she married Father, she was ostracised by her family and everyone from her class. It didn't matter that Father was by then a prosperous man.' She sighed again. 'And it didn't help, I suppose, that Father never made any effort to fit in with the aristocracy. He spoke the same way as he'd always spoken, mixed with the same people, and Mother's family couldn't cope, especially as he never deferred to them or acted as if they were any better than him.'

Good for him.

Nellie was admiring this man more and more and couldn't see why his son should disapprove of him, unless Mr Lockhart was a complete snob and ashamed of a man because of his origins, even though he had achieved so much.

'But it did get a bit hard for Dominic,' Miss Lockhart continued. 'When he was sent off to boarding school, he got into so many scrapes because of people making fun of Father's accent and his background. That's why he's so determined to move up in the world. He doesn't want anyone else in the family to be looked down on. After his marriage to Lady Cecily our family will be reconnected with the aristocracy. And he's hoping it will mean I'll be able to marry a man with a title. This is my fourth Season, you know, and Dominic's worried I might never marry anyone, but he particularly wants me to marry a titled man.'

She shrugged her shoulders as if this was no real concern of hers. 'And next year one of my younger sisters, Violet, will come out. Dominic's hoping she'll be presented at court and that can only happen if someone who has already been presented at court arranges it, such as Lady Cecily.'

She shrugged again. 'So, you see, his marriage to Lady Cecily will mean we might marry men with titles, then our children will have titles and the so-called shame of Father's background will be erased.'

'I see,' Nellie said, failing to keep the note of disapproval out of her voice. It was starting to look as if Mr Dominic Lockhart was indeed a complete snob after all. It was just what she would have expected from a man in his position.

'But I wish he wouldn't think he has to sacrifice himself in order to achieve all that on our account,' Miss Lockhart said and sighed lightly.

'Sacrifice? How so?' Despite her growing disapproval, Nellie was still interested in hearing all about Mr Lockhart. But just to confirm her belief that he was an insufferable snob, that was all.

'Well, this marriage. Cecily Hardgrave is such a... well, she's not for Dominic. Dominic has such a strong personality he needs someone intelligent who will challenge him, who'll stand up to him, and I'm afraid that's not Cecily Hardgrave. She's nice enough, lovely really, but she's not the woman for Dominic.'

'And what does Lady Cecily think of this?'

'Oh, she'll do whatever her father tells her to do.'

'So, is she in love with Mr Lockhart?' Nellie knew she was getting far too familiar. How Lady Cecily felt about Mr Lockhart was hardly the business of the woman who had come to style Miss Lockhart's hair. But Miss Lockhart gave no appearance that she was offended. She furrowed her brow as if giving the question serious consideration.

And Nellie was desperate to hear the answer. Lady Cecily had spoken to Nellie of love, that wonderful, devastating emotion that changed everything, so, despite her cool behaviour, she must be in love with Dominic.

'I don't know,' Miss Lockhart finally said. 'It's hard to tell what she thinks, she's so guarded. But her father arranged this marriage for her and she seems to be happy to go along with it.'

Nellie shook her head, not sure if it was the answer she wanted to hear or not. But it hardly mattered. They were engaged, they were to marry and there was no reason why Nellie should concern herself over whether they were in love or not. But the griping of her stomach and the burning in her throat suggested she did care, far too much.

'It sounds like a very suitable marriage for all concerned,' Nellie forced herself to say, trying to console herself that in one area she was more fortunate than Lady Cecily. Women from Nellie's class could marry whoever they wanted. Well, she couldn't marry a man like Mr Lockhart obviously, but within her own class she could marry for love. Whereas for the aristocracy and gentry it was all about jostling to achieve the best match possible for the family. As Mr Lockhart said, love and happiness had nothing to do with it.

Nellie stood back to admire her handiwork as Miss Lockhart smiled at herself in the mirror. 'Oh, Miss Regan, that's wonderful. My lady's maid could never do such an intricate style. Dominic said you're now running a very successful business in London and I can see why you're doing so well. The women in London are so lucky they can use your services.'

'Really, Dominic... I mean, Mr Lockhart said that?'

'Yes, he was very impressed.' Miss Lockhart moved her head from side to side to inspect her hair. 'And so am I. And not just because you're so good at what you do, but because you're so independent. It must be wonderful to be an independent woman, to be able to do what you want when you want.'

Nellie smiled at Miss Lockhart's reflection. 'Yes, it is.'

'You've got your own business, your own place to live, your own money. You must be so proud of what you've achieved.'

Nellie's smile grew wide and she nodded. 'I've been very lucky, and I've had lots of help, but, yes...' She gave a slightly embarrassed laugh. 'I am rather proud of how well the business has done and I've got lots of plans for the future. I'm training my two assistants and teaching them everything I know about hairdressing. Soon they'll be able to take charge of their own hairdressing parlours. And who knows, maybe one day I'll have parlours and training schools throughout England.'

'Oh, that's wonderful. I'm sure you'll achieve your dream.'

'Anyway, enough of that. Let's see what you are going to wear for the ball.'

Miss Lockhart rushed to the wardrobe, removed a pale lemon dress and, smiling, held it up for Nellie's inspection.

'Are you sure you want to wear such a light colour? I think you'd suit something in a darker shade.' Nellie looked in the wardrobe and saw that all the dresses were of a similar hue.

Miss Lockhart's smile faded. 'But my lady's maid said that I suit pale colours.'

'Hmm.' Nellie suspected the lady's maid had dark colouring and it was she, not Miss Lockhart, who suited pale colours. Like most mistresses, Miss Lockhart no doubt passed last Season's gowns on to her lady's maid, so the maid was making sure those dresses suited her by giving Miss Lockhart false advice.

'Well, I'm sure you'll look lovely in it. But perhaps we should liven it up a bit. Do you have any jewellery or scarves in a stronger colour?'

Miss Lockhart looked through her jewellery box and removed a dark red garnet necklace and frowned. 'This belonged to my mother, but I never wear it. The colour always seemed a bit bold for me.'

'Nonsense. You're a very bold young woman and everyone at the ball tonight should be made to know it.' She put the necklace round Miss Lockhart's neck and clipped it closed. 'See how the gems bring out the colour in your cheeks. Do you have the matching earrings?'

Miss Lockhart rustled through her jewellery box and brought out a pair of stunning garnet and diamond earrings.

'Perfect,' Nellie declared and attached them to Miss Lockhart's ears.

Miss Lockhart smiled. 'Oh, Miss Regan, you're a gem as well, they look perfect. Even if this ball is as boring as every other ball I've been to this Season, this one will be different because I'll be the envy of the other women. When they see my hair, they're all going to be so jealous and wish they had a lady's maid who can create the latest French fashions with such flair.'

'You find balls boring?' Nellie had always liked the idea of dressing up in a beautiful gown, listening to wonderful music and being whirled round the dance floor by a man dressed in formal clothing. But, she supposed, if it was something you did all the time, it could perhaps become boring.

Miss Lockhart nodded and sighed. 'Deadly. The men are all dull and the women are such snobs. When I came out at eighteen I was really excited, but I soon realised that the men weren't interested in me and that Season was just horrible. And the women were just as bad. They saw it as a chance to let me know I wasn't really one of them. Each Season has been worse than the one before and now the only way I can endure it is to get the polite chit-chat over as quickly as possible, then find myself a quiet corner where I can sit out the horrid thing.

'And tonight's ball is going to be even worse than all the rest. Dominic is going to expect me to land myself a husband before the end of the Season. After all, one more Season and I'll be officially on the shelf. That's why he's hosting this ball. He's invited just about every eligible titled man in the land. It's all so demeaning, really, like being inspected at a cattle market.'

Nellie smiled at the sad face reflected in the mirror. 'It doesn't have to be demeaning nor does it have to be boring. There'll be music and dancing, and, as you said, the other women are going to be envious of your new look. Just have fun and enjoy yourself. And don't see the men as there to inspect you, see it the other way round. You're a wonderful catch, you're beautiful, intelligent and vibrant. Any man who's got a brain in his head will realise that. So, tonight is your chance to make a careful inspection of what's on offer to see if any of these men are worthy of you. And if none of them are, well, who cares? It's hardly your fault if you're too good for them, but that shouldn't stop you from having fun.'

Miss Lockhart looked at her as if she had just said something outrageous. 'But Dominic really wants me to find a husband.'

'Who cares what Dom…what Mr Lockhart wants? You, too, are an independent woman. So, all that's important is what you want. And tonight, if I'm not mistaken, you want to have a good time and not worry about all this foolish husband-hunting business.'

Miss Lockhart's restrained smile soon turned into a full, beaming grin. 'You're right. I am an independent woman and I will enjoy myself. After all, what do I have to lose? I've had a miserable time at every other ball and not found a husband. If I have a good time and still don't find a husband, it will make no difference, but I'll have had a good time anyway.'

'Exactly.'

Miss Lockhart stood up and took off her day dress. Nellie gave her corset laces a tight tug to cinch in her waist a bit more and helped her into her silk petticoat. Miss Lockhart then stepped into her gown and Nellie buttoned up the small ivory buttons running up the front. She helped her into her white satin shoes, then stepped back and admired Miss Lockhart's appearance and smiled.

'You look beautiful, Miss Lockhart.'

Miss Lockhart moved over to the full-length mirror and did a little twirl, the long train of her satin gown swirling around her ankles. 'Oh, Miss Regan, it's wonderful and you're so right about the garnets. In future I'm going to get all my gowns made in much bolder colours.' She smiled at Nellie. 'Now let's go and show Dominic what you've done.'

She pulled on her elbow-length gloves, picked up her lace fan, then grabbed Nellie's hand and led her towards the door. It was as if they were now the best of friends, both excited about the night to come.

'Dominic,' Miss Lockhart called out from the top of the stairs. 'What do you think of my new look? Nellie's completely changed the style and she's given me lots of good advice about what colours I should wear. Oh, thank you so much for arranging this, Dominic.'

Nellie looked down to see Mr Lockhart standing at the bottom of the stairs. Her stomach clenched, her heart skipped a beat. His face had recovered substantially over the last month and from this distance there was no sign of the bruises and swelling that had distorted his handsome appearance. Now he was back to how he looked when she had first seen him. All smouldering intensity, dark good looks and upright bearing.

Like a buzzing noise beside her she could hear that Miss Lockhart was still chattering, but her attention was focused on the man staring up at her. She fought not to react. To achieve that goal, all she had to do was stop her heart from pounding as loud as a big bass drum, extinguish the fire that had burst on to her cheeks and release the small trapped bird that seemed to be fluttering inside her chest.

You're not some little shop girl, Nellie Regan, who has fallen for a rich gentleman. You're a sensible businesswoman. Now start acting like one. This man is not for you.

She leant down and brushed the train of Miss Lockhart's gown, even though it was perfectly straight. When she stood up, she had expected...*had hoped*... Mr Lockhart would have looked away, but he was still staring straight at her with those pitch-dark eyes. She held his gaze, unable to look away. How had she ever thought his eyes were cold? They were not cold. Like black velvet they were rich and warm. They were eyes that could draw you in, deeper and deeper, until you willingly surrendered to their dark depths.

Nellie shook her head to drive away such fanciful thoughts and to break the forceful hold of his gaze.

She held herself erect and tried to act as if seeing him again was having no effect on her whatsoever and started to descend the stairs, but the silly shop girl still wouldn't listen and the pounding and fluttering raging in her body would not be stilled.

Her descent was halted when a young girl of about seventeen and a child rushed past her, flying down the stairs as fast as they could and screeching to a halt in front of Mr Lockhart.

'We want to go to the ball, too,' the youngest cried

out in an excited voice. 'Please, Dominic, please.' She jumped up and down, holding on to his hand.

'We've already talked about this, Emmaline.' He looked up at Amanda, who shrugged her shoulders as if to say it was his problem. He sighed loudly and looked back at the excited child.

'All right, Emmaline,' he said, his voice stern. 'You and Violet can stand in the reception line, but you have to promise to go to bed immediately after the guests have arrived.'

Emmaline squealed her delight. Violet clapped her hands together with glee, then kissed him on the cheek. He kissed the younger child on the top of her head and the two girls departed, hand in hand, talking loudly and excitedly.

Nellie found herself smiling and for a moment she forgot her resolve to not let anything Mr Lockhart did or said affect her. His affection for his sisters was obvious. No wonder he had come all the way to London, then followed her to The Hanged Man, all so his eldest sister could have the hairstyle she wanted. It seemed he would do anything to make his sisters happy.

How could she not be attracted to such a man? His gaze turned back to her and she quickly remembered her earlier admonition. She was not a silly shop girl. She was a businesswoman who was here to do a job and she would behave in a completely professional manner at all times. She stood up straighter, forced that silly grin off her face and descended the stairs with as much decorum as she could muster.

Now, remember, Nellie, best behaviour. No imita-

tions, no rude comments. Act like a lady at all times and make sure you do not do or say anything that you will later regret.

It must be the effect of taking a beating last month. He wasn't thinking straight. Otherwise Dominic would not be standing at the foot of the stairs, staring up at Nellie Regan like some lovestruck puppy or adolescent boy with his first crush.

He coughed lightly, drew himself up taller and forced his gaze to move to his sister, who did indeed look beautiful this evening. He assumed something had changed with her hair, or perhaps it was what she was wearing, or was it because it was the first time he had actually seen her smiling before a ball and giving every appearance that she was actually looking forward to it.

Whatever Miss Regan had done it had obviously worked. Amanda looked radiant. Despite his reluctance to see Miss Regan again it seemed it had been worthwhile having his sister's hair styled by the former lady's maid, if it could give her so much pleasure.

'Yes, Amanda, you look beautiful,' he said and his sister beamed with joy. 'The first guests will be arriving soon, so we need to be ready to greet them.' *And I need to get away from Miss Regan before I say or do anything foolish.*

Amanda kissed Miss Regan on the cheek as if they were now friends and rushed down the remaining steps and through to the ballroom to join her sisters. His gaze returned to Miss Regan. She also looked stunning in a plain cream blouse and dark green skirt. So stunning he had no choice but to watch her as she descended at a more leisurely pace than his excitable sister. She was so elegant, so aristocratic in her bearing. But she wasn't an aristocrat, she was an ex-servant, someone now in trade, and she was here to tend to his sister. That was something he should not forget.

As she neared the bottom of the stairs, he heard the rustling of her skirt and her undergarments, a sound that evoked images of silk, of her silk-like complexion, her silk stockings, the silky softness of her skin at the top of those stockings, the…

He coughed to drive out that uninvited but tantalising image. 'Miss Regan, thank you for coming tonight. My sister obviously appreciated it.'

She reached the bottom of the stairs and smiled up at him. 'You're very welcome and your sister is a delight.'

He nodded. 'As promised, I have instructed the servants to prepare a suite for you and a meal will be brought up to your room. The coachman has been instructed to take you back to the station at a time of your choosing. I've also instructed my steward to provide you with sufficient remuneration to compensate you for the time you have taken away from your business. I hope that is satisfactory.'

Dominic's voice sounded suitably professional. Good. He felt much more comfortable now that they were discussing business terms, although he'd feel even more comfortable if she wasn't gazing up at him with those bright green eyes, or if those soft pink lips weren't slightly parted, as if encouraging him to imagine what it would be like to kiss her.

She gave a little laugh, as if he had made a joke, although he suspected she was laughing at his formal manner, not anything amusing he might have said. 'Very satisfactory, thank you.'

'Good. Then I hope you have an enjoyable night.'

'And you as well. I hope your ball is a rip-roaring success, just like your engagement party.' She bit her lip and blushed slightly, although he doubted it was from embarrassment.

He suppressed an exasperated sigh. Of course she wouldn't be embarrassed. She enjoyed mocking him and it seemed she was doing it again. Although he had to admit she was right. His engagement party had been somewhat staid, but that was in keeping with the occasion. It was an event to announce the advantageous joining of two families. And his own ball would not be a *rip-roaring affair* either. It would be one of his sister's last chances to find a suitable husband before the end of the Season and would be conducted with all the necessary decorum.

'You're right, Miss Regan. My engagement party was nothing like a night out at The Hanged Man.' He knew he was sounding pompous, but he would not let her mock him in that manner without any repercussions.

Any hint that she had embarrassed herself with her jibe about his engagement party disappeared. Instead, she thrust her chin forward, in that defiant manner with which he was becoming familiar. 'No, you wouldn't want to host a ball where there was laughing and merry-making. You couldn't expect the gentry to do something as common as actually enjoy themselves.'

It was Dominic's turn to bristle. 'Indeed, the gentry do tend to aim for a level of refinement and decorum that would be out of place at The Hanged Man.'

Her lips tightened into an irritated line. 'Well, I suppose decorum and refinement is one way to describe it.' She exhaled loudly. 'Although I'd call it boring and passionless,' she murmured, but loud enough so he could hear.

Dominic's teeth clenched tightly together. He drew in a deep breath and released it slowly through flared nostrils. He would not rise to her bait. He would not be seen arguing with an ex-lady's maid when his guests arrived, no matter how insulting and ill mannered her behaviour.

'Well, if you'll excuse me, Miss Regan, I have a rip-roaring ball to attend.' With that he took Miss Regan's hand and kissed the back of it. Why he felt the need to do that when even a formal bow was more than he would usually perform for a servant or a person in trade, Dominic did not know. Perhaps it was because she was the most irritating woman he had ever met and such irritation had upset his equilibrium and caused him to act so oddly. Or was it because despite everything, he just found her so damn attractive and wanted to feel the touch of her skin against his lips?

Whatever his reason, Dominic took some satisfaction at having removed that superior look from her face. Her mouth had fallen open, her eyes had grown wide and she was staring at her hand as if she no longer knew what this strange thing was attached to the end of her arm.

Good. Dominic smiled to himself as he walked through to the ballroom. It hadn't been his intention to shock her, but shocking Miss Regan was indeed a very satisfying thing to do.

Chapter Fourteen

Dominic stood in the reception line at the entrance to the ballroom, greeting his guests. This ball was important. He had to remember that and not get distracted. It was nearing the end of the Season and Amanda needed to secure some interest from at least one of the titled men present. And as the host it was also his opportunity to make an impression on the guests, members of England's elite, men who would now see him as the future son-in-law of the Duke of Ashmore, not as the son of a former stable boy.

Focusing on the task of meeting and greeting would be made a lot easier if he wasn't still thinking about Nellie Regan. Somewhere in his house she was no doubt wreaking havoc. Either that or she was flirting with one of the servants. He looked over at the line of footmen, standing tall and straight along the far wall. No, she wouldn't be doing that. They'd be busy until the ball was over. Not that he should care who she chose to flirt with. She could flirt with as many footmen, coachmen or whomever she wanted to. It was none of his business. He bowed his head as another aristocratic couple was announced.

It was the present company he should be concentrating on, not some disrespectful ex-lady's maid. These people were all closely associated with his future in-laws and it wouldn't be long before they would be associated with him. His sister would hopefully soon be married to a titled man. Thanks to his marriage to Lady Cecily, his younger sisters, Violet and Emmaline, would be presented at court when they came out and their opportunities for a successful marriage into the highest ranks of English society would be all but assured.

It was all perfect. Everything was going to plan, exactly as he had hoped. He glanced at Amanda, who was greeting Lord Westcliffe, Marquess of Peningdale, the eldest son of the Duke of Castlemere. She looked so happy and was sending the Duke's son coy, flirtatious glances, which were being received with enthusiastic smiles.

It was strange how a hairstyle could change a woman so radically, or was it due to Miss Regan's influence? Had she said something to Amanda that had brought about this transformation from a young woman who always looked bored and sat in the corner as if she'd rather not be noticed, to someone who wanted to shine and be the centre of attention?

If she possessed a skill like that, he could see why her business was prospering. He turned back to greet another couple, who, prior to the announcement of his engagement to Lady Cecily, would not have deigned to attend a social occasion hosted by someone as lowly as him.

They swept past him and he looked back at his radiant sister, still sending smiles at Lord Westcliffe as she absentmindedly greeted more guests. There was no doubting that a few hours in Miss Regan's company had had a positive effect on his sister. But wasn't that what he had paid her for. She had simply done her job and he should be giving it no more thought than he did to the people who had decorated the ballroom for tonight's occasion, or the musicians waiting patiently for his signal to begin playing. Miss Regan had done the job he had paid her for, nothing more. That was the only reason she was here in this house and he would give her no more thought this evening.

He flicked a gaze around the room. At his engagement party she had secretly watched from the minstrels' gallery. The ballroom at Lockhart House did not possess a gallery, but he wouldn't put it past her to be hiding behind one of the many large potted palms or bouquets of flowers so she could later mock the proceedings.

But the palms and flower arrangements were all free of nosy ex-lady's maids. Nor could he see her lurking behind the marble columns that edged the ballroom or peeking out from behind the musicians seated on the elevated stage at the far end of the room.

He briefly wondered if she might be secreted under the refreshment table. But now he was being absurd.

He smiled to himself. She could be outrageous, but even Miss Regan would not go that far.

The final group of guests arrived and he signalled to the band to start playing the first dance of the evening. Dominic turned to his fiancée and smiled politely. 'May I have the pleasure of the first dance?'

She sent him a small nod, as if she were performing a duty rather than taking part in a pleasurable activity. Cecily placed her gloved hand on the back of his hand and with stiff formality allowed him to lead her on to the dance floor. Images of Nellie's performance in front of the servants invaded his mind. She had been exaggerating, but not by much.

Nellie had mocked the lack of passion between him and Cecily and she was right. They were little more than acquaintances when they had agreed to become engaged. He had assumed that lack of familiarity would decrease over the course of their engagement, but if anything, they were more like strangers now than they had been before they had agreed to marry.

Whereas with Nellie Regan he had felt immediately relaxed in her company. He had laughed, had talked, he'd even shared details of his life that he rarely discussed with anyone.

But he most definitely should not be thinking of that now. Not when he had his fiancée in his arms. Or should he say, almost in his arms. Once again Cecily was making sure there was plenty of space between them, despite the intimacy of the waltz.

'Cecily, you seem very distracted this evening. Is everything all right?'

She looked up at him, almost startled that he had spoken to her, then seemed to force herself to smile. 'Oh, yes, perfectly all right, but thank you for asking. And you, I assume you are also well this evening?'

The level of politeness was almost absurd and the falsity of her smile was at odds with her claim that she was *perfectly all right*.

'You're not having doubts about our engagement, are you? If you are, please do not feel under any obligation.'

Was she having doubts, or was it he who was starting to question this arrangement?

Her smile remained frozen on her face. 'No, I'm not having doubts. Not at all. As Father says, our marriage will be the perfect match. It was a great honour that you asked my father for my hand and once we have had the opportunity to get better acquainted, I am sure we will have a perfectly happy marriage.'

Her tone of voice and that forced smile suggested she was repeating a well-rehearsed speech, one perhaps that her father had given to her. His engagement *was* an ideal arrangement for him and for the Hardgrave family, and he had assumed it was what Cecily wanted as well. But whether she had any actual feelings for him, that was impossible to discern.

And she was wrong. He hadn't asked the Duke of Ashmore for Lady Cecily's hand. The arrangement had been suggested by the Duke himself and he had been told that Lady Cecily had expressed interest in him. It seemed that was not entirely the case—either Cecily was mistaken or she had been misled by her father.

Courting Lady Cecily hadn't occurred to Dominic

until her father had suggested the arrangement, but he had immediately seen it as an excellent idea. She was refined, attractive and the daughter of a duke, the sort of woman any man would want for a wife. Until a month ago he had not questioned that decision.

But now he was wondering if he had been blinded by his desire to advance his family's position in society. And what of Lady Cecily? Was this marriage really what she wanted, or was she merely doing what her father told her to, against her own wishes?

He had thought that she was equally in agreement— after all, she had claimed she couldn't be happier when he had asked for her hand. But nothing in her actions since that day suggested she was genuinely happy. Had he been blinded to what she really wanted because their marriage suited him perfectly? Was he now seeing signs of reluctance on her part because that, too, suited him? Dominic was never confused about what he wanted. Usually he knew exactly what he wanted, made a decision and stuck to it. But suddenly his engagement to Cecily Hardgrave was becoming increasingly confusing and causing him to question the wisdom of his decisions.

'You should do what makes you happy, Cecily,' he said. 'Don't worry about what anyone else wants, your father, or me. Do what makes you happy.' He was starting to sound like his parents, or, worse than that, Nellie Regan, with all this talk of happiness, but he could not see this young woman suffer if marriage to him was not what she wanted.

She looked up at him, her eyebrows drawn together,

her false smile wavering. The band finished playing and they stopped dancing.

'Thank you, Dominic.' He was unsure whether she was thanking him for the dance or for what he had just said, or merely making polite, meaningless conversation.

He offered her his arm. She placed her gloved hand lightly on his forearm and he led her off the dance floor. Cecily immediately excused herself, muttering something about a problem with the servants she needed to sort out. Dominic watched her leave the ballroom. He'd never met anyone who had more problems with their servants. It seemed every time they were together, she had to rush off to sort out some problem or other.

Cecily and her parents were staying at Lockhart Estate overnight, so had brought Cecily's lady's maid, along with the family's coachman, a footman and her parents' personal servants. With so few servants in attendance Dominic could hardly see what problems would demand her immediate attention. But it would seem he was wrong.

He looked around and saw Amanda was dancing with the Duke of Castlemere's son. This was even more than he had hoped for when he had decided to host a ball. He smiled with satisfaction. When the other guests saw she had drawn the attentions of someone so high up in the social hierarchy it would certainly spark interest among the unmarried men. Dominic was sure he would soon be getting visits from one or more of the young men, with requests to keep company with his sister.

With the main reason for this ball taken care of, he could attend to the other reason for hosting this occasion. It provided him with the opportunity to mix with influential people who would further advance the family's position in society. He crossed the ballroom floor and joined a group of eminent men, which included a member of the House of Commons and two members of the House of Lords, just the sort of men with whom he should be associating.

He shook their hands and listened as they discussed the new horseless carriages and a recent motor-racing competition that had taken place in France where automobiles had reached a staggering twenty miles per hour. The men were all excited about the prospect of being able to drive their own vehicles at such speeds and several had already put in orders to have a horseless carriage built.

Dominic was also interested in the possibilities of this new technology and the changes it would make to society, but he couldn't stop his gaze from straying again as he searched the room to see if Nellie Regan was watching.

He couldn't see her anywhere and knew he should not be looking. He forced his attention back to the group of men and tried to pay attention as they moved on to discussing the latest bills before the House.

Would she be condemning him for talking to this group of older men when he should be dancing with his fiancée and enjoying himself? Once again, he reminded himself that he did not care one iota what this former lady's maid thought of him. She might be enterprising, with energy that most businessmen would envy, and she might be so attractive and graceful that she could easily pass as a member of the aristocracy, but she was still little more than a servant. A person in trade at best. And he was wasting his time even thinking about her.

And he *wouldn't* think about her. He cast one more glance around the room. He wouldn't imagine what she would say about him attending a ball and spending his time talking politics rather than dancing.

After all, he could hardly dance and have fun if his fiancée was absent, so of course he would spend the evening talking to a group of men. It had nothing to do with being boring or lacking passion.

He looked around the room again. Cecily had not come back either. She had been absent for a considerable amount of time. Surely any problem with the servants would be settled by now.

He excused himself from the circle of men. He had been remiss and should have thought to check earlier, or even offered to help her with whatever problem she was encountering.

He skirted round the dance floor and asked a footman if he knew where Lady Cecily had gone. The footman informed him that she was last seen heading towards the servants' hall. Dominic rarely went below stairs, even in his own home. He discussed the running of the house with the head butler, but that was always conducted in his library. And his sister held similar discussions with the housekeeper, again in her own drawing room. Then they left the running of the household to the senior servants. While he had spent a lot of time below stairs as a boy, the goings on down there were increasingly becoming a mystery to him.

But it was an area that Nellie Regan would know well. He thought back to when he had first seen her, entertaining the servants with an imitation of himself and Lady Cecily in the servants' hall at Ashmore House.

He smiled at the memory of how she looked when she realised he was watching her. How her face had quickly turned from embarrassed to defiant. How he'd seen that defiant look again when he'd visited her shop and once more when he'd appeared at The Hanged Man. Then another image entered his mind. One he knew he shouldn't think of, the image that had been tormenting him for the last month. The image of her beautiful body visible beneath her nightgown, her red hair flowing down her back. How could he not think of that? How could he not want to see such tempting beauty again? She had literally taken his breath away and it was a sight he knew would be etched on his brain for ever.

He paused, breathed deeply to try to clear his mind. What he should be focusing on was finding his fiancée and helping her with whatever problem it was that had taken her away from the ball. He strode towards the back stairs that would take him down to the servants' hall, reminding himself that he would not think of Nellie Regan again. He would not remember the way she looked in the morning light, with the sun shining through her nightgown. He would not think of her soft skin, her sparkling green eyes, her lips. And he certainly would not think of her curvaceous body.

He passed the open door of the library, glanced in and there she was. Nellie Regan. Standing beside a bookcase, her head bent, a book in her hand, a smile on her face.

He stopped walking and stood in the doorway, staring at her. Like a willing captive he could not walk away. Nor did he want to.

Chapter Fifteen

As if pulled by a magnetic force he walked into the library. She looked up. Her green eyes held his gaze. Slowly, she closed her book. 'I'm sorry. I hope you don't mind, but I can't walk past a library without going in and seeing what books it contains.'

'I don't mind at all.' His voice came out as a low growl. He coughed to clear his throat. 'What are you reading?'

She smiled at him and looked down at the book in her hand. 'A very well-thumbed copy of *The Adventures of Tom Sawyer.*'

Dominic laughed and leant over her shoulder to look at the cover. 'It was my favourite book as a child. I envied Tom his freedom and the way he happily got himself into all sorts of trouble.'

'I knew it was yours. I saw your inscription in the front.' She opened the first page of the book and showed it to him. There was his childish scrawl, announcing that the book belonged to Dominic Lockhart and everyone else, especially his sister, were banned from reading it. She laughed. 'I hope that ban doesn't still stand and you don't mind me reading it.'

'I'll make an exception for you.'

She smiled again and his gaze was drawn from her laughing eyes to those full, pink lips. Pink lips that he had often thought of kissing. She stopped smiling and his gaze moved back to her eyes. She was staring at him, her eyes soft. Like a prisoner held by invisible restraints he couldn't look away. Her lips parted slightly as she drew in a rasping breath and her tongue slowly moved along the full lower one, as if relieving suddenly dry lips. It was a simple gesture, but Dominic was captivated.

'I'll make an exception for you,' he repeated, his voice husky and constricted. Before he could register what he was doing he had leant forward and was kissing those tempting lips.

He had first imagined doing this when he had seen her standing at her washstand, her curvaceous body on display. And he had repeatedly dreamt of doing it ever since. Now his dream had become an intoxicating reality and he was drunk with the pleasure of it.

His arms enveloped her. He pulled her towards him. What he was doing was wrong. He knew he should stop. He waited for her to react with horror. To push him away. To slap his face as he deserved. To let him know his kisses were unwanted. Then he would stop, but he couldn't do it by himself. He was incapable of stopping, even though he knew that was exactly what he should do.

But how could he stop now? How could he pull away from her, now that he had experienced the touch of her lips, the silky feel of her skin? That alluringly feminine taste of her lips had stripped away his last vestige of control. He had been robbed of the power to do what he knew was right.

She moaned lightly. Her lips parted. Exhilaration coursed through him. She did not want him to stop. She wanted this as well. This was more than he could have dreamt of.

He pulled her even closer, held her tighter, kissed her harder, his hand lightly stroking the soft skin of her neck. He wanted this woman. Wanted her right here, right now. He ran his tongue along her full bottom lip, tempting her to give him what he wanted. And she did. Her lips parted wider, letting him in. His tongue entered her mouth, savouring the intimacy of the act.

To his immense pleasure her arms encased his shoulders. Her hands ran up the back of his neck, to his head and through his hair, holding on to him tightly. She kissed him back with a fervour that matched his own. Her breasts were tight up against his chest as she moulded herself into his body, every inch of her touching him. Dominic intensified the kiss as he registered her tight nipples pressed into his chest, her body telling him what he wanted to know. She wanted this as much as he did.

And he wanted her with an intensity that had driven all thought from his mind. As he trailed a line of kisses down her throat, she tilted back her head, exposing the creamy white skin to his lips, and moaned gently.

He wanted to kiss and caress every inch of her beautiful body, to make her moans come louder and faster, to cause her to writhe with pleasure under his touch. Her breath becoming quick gasps, his kisses returned to those waiting lips, kissing her hard, parting her lips and entering her mouth again.

But he wanted more than just her kisses, more than just caresses. He wanted this woman, wanted all of her, wanted her with a desperation that defied all reason. His aching need for her was pounding within him, his erection straining against his trousers, he needed to be deep within her, needed the release that only she could give him.

His hands moved down her back to her buttocks, those beautiful round buttocks. But he did not want to feel them through her layers of frustrating clothing. He wanted her naked. He wanted to be able to observe her beauty laid out before him.

His hands moved up to her slim waist and he lifted her up on to the table. With desperate fingers he pulled at the buttons of her blouse with more haste than finesse. To his immense relief she helped him, unbuttoning her blouse and letting him know that this was what she wanted as well.

The blouse parted. He pulled down her chemise in one firm tug and was rewarded by the sight of her full, round breasts exposed, lifted up towards him above her corset. He took a moment to stand back and admire the glorious sight. Her hands dropped to her sides, giving him an unimpeded gaze. She was enjoying being looked at as much as he was enjoying the sight of her naked breasts. Her breath was coming in increasingly rapid gasps, while her breasts moved up and down, and her tight nipples were pointed invitingly at him. It was an invitation he could not refuse.

She reached her hands towards him, her full lips parted. 'Dominic,' she whispered. It was the first time she had used his given name and it felt good, very good. He wanted to hear her say it again. He wanted to hear her calling out his name as he made love to her, to scream it out as he made her writhe with ecstasy. He wanted to make her lose herself in pleasure, the pleasure he was giving her.

Taking her beautiful breasts in his hands he teased and tormented the hard buds and watched her reaction. She closed her eyes, her lips parted, and she placed her hands over his, encouraging him in his caresses.

Her rapid breathing became moans, then gentle cries as he continued to rub his thumbs over the tight, sensitive nubs. Her cries coming faster and faster, he kissed her neck, his lips moving slowly, teasingly down her neck, to her shoulders, her chest, and across the soft, swelling mounds of her breasts. When he reached his destination, he took one tight bud in his mouth, licking it, sucking it, nuzzling it, while his hand continued its tormenting caress of its beautiful twin. Her hands clasped his head, her fingers wove their way through his hair, holding him to her breast as her breath came in increasingly rapid pants.

Urged on by her obvious signs of pleasure, he reached down and grabbed the bottom of her skirt, bunching up the soft material. He heard her breath catch. Stopping what he was doing, he looked up at her face. Had he gone too far? But it was not a gasp of protest. Her head was thrown back, her eyes were closed, her lips parted. She had the beautiful expression of a woman caught up in the raptures of desire. He smiled down at her. She was just as incapable of stopping as he was. And he had no intention of stopping.

Kissing those parted, gasping lips, he ran his hand up the inside of her leg along her silk stocking, under her loose undergarments to the soft naked flesh above her garter.

Her gasps grew faster, louder, urging him on. It was all he needed. When her legs parted, giving him easier access, he released his own deep moan of pleasure. His stroking hand rose teasingly, slowly up the silky flesh of her inner thigh. Another growl of pleasure escaped his lips as she parted her legs even wider in invitation.

His caressing fingers reached their destination and he ran his hand along the soft, intimate folds, then pushed his fingers inside her. If he'd had any doubts that she wanted this as much as him they would now be completely swept away. She was so wet for him, so ready for him to enter her and make her his own.

Watching her face, he gently rubbed her sensitive nub, his fingers moving deeper within her with each stroke. Each one brought more moans of pleasure from her lovely lips. She was completely lost in the experience. She gasped in rhythm with his stroking hand. Harder and harder, faster and faster he stroked, while watching her beautiful face. One long gasp escaped her lips, tears slid past the edges of her closed eyes, and he felt the completion of her pleasure wet on his fingers.

She looked so beautiful. So beautiful he knew he had to be inside her. Now.

His erection so hard it was almost painful, he desperately needed to feel her encasing him. He had to relieve the throbbing desire for her that was possessing him, that had taken him over and driven away the ability to think.

She opened her eyes and gazed at him as if in a trance. Her green eyes appeared black. A rose-coloured blush had consumed her cheeks, her neck and naked breasts. She reached out to him. Her swollen lips parted, as if she was struggling to form words, but had lost the ability to speak.

'Oh, Nellie. I want you so badly,' he murmured as he kissed the side of her neck. 'I have to have you. I want to make love to you.'

Her body suddenly went rigid. Her hands gripped his shoulders, her fingers digging in deeply, and she pushed him away. He looked at her stricken face and shame washed through him. His actions had been so wrong, so selfish.

Her previously hooded eyes were now large and startled. Her once-panting lips were now closed in a tight line as she scrambled to clasp her blouse together and pull down the fabric of her skirt.

He should not have given into his primal need to make love to her. It was unforgivable. He had wanted her so desperately he had forgotten what was right. He had only been thinking of himself, of his desperate need for her. He had thought it was what she wanted.

'I'm sorry, I'm so sorry,' she said, staring over his shoulder.

'No, Nellie. You have done nothing wrong. I'm the one who should be sorry. Please forgive me, I should have used more self-control. Please, can you ever forgive me?'

'No, no,' she gasped and pointed at the doorway.

Dominic turned to look where she was pointing. Lady Cecily was standing at the door. Staring at them. Her face showing no emotion, giving no indication of what she must be thinking about the shocking scene she had just witnessed.

Chapter Sixteen

'Go to her.' Nellie pulled down her skirt and wished her emotional state could be restored as easily as her clothing. Her heart was still pounding so hard within her chest she was sure Dominic must be able to hear it. Her skin tingled as if every inch of it was still being stroked and caressed. Her lips still burned with the imprint of his impassioned kiss. Her body still ached for him, longing for him to once again give her that ecstatic satisfaction, longing to finally have him deep within her.

She did not want him to leave, but he had to. To stay would be cruel, selfish, even more unforgivable than what they had already done. If such a thing was possible.

They had been caught up in the moment. But they should not have allowed that to happen. Nellie should have stopped it, stopped herself, stopped him. To her shame she had done nothing to prevent this happening. Instead she had encouraged him in his exploration of her body. Had enjoyed every sensual moment of it. And to her shame she wanted him to continue, wanted to feel his hands caressing her, wanted to feel his lips on hers, wanted to wrap her legs tightly around his firm thighs. Wanted him to make love to her.

Her heart hammering in her chest, her body still throbbing with the memory of his caresses, she tried to control her body's reaction, tried to suppress her need for him.

She swallowed and drew in a series of ragged breaths. It had all been wrong. So wrong. It should never have happened. When she had seen Lady Cecily standing at the door it had been a tidal wave of guilt that had crashed over her, instead of another tidal wave of ecstasy.

Yet, despite the shock at seeing Lady Cecily standing at the doorway, a shameful part of her had, for one brief moment, been tempted to close her eyes again, to pretend she had not seen her. She had been tempted to ignore the other woman's presence. She had been so caught up in the rapture of the moment, she had wanted to ignore what her eyes were seeing, to only focus on the euphoric pleasure her body was feeling. It seemed her selfishness knew no bounds.

And Lady Cecily wasn't just another woman. She was Dominic's fiancée. Nellie knew he must go to her. But even though her words were telling him to leave, her body was screaming out for him to stay. Part of her wanted to ignore the guilt that was consuming her. She was tempted to beg him to take her in his arms, to kiss her again, to caress her again, to continue what he had started and make love to her. To bring her once again to that pinnacle of pleasure. And that only showed just what an appalling woman she was.

Despite what her body was crying out for, she had to fight against that desire, that overwhelming temptation. Despite her burning need for him, she had to extinguish the inferno that had engulfed them and try to put this right, as impossible as that goal was.

'Go to her, Mr...' Nellie repeated and paused. 'Go to her, Dominic.' He looked down at her, his dark eyes still glazed by a fog of desire, but like herself, she could see that the full, shameful realisation of what they had done was starting to cut through the fog.

She lowered herself from the table. Holding her gaping blouse together, she took a step away from him. 'Go to Lady Cecily. Go to your fiancée,' she stated more forcefully.

'I can't leave you, Nellie,' he murmured, taking a step towards her and reaching out his hands.

Nellie looked down and took in a deep, slow breath, determined to be strong. 'Yes, you can.' She looked up at him with more resolve than she felt. 'Yes, you will. She needs you. She must be in shock after what she has just witnessed.' Although the expression on Lady Cecily's face did not seem distressed in the slightest. Her head had been inclined slightly, her gaze had been calm, her face expressionless. It was as if she was observing a mildly curious scene that had no real relevance to her. But then, the upper classes were notorious for refusing to show any emotion. She might not have looked it, but how could she not be distressed by what she had witnessed?

'You need to go to her,' Nellie repeated more forcefully. 'I can take care of myself.'

After all, isn't that what I've always done?

'But, Nellie, I...'

'I said go to her.'

'But we need to talk. We have to talk. This has changed everything between us.' He gestured towards the table.

Nellie nodded, but pointed towards the door. 'All right. But first you need to find Lady Cecily. You need to talk to her first.' He nodded, but remained rooted to the spot. Nellie gave him a small push. 'Go.'

He nodded, paused, then headed towards the door. 'Wait for me, Nellie. We must talk about what has happened,' he said over his shoulder as he departed.

Nellie leant back against the table, her legs weak, her body completely drained of all energy. She closed her eyes and tried to breathe slowly and deeply. She needed to compose herself, to try to make sense of what had just happened and think about what she was going to do now.

Slowly her racing heartbeat returned to its normal rhythm. She opened her eyes, looked down and saw her blouse, the buttons undone, her chemise pulled down below her breasts. If Nellie needed a reminder of her slatternly behaviour, her dishevelled clothing would provide it. But she didn't need a reminder. She knew what she had done was wrong. She pulled up her chemise and quickly buttoned up her blouse.

Then she saw the innocent book, abandoned on the Persian rug. It had fallen from her hand when she had kissed the man she shouldn't have. She picked it up and replaced it on the shelf, wishing the damage she had done could be mended just as easily.

How long Lady Cecily had been standing at the door watching, Nellie had no idea. But even if Nellie had seen her the moment she had arrived, Cecily still would have seen enough to know what was going on.

The burning on Nellie's cheeks burst into an inferno of shame. The Duke of Ashmore had accused her of being Dominic's mistress. She had been outraged by his suggestion, yet how she had behaved had exceeded even the low standards that the Duke considered acceptable behaviour. He had said he didn't object to Dominic having a mistress, even expected it of him, but the Duke did expect discretion. And discreet was one thing their behaviour most definitely had not been.

Nellie placed a trembling hand on the table. This was terrible. Lady Cecily had never done her any harm and now she had caused her such distress, she had probably ruined Dominic's chances of making a good marriage. Something he wanted so much. She'd probably brought shame on him and the family, ruined Miss Lockhart's chances of making a successful marriage and the younger sisters' chances of being presented at court. All because she couldn't resist a man who could never be hers.

She might not approve of the way the upper classes bargained and manoeuvred to secure the best possible marriage deals, but it wasn't her place to ruin other people's lives. Dominic wanted to marry Lady Cecily. He wanted his sisters to move in higher circles than they already did. Whether Nellie approved of such aspirations was neither here nor there. She shouldn't be ruining other people's lives just because she couldn't resist an attractive man. She should not have succumbed to her passions, not when it could cause so much damage to so many people.

Nellie could not imagine what the conversation between Dominic and Lady Cecily was going to be like. If she was Lady Cecily, she would be tearing him limb from limb before leaving and never seeing the rascal again. And as for how she would behave towards the slattern who was caught in a compromising position with her fiancé, well, Nellie would show no mercy towards such a woman.

But she could not imagine Lady Cecily doing such a thing. High emotion was something she would not expect from her. The way Lady Cecily had just stood at the doorway as if watching a slightly unexpected scene that she was too polite to interrupt suggested she was unlikely to vent her anger on either Dominic or Nellie. But who knew how people would react when in an emotional state?

Her behaviour tonight had proven that. She had come into the library to find a book to read and had ended up in Dominic Lockhart's arms. She had most certainly acted against her better judgement because she was caught up in an emotional state, an emotional state she felt powerless to control.

She ran her finger gently along the spine of Dominic's childhood book. It had been such a delight to handle a book that he had loved so much as a boy and to see the playful note he had written in the front. He had once been a naughty child who loved reading a book that featured a mischievous imp. But that wasn't who he was now. He was a man with responsibilities, with sisters whose futures he needed to take care of.

Her hand dropped to her side. Once again, her impulsive behaviour had detrimentally affected Dominic's life. Her reckless behaviour had resulted in him being beaten black and blue. Now her inability to control her desires had put him in a compromising position. While she couldn't take full responsibility for what had happened between them, she had certainly been a willing participant.

She looked around the library and sighed. What was she to do now? Acting as if nothing had happened was certainly out of the question. She could hardly do what she had originally planned, find a book to read and retire for the night. With so many confused thoughts whirling through her head, reading would demand more concentration than she was capable of. How could she possibly settle down and read a book when she was so racked with guilt? How could she concentrate on anything when the memory of that kiss, those caresses was still so clear in her mind's eye, still imprinted on her body?

Dominic had kissed her like a man possessed. A man who wanted to possess her. Nellie lightly touched her lips. There was no doubting that the man lusted after her. Desired her as much as she desired him. But that meant nothing. He was engaged to another woman. He planned to marry another woman.

All she could ever hope for was to be Dominic's mistress, just as the Duke of Ashmore had assumed. Despite her protestations to the contrary, hadn't she proven that she was just the sort of woman who would become a man's mistress? The shame consuming Nellie increased its painful grip. It seemed she wasn't the woman she thought she was. She was a woman who could let her passions control her and cause her to make foolish decisions.

She had been a fool to let her desires possess her in such a reckless manner. She should have controlled herself. Or at least tried, but she hadn't even done that.

And if Lady Cecily hadn't appeared at the doorway, would they still be making love? She looked over at the library table. An excited tremor rippled through her body, answering that question for her. She closed her eyes. Wasn't that something she had been dreaming about since she first laid eyes on Mr Dominic Lockhart? Something she thought would never happen. Something she knew should never happen. Something that *must* never happen again.

There was no denying the attraction between herself and Dominic. She desired him, more than she would once have thought possible. And that look in his eyes when he kissed her, the insistency of that kiss, that demanding need she felt when he was holding her close, made it clear just how strong his desire for her was.

But all there could ever be between them was something physical. And for her that could never be enough.

As much as her body craved him, she would not be his mistress. She did not want to be some wealthy man's bit on the side, even if that wealthy man was Dominic Lockhart.

Such an arrangement would be insulting to Nellie and insulting to Lady Cecily. And if it was something that Dominic would countenance, then he wasn't the sort of man she had assumed him to be.

She placed her finger back on the spine of his childhood book. If she was being completely honest, she could never be his mistress because that wasn't what she really wanted. It wasn't just that it would be morally wrong. It was because it would not be enough. Giving herself to Dominic had been about more than just lust. It was much more than that.

Her hand dropped back to her side. She had done the stupidest thing she could imagine. She had fallen in love with Dominic Lockhart, a man so unattainable it was ridiculous to even think about such things. Only a stupid, stupid woman from her class would fall for a man from Dominic's class. Nellie had always arrogantly thought herself smarter than most women, less gullible, and certainly less naive to the ways of the world. But it seemed she was wrong. A smart, sensible woman would never be so foolish as to fall in love with an unattainable man from the wrong class who was already engaged to be married. It was obvious Nellie was neither smart nor sensible.

She leaned against the table and took her head in her hands. Hopefully, Dominic had no idea what she felt for him. She would hate to think that he knew she was in love with him. That would cause too many complications. Despite what had just happened, she knew that Dominic was still an honourable man. If he knew she was in love with him it would make things even more complicated than they already were. He would feel responsible for her as much as he did for Lady Cecily. And she couldn't have that. Much better if he just saw her as a wanton woman who was easily seduced.

Nellie's choices were becoming obvious. She was in love with Dominic Lockhart, but the most she could ever be to him was a mistress. She did not want to be his mistress. But she was incapable of resisting her passion for him—hadn't she just proven that?

She quickly stood up from the table as if it was burning into her and looked down at the inoffensive piece of furniture as if it was somehow partly responsible for what had happened. The moment he had kissed her she had been lost. If he wanted her again, could she ever find the strength to deny what she also wanted? Were her protestations that she would never become any man's mistress genuine? No matter how much her rational mind told her it was wrong, the driving desires of her body were stronger than her rational mind. The truth was she could not resist Dominic Lockhart.

If she was to avoid becoming the mistress of a rich man, there was only one thing she could do. Never see him again.

She turned from the table and faced the door. And never seeing him again would be the kindest thing she could do for Dominic. All she had done since she had come into his life was cause problems for him. The only reason she was in his home was because she was trying to repay her guilty debt to him for causing him to be beaten by thugs. She had styled his sister's hair as promised, so that guilty debt was paid. Now the best way she could repay this latest guilty debt to Lady Cecily, and to allow Dominic to have the life he wanted, was to get out of his life and stay out.

The next morning Nellie stood on the platform of the small local railway station and anxiously waited for the early morning train that would take her back to London.

It seemed fleeing from Dominic Lockhart was becoming a habit, but it was a habit Nellie was going to have to break. This would be the last time she would flee because she would never see him again. Leaving Lockhart Estate last night had been the most sensible thing she had done in a long time. She knew that if she had seen Dominic again her firm resolve might have unravelled. Especially with his kisses still fresh on her lips, her skin still aware of the caressing touch of his hands, her body still burning for him.

Last night the coach driver had been reluctant to take her into the local village so she could find lodgings for the evening. He didn't want to go to the trouble of hitching up the carriage in the middle of the night and was no doubt looking forward to his bed after a long day's work. It was only when she reminded him that he had been instructed by Mr Lockhart to do exactly what Nellie wanted that he had resentfully relented.

Then she had spent a restless night in the rooms

above the local inn, tossing and turning without sleeping. It hadn't been the sound of revellers in the tavern below that had kept her awake, she was used to sleeping in a noisy city, it was the thoughts in her head, going around and around.

She looked along the track and willed the train to hurry. She was emotionally shattered and wanted to return to the refuge of her business and her own rooms.

The uniformed station master walked past, looking at his fob watch. 'Not long now, ma'am. The early train to London is never late,' he said proudly, as if he was personally responsible for the efficiency of the train service.

Nellie looked up at the station clock. Five minutes to go until the train was due. Five anxious minutes and this would all be over.

She paced the empty station. No one else was getting on the early morning train. It would be stopping to pick up one lone passenger and the trollies that were piled high with goods and the bulging bags of mail waiting on the station to be loaded on board.

She turned to pace her way back along the station and was stopped in her tracks. She wasn't alone after all. Dominic was running along the station and he didn't look happy.

'Nellie, what are you doing?' he shouted, still halfway down the platform. 'Were you going to leave without speaking to me? We need to talk after what happened between us.'

Nellie anxiously looked around the station. Was there anywhere she could flee to? No, she was being ridiculous. Soon the train would arrive. Then she could go back to London, back to her real life, but for now she was going to have to endure one more conversation with Dominic.

He stopped in front of her and grabbed her arms tightly. 'Nellie, you can't leave, not now, not like this.'

She drew in a shaky breath and looked up at him. The dark smudges under his eyes, his unshaven face and the grey tinge to his skin suggested he, too, had spent a sleepless night. And it was all her fault. Thanks to her he had lost everything. Lady Cecily had presumably given him his marching orders and how could Nellie blame her? There would be no connection to the Ashmores, no presentation at court for Violet and Emmaline, no royal balls, no dukes coming a'courting for his sisters, and all because Nellie Regan couldn't resist this irresistible man.

And he was wrong. She *could* leave without speaking to him and that was exactly what she had planned to do. But that was now an impossibility. She was going to have to have one last, painful conversation with him, one that would end everything between them, one from which there would be no turning back.

She shook her head, lifted her chin and forced down all silly emotions, all unwanted desires. She hadn't been strong last night, but she had to be strong now. 'There's nothing to say, Dominic, so don't waste your breath.'

He reached down for her hands, but she placed them firmly behind her back. 'Nellie, you can't leave me, not without discussing what happened between us last night. Last night changed everything for us. We have to talk about it.'

She shook her head again. Last night *had* changed everything and that was why it should never have happened, that was why she had to leave. And Dominic needed to understand that. They had both succumbed to their passions, but in the cold light of day, she knew there was no future for them.

She forced herself to give a light laugh. 'There's nothing to discuss. We had a quick kiss and a fumble in the library. It wouldn't be the first time that had happened between a master and a servant and I doubt it will be the last. There's nothing more to talk about.'

Further colour drained from his already ashen face and he recoiled as if she had slapped him. The hands that were reaching out to her dropped to his sides and he took a step backwards. Nellie wanted to take him in her arms and soothe away the pain that was written on his face. She wanted to tell him that was not how she saw him, that she loved him. But her cruel words had the intended effect. They had made him see that he was better off without her in his life, causing him constant problems.

He had to realise the truth. There was no future for *them*, but that did not mean that Dominic needed to ruin his own future, and the future of his sisters, just because he had allowed his passions to rule his head for one foolish moment. Lady Cecily might have rejected him last night—Nellie could only assume that she had, it was certainly what Nellie would have done—but another aristocrat with the necessary pedigree and connections was sure to see the advantage of marrying his daughter to the wealthy and extremely suitable Mr Dominic Lockhart.

'It wasn't like that,' he finally said, his voice quiet and strained.

Nellie pushed her chin forward and shrugged her shoulders. 'Well, it hardly matters what it was like. I'm leaving. That's the end of the matter.'

After all, I've done enough damage already.

'Now, I'd appreciate it if you went back to your guests. I've a train to catch and a business to run.'

'But, Nellie…'

'Miss Regan,' she forced herself to say to him. 'I'm not your servant, you can call me Miss Regan. You may have wanted to do what countless other men in your position have done with servants, but that doesn't mean we're on equal terms.'

Nellie knew her harsh words and tone had hit home. Shock and pain seemed to wage a war on his face, until it finally set into that stern, arrogant expression he had worn when she first saw him. As cruel as her words were, they were right. They could never be on equal terms. They came from different classes and nothing could ever change that.

'As you wish, Miss Regan. Then this is goodbye.' He remained standing in front of her.

Nellie leaned forward and looked along the empty track as if more concerned about when the train would arrive than what had just happened between herself and the man she loved.

'Yes, goodbye, Mr Lockhart.'

He turned and strode off down the station, his back rigid. Nellie watched him walk away. She took a few steps towards him. Should she chase after him? Should she tell him that she didn't mean the harsh things she had just said? Should she go to him and tell him she was sorry, that she didn't think he was like countless other men who had tried to take advantage of a servant?

But then what would she say? She halted. Would she tell him she loved him, that she didn't care if she ruined his life as long as she could be with him?

She took another, hesitant step in his direction, just as the train puffed its way into the station. The train that would take her away from the man she loved. Despite her firm resolution she cried out to him to come back. The hissing engine stopped in front of her, releasing a billowing wall of steam that engulfed the station and drowned out her cries.

He disappeared around the corner of the station and, with tears coursing down her cheeks, Nellie entered the train that would take her away from Dominic Lockhart.

Chapter Seventeen

It was over. Nellie was determined to put the past where it belonged, firmly behind her, and get on with her life. But that would be so much easier if she wasn't constantly thinking about Dominic Lockhart, if she wasn't forever remembering the way he looked, the sound of his voice, the heady masculine scent of him and, worst of all, the touch of his lips, the caressing stroke of his hands.

Fight it as much as she could, those memories kept invading her thoughts. Not for the first time, she shook her head as if she could physically drive out those memories. She should not be thinking of him now, not when she was working. She had to concentrate on what she was doing.

Forcing herself to focus, she continued to curl and clip her client's hair into place. The customer had been chatting while Nellie had styled her hair, but Nellie had heard hardly a word, too preoccupied with her own whirling thoughts. Fortunately, the client had been content with the occasional nod of encouragement from Nellie and seemed oblivious to the fact she had not been listened to, but this would not do.

She stood back to inspect her work, hoping her distraction was not too evident in the woman's hairstyle. She could not afford to let her high standards drop, no matter how distracted her mind was becoming. It was vital that she think about her work and not that man.

Her client turned her head from side to side and smiled. 'Oh, Miss Regan, you are a wonder. I can't thank you enough.'

With relief, Nellie smiled her thanks and escorted the young woman out to the front room, where Harriet took her money and, like the good saleswoman Harriet was, pointed out some interesting hair adornments and cosmetics the lady might like to purchase as well. Nellie smiled at Harriet and pushed aside the silk curtains to return to the parlour. As soon as the curtains fell back into place her smile died, her shoulders slumped in dejection.

She had intended to tidy up before the next customer. Instead she collapsed into an armchair, exhausted from all this pretence. It was hard to maintain a façade of happiness when your heart was breaking, hard to act as if all was right with the world, when your world had been turned upside down and you no longer knew what to think or feel.

She put her head in her hands. Free of the strain of pretending to be happy in front of her client, the full extent of her misery overtook her. It had only been a week since she had left Dominic at the train sta-

tion, so it wasn't surprising that she still felt distraught.
But how long was she going to have to suffer this torment before she got that man out of her system? How
long before Dominic ceased to be permanently in her
thoughts? How long before he stopped invading her
dreams? How long until she could do what she was
determined to do: put this unfortunate episode behind
her, forget all about it, pretend it never happened and
just get on with her life?

Nellie knew that wasn't going to happen until he
stopped possessing her thoughts. But he was always
there in her mind, no matter how she tried to divert
herself. He was there when she made polite conversation with her clients. She couldn't help but wonder
what he was doing when she was taking a drink after
work at the local public house. But, worst of all, she
couldn't stop herself from obsessing over him when
she was back in her rooms. Then all she could think
of was the memory of him in her bed, with his muscular chest naked except for the bandages. And once she
had thought of that there was no way she could stop
her mind from straying to the memory of that kiss, the
way he had taken control, had lifted her on to the table,
had kissed and caressed her.

She ran her tongue along her lips, remembering
that kiss, remembering the masculine taste of him,
remembering his intoxicating scent, all musk, leather
and sandalwood.

How could she have not reacted the way she had?
How could she not have become consumed by passion
and desire by such a kiss? Once again, she became

completely lost in the memory. Her body reacted as if he was kissing her again, caressing her again. Like the foolish girl she was, her lips throbbed with the memory, her heart pounded faster, her skin tingled, craving his touch.

A touch that would never come.

Nellie wiped away her tears, shook her head to drive away those tormenting memories and stood up straight. This would not do at all. She needed to get her thoughts under control. She placed the combs into a solution to be washed, determined to try to act as if she was a professional businesswoman, not some silly shop girl who had fallen for the wrong man.

Harriet entered the parlour and handed Nellie a white calling card with embossed gold lettering. When Nellie saw the name on the card her legs went weak beneath her and she grabbed the back of the nearest armchair to stop herself from falling. She had to fight to remain upright. It was essential to remain calm and at least pretend a whirlwind of emotions hadn't been released within her at the sight of that name.

'There's a lady outside who says she'd like to have a word with you,' Harriet said.

Nellie gripped the card tightly and drew in a few breaths to steady her rampaging heartbeat. 'Thank you, Harriet. Ask her to come through here, will you, please?'

Harriet disappeared behind the curtain. Nellie stared at her startled reflection and forced herself to breathe in and out, slowly and deeply. Whatever Lady Cecily had come to say to her she would just take it. For once in her life she would accept every remonstration that was thrown her way. She would say nothing in her defence. After all, how could you ever justify behaviour that was indefensible?

Lady Cecily pushed past the curtain and smiled at Nellie. It was not the expression Nellie expected to see. It was the first time she had seen Lady Cecily smile and it transformed her usually dour countenance, both softening and lighting up her face. But why she should be smiling now, of all times, was a mystery. And why should she be smiling at Nellie, of all people? That was even more mysterious. She should be consumed with anger, snarling at Nellie, not smiling.

'Nellie, I am so pleased to see you again,' she said, still smiling.

Nellie knew she should curtsy and attempt a polite smile back, but instead she stood in the middle of the room, too surprised and wary to move. They stood staring at each other, one smiling, the other frozen to the spot. Then Nellie remembered her manners. She bobbed a quick curtsy and gestured towards an armchair.

Lady Cecily sat down, tucking her skirt underneath her. Nellie remained standing until Lady Cecily gestured for her to also sit. Slowly Nellie lowered herself into the chair, still holding her breath, her stomach clenching, her shoulders tense.

She was desperate to hear what Lady Cecily had to say, to get it over and done with, but also dreading what was to come. All Nellie knew for certain was that for probably the first time in her life she was going to have to remember her place and not speak until asked to.

'Oh, Nellie, I've come to thank you,' Lady Cecily said, her smile growing even bigger.

Nellie nearly fell off her chair but managed to stop herself by gripping the arms. But she wasn't able to stop her mouth from falling open.

Slowly, she closed her gaping mouth and swallowed. 'Thank me?' she asked, her voice strangely high pitched.

'Yes. My life has changed completely and I couldn't be happier. And it's all thanks to you, Nellie.'

'Oh?' Nellie said, as much a question as a statement. Presumably she had given Dominic his marching orders and quite right to. Nellie would have done exactly the same if she had seen her fiancé kissing another woman. But why should she be so happy about her engagement coming to an end and in such scandalous circumstances? And why should she be thanking Nellie, of all people?

'Well, I…' Lady Cecily paused, her face serious as she looked at Nellie.

Nellie braced herself and gripped the crumpled calling card in her hand more tightly. Now she was going to get the reprimand she so rightly deserved.

'You don't mind if I call you Nellie, do you?'

A strange buzzing sound erupted in Nellie's head as she tried to order her confused thoughts. 'No. No, I don't mind at all,' she said. She deserved to be called much worse names than her own given name.

'Good, thank you.' Lady Cecily's smile returned.

'Yes, I took your advice and it's changed my life. I'm a free woman now and I'm so happy.'

Nellie swallowed. 'Advice?' She had given no advice to Lady Cecily, had barely spoken to her. And even if she had given her advice, she doubted it would have been anything sensible and certainly should not be followed. After all, who in their right mind would listen to advice from a woman like Nellie, a woman whose own behaviour was beneath contempt? A woman who couldn't stop herself from falling for a man she could never have.

'Yes. I was so intrigued about what you said about America being a place where people can reinvent themselves, become who they want to be. And that's exactly what I'm going to do. I'm going to go and live in America and reinvent myself as the woman I really want to be.'

Nellie closed her eyes and rubbed her hand across her forehead. This was a disaster. How much more destruction could her behaviour bring to these people's lives? She had caused Dominic to be beaten black and blue. She had ruined his chances of making a suitable marriage to Lady Cecily. She had destroyed Dominic's sisters' chances of marrying well. And now a few foolish words, words she could hardly remember saying, had caused Dominic's fiancée to flee from him across the ocean. She had said a few stupid words, kissed the wrong man and that had caused this lovely young woman to take drastic actions that would change her life for ever. All because Nellie couldn't keep her passions under control.

'I'm not sure if that's such a good idea,' Nellie said quietly.

She wasn't sure whether she should be trying to give Lady Cecily any more advice, not when her last, which she couldn't even remember giving, had caused such problems. And not when her own behaviour was so despicable, but she had to try to undo some of the damage she had done.

'Perhaps you shouldn't end your engagement to Mr Lockhart until you've had some time to think about it. After all, until I came along you were looking forward to marrying him. And I know what I did was unforgivable, but it was just one…just one kiss. What happened between Dominic and me meant nothing to either of us.'

Well, it meant a lot to me, but it shouldn't have.

'You shouldn't call off your marriage just because of one kiss. And I promise you, it will never happen again. I will never see Mr Lockhart again. And even if you don't want to stay engaged to him, you certainly shouldn't give up everything you have here in England and go all the way to America, where you know no one, where you'll have nothing.'

Lady Cecily continued to smile throughout Nellie's speech. Even when she had mentioned *that kiss* her expression hadn't faltered.

'Oh, I won't be on my own. I will have someone with me. I'll have Charlie.'

This was getting more and more confusing. 'Charlie—who's Charlie?'

'Charlie Armstrong. He is… I mean he was the head footman at Hardgrave Estate.'

Nellie stared at her, momentarily dumbstruck. Charlie Armstrong the footman, the man who was the only servant who hadn't laughed when Nellie had done her rather rude impersonation of Dominic and Lady Cecily's wedding night. Colour rushed to Nellie's face at the memory of that other piece of bad behaviour on her part. Charlie Armstrong was obviously very loyal to his mistress, but even a loyal servant would not be enough in a country where Lady Cecily knew no one.

'But, Lady Cecily, even with your own footman I still think going to America is an unwise decision. I urge you to reconsider.' Nellie sounded as if she was talking to a rather dim-witted child. She knew she was being rude. Lady Cecily was not dim-witted, nor was she a child, but she was certainly behaving like one. Perhaps this was how she expressed anger and grief, by making rash decisions, by doing things that would cause her further harm. Instead, she should be yelling at Nellie, trying to ruin Nellie's life, not ruining her own.

'Please, Lady Cecily, I beg you to reconsider.'

'Oh, Nellie, you don't understand, do you? Isn't it obvious?' She continued to smile at Nellie and waited for a response.

Nellie slowly shook her head. Nothing about this woman's behaviour was obvious.

'I'm going to marry Charlie. I'm in love with him.' She was beaming. 'I didn't think we could ever be together, so I agreed with Father when he said I should marry Mr Lockhart.' She stopped smiling and her brow furrowed. 'Dominic is such a good man and I thought perhaps one day I'd come to love him. I thought when I married him and moved to his estate, away from Charlie, I'd be able to forget the man I really loved. But when I saw you in Dominic's arms, when I saw the two of you kissing, I knew how wrong I was.'

Nellie swallowed, her cheeks burning in shame at the memory of what Lady Cecily had seen. 'I'm sorry I...'

Lady Cecily smiled at her and held up her hands. 'Don't worry, Nellie. You have nothing to apologise for—quite the contrary. It was seeing the two of you together that made me realise I would never love Dominic the way I love Charlie. The two of you were kissing with such passion, such abandonment. I could never feel that way for any other man but Charlie.'

Lady Cecily shook her head, her smile fading. 'I stood at the door watching the two of you and I felt nothing, absolutely nothing.' She looked at Nellie, her eyes wide as if appealing to her for understanding. 'I was watching another woman kissing my fiancé with such fervent passion and I didn't care. I realised that if you had been kissing Charlie I wouldn't be just standing there, watching and feeling nothing. I would have been furious, heartbroken, desolate. Even the thought of it is making me feel angry.'

She closed her eyes, shook her head slightly, as if trying to drive out the emotions surrounding that imagined scenario, and her smile returned. 'That's when I realised I couldn't give up Charlie. I immediately rushed back down to the servants' hall to find him and tell him what I felt.'

Nellie stared at her, trying to absorb what she was saying.

Lady Cecily blushed slightly. 'That's where I had been coming from when I saw the two of you in the library. I'd made up an excuse to talk to him. When I'd become engaged, we'd agreed to have as little to do with each other as possible, but I was always making up silly excuses to see him. I couldn't keep away from him. It was because of me that he was at the Lockhart Estate that night. I had insisted to Father that the head footman needed to accompany us to the ball. I just had to keep seeing him, despite our agreement to try to avoid each other.'

She smiled coyly. 'Anyway, when I saw you and Dominic together, I knew that I couldn't give up on Charlie, that I had to find a way for us to be together. It was then that I remembered what you said to me about America, here in this very room.'

She looked around as if the parlour held some marvellous qualities that could transform people's lives. 'So, I rushed back down to the servants' hall and asked Charlie to run away with me and start a new life in America. He didn't need much persuading. Especially after I told him how much I loved him, how I couldn't live without him.'

She smiled at the happy memory. 'Charlie gave in his notice immediately. We crept away that night. Charlie took our carriage and we drove through the night down to London where we found somewhere to stay and booked our passage to America. We've been hiding out in London ever since, pretending to be a newly married couple.' Her cheeks reddened slightly and she gave a little laugh. 'It's been such fun, I can tell you.'

Lady Cecily tried to pull her face into a more serious expression, failed and went back to smiling. 'Anyway, we leave today for our new life together. We plan to marry as soon as we arrive in America, then we can start our new life as man and wife. But I couldn't leave before coming to see you and thanking you. If you hadn't kissed Dominic, I would never have come to my senses. So, thank you, Nellie.'

She stood up, leaned down and kissed the speechless Nellie on her cheek. 'I have to run now. In a few hours I'll be on a steamship heading for America and a new life with my future husband, Charlie.' Her voice softened every time she mentioned Charlie's name and she continued smiling as if incapable of containing her joy.

'Goodbye, Nellie.'

She swept out of the parlour, leaving Nellie still sitting in her armchair, staring straight ahead and wondering what Lady Cecily's revelation would mean for her and Dominic.

Chapter Eighteen

Dominic stared down at his uneaten breakfast. He wasn't hungry. A few short weeks ago his life was going according to plan. He knew what he wanted and how to get it. Then along came Nellie Regan. She had turned everything upside down and around and about and left him shaken up and disorientated. She had caused him to question everything: who he was, what he wanted and why he wanted it.

Now he was left reeling as if battered by a fierce emotional storm. Kissing her, holding her, caressing her lovely body had felt so right. Then she was gone.

On the night that they had kissed, she had been right to tell him to try to find Cecily. It was the right thing to do, to try to explain what had happened, to try to undo the damage they had done. But would he have done the right thing if he had known that Nellie would not be waiting for him when he returned? Dominic didn't know. And now he never would.

After he had left Nellie in the library, he had

searched Lockhart Estate for Cecily, but she had been nowhere to be found. Finally, when he had all but exhausted his search, he had gone down to the last place he would expect her to run to, the servants' hall. There he had been told she had left, along with her footman. It had been too late to pursue her back to Hardgrave Estate and, if he was being perfectly honest, he was relieved that she had left. He could talk to her once tempers had settled. In the meantime, he could return to Nellie. After what had happened, he had so much he needed to say to her, so much he wanted to ask her.

He had gone to her room, expecting to find her waiting for him. But she wasn't there and neither were her bags. Once again, he searched the house. Had she moved to another room? Had she decided to stay in the servants' quarters after all? He didn't know. Frantically he had searched the entire house and grounds, but she was nowhere to be found. It was only when he saw his coachman coming up the drive and he had questioned the tired man that he discovered her whereabouts. He was informed that the coachman had taken her to the nearby village and she was staying the night in a local inn.

Dominic had wanted to leave immediately, to follow her. He could not let her go, not like this, not ever. But he had seen the fatigue etched on the coachman's face. It was the small hours of the morning, the man needed his rest, as did the horses.

Instead he had arranged for a horse to be made ready for him first thing in the morning. After a sleepless night he rode to the inn, only to find she had already left to take the first train to London. With only minutes to spare he had ridden to the station, but their meeting hadn't gone as he expected. Instead of running into his arms as he had hoped, she had told him there could never be anything between them.

He had been shocked, angry, but deep down he now knew she was right. He hadn't been thinking straight when he had kissed her. He hadn't been thinking straight since he'd first met her. When he had seen her at the train station, all he wanted to do was hold her, to kiss her. He had not been thinking of Lady Cecily. He had not been thinking of his sisters and their chances of making good marriages. He had not been thinking of his family's position in society. He had been thinking of nothing except his own needs, of having Nellie back in his arms. He had let his passions rule his head. But Nellie had a cooler head than him. She had been the one to act rationally.

But it had all been for nothing, anyway. After what had happened between himself and Nellie, he knew he could not marry Cecily. But before he had a chance to tell her and her father that the engagement was off, he discovered that she had run off with her footman.

He moved the uneaten breakfast around on his plate. It appeared he had never really known Cecily Hardgrave. Her reserve and coolness towards him were not due to her aristocratic bearing, nor was it because they had yet to get to know each other properly. It was because she was in love with another man. Yet she had been willing to marry him because that was what her father wanted, what society expected. In one way he and Cecily Hardgrave were alike. They had both been trying to do what was right, to do their duty by their family and conform to society's expectations.

Before the Duke of Ashmore had told him that Cecily had gone to America with her footman, Dominic had tried to write to her, but had been unable to compose a letter to express or explain what had happened. He'd been unable to do that because he was still trying to make sense of it himself. All he could write was that he was profoundly sorry and that was true. Sorry for what she had seen, sorry that he no longer wanted to marry her, sorry for how he had treated her, sorry for the whole damn episode.

He had never sent the letter because a crestfallen Duke of Ashmore had arrived at his home. Dominic was sure that Cecily had told him everything she had seen in the library. He had been unsure how the Duke would have taken the news that the man he expected to be his future son-in-law had been caught with another woman. The Duke had suspected Nellie was Dominic's mistress, even though it wasn't the case. The Duke had even said he had no objection to Dominic having a mistress as long as he was discreet. But a lack of discretion was one of the many crimes Dominic had committed.

The Duke had been within his rights to call off the engagement—after all, such a marriage would be an insult to his daughter after what she had witnessed. Dominic was prepared to extend him the privilege of ending the engagement and of telling society whatever he liked about the reasons—it was no more than Dominic deserved.

But instead of reprimanding Dominic for his lack of discretion, he had come to apologise. The Duke had told him, with great shame, that Cecily had run off with her footman and no one knew where she had gone. She had left a note to say she loved the man, wanted to marry him and begged her father not to try to find her.

The Duke was deeply embarrassed by his daughter's behaviour and kept apologising. Dominic had assured him, repeatedly, that there was nothing to be sorry for. Throughout their conversation Dominic had been forced to keep his face serious and suppress the smile that was threatening to reveal the happiness he was feeling. He was so pleased for Cecily. She had not been hurt by his behaviour. If anything, it had freed her. It might not make sense for the daughter of a duke to marry a footman, but who was Dominic to judge anyone? Particularly when Cecily had proven she had the courage to do what she wanted, rather than what society demanded. Once he would have scorned such behaviour, but now it brought him immense pleasure and he quietly wished Cecily every happiness with her footman. The pursuit of happiness—that was something else he would have scorned just a few months ago.

But even if he admired Cecily, it did not mean it was an example that he could follow. Unlike Cecily he had other people to consider. When he'd chased Nellie to the train station he had been prepared to throw in everything for her, his position, his sisters' futures, everything. It was only her good sense that had stopped him from making a rash, regrettable mistake.

Unlike Cecily he had three sisters who needed to

make good marriages. He could not subject them, or their children, to the scorn of being an outsider, someone who was looked down on because of their lowly position in society. He could not let history repeat itself by marrying someone from Nellie's world.

His mother had caused a scandal when she had married an ex-stable boy. For that action she'd been ostracised from society, and so had her children. How much more damage would be caused if he married a former servant, someone in trade? His sisters' chances of making good marriages would go from slim to nonexistent.

That only left Dominic with one choice. He had to put all thoughts of Nellie Regan out of his mind. He had to still the tempest of thoughts that were storming around inside his head, had to banish memories of her eyes, her lips and her luscious body.

He pushed away his untouched breakfast, picked up the silver coffee pot and poured himself a cup. But driving out thoughts of Nellie Regan wasn't going to happen if he kept replaying over and over again what it was like to take her in his arms, to kiss and caress her. Only action would still his thoughts and allow him to be free of this self-inflicted torment. He had to fill up his days with activity so he had no time to think. No time to do what he was doing right now, staring down at the thick black liquid in his coffee cup, while he ruminated on what might have been.

The door flew open and Amanda rushed into the breakfast room. She served herself from the silver terrines lined up on the sideboard, the spoons clinking loudly against the serving dishes as she filled up her plate. Smiling, she sat down opposite and began eating a hearty breakfast. 'Good morning, Dominic,' she trilled. 'Isn't it a beautiful day?'

He looked up at the floor-to-ceiling windows and out to the gardens and parklands of Lockhart Estate. The sun was indeed shining brightly in a clear blue sky. He hadn't noticed until now.

He forced himself to smile at his sister. 'And what do you have planned for today, Amanda?'

Her smile grew brighter. She shuffled around in her seat as if unable to contain her excitement. 'Thomas… Lord Westcliffe is going to come by today and he's going to want to speak to you.'

Dominic raised his eyebrows. 'He is?'

'Oh, Dominic,' she cried out in joy. 'He wants to court me. I know it's very sudden and we've only just met, but he's so wonderful. He's funny, witty, clever, he's just lovely. And he's so handsome.'

Dominic's forced smile became genuine. 'And he's the son of a duke.'

Amanda flicked her napkin in his direction before placing it back on her lap. 'Oh, who cares about that. I'd want to be with him no matter who his family was.' She bit the edge of her lip. 'I think I'm falling in love with him. Can you fall in love with someone when you've only just met them?'

Dominic didn't know the answer to that question, but he kept on smiling. 'That's wonderful news. Of course I would be more than happy to meet with him.'

Amanda smiled at him across the table. 'It also

means you don't have to worry about us any more. If I do marry him, all your problems are solved as well, aren't they?'

Dominic raised his eyebrows once again in question.

'Well, if I marry Thomas…' She smiled and closed her eyes briefly. 'If I marry Lord Westcliffe, the family will be connected to an old, aristocratic family. I'll be able to arrange for my sisters to be presented at court. And you'll be free to marry whomever you want.'

Dominic knew his sister was trying to be kind, but things were never as simple as that. 'A marriage to Lord Westcliffe will certainly be excellent for your sisters and the family. It is a very favourable arrangement and I am pleased for you, Amanda.'

Amanda put down her knife and fork and glared at him. 'Dominic, if I marry Lord Westcliffe, it will be because I love him, for no other reason. I'd do it whether he was the son of a duke or a dockworker. All I'm saying is that as he *is* the son of a duke it makes things easier for you, because you alone in this family care about such things and I know you feel you won't have done your duty until you've married us all off to aristocrats.'

'That's not true. I…'

Amanda picked up her napkin and waved it at him, as if shooing away his words. 'It is true and we're not like you, Dominic. My sisters and I have always wanted to marry for love, not social position, just like Mother and Father did.'

Dominic could hardly believe what he was hearing. How could she say she did not care that the family had become pariahs, that their mother had lost all contact with her family and friends, that everyone looked down on them? 'Amanda, that's a foolish, sentimental…'

She waved her napkin again. 'Mother and Father were in love, they were happy. Mother never really cared that her family had turned their backs on her. It was a sacrifice she was prepared to make in exchange for love. And she could see what sort of marriages her sisters had made and was pleased she had escaped their fates. Her sisters might have maintained their position in society by making supposedly good marriages, but they were miserable. Mother didn't feel sad that they wanted nothing to do with her, she felt sorry for them. And she never wanted that for us. She always told me that I should follow my heart and marry for love, nothing else.'

Dominic stared at his sister as he tried to formulate an argument to prove to her just how absurd she was being.

'And that's what she would have wanted for you as well, Dominic.' She replaced her threatening napkin and reached her hand over the table towards him. 'I think she always assumed that as a man you would have choices and would choose to marry someone you loved, so perhaps that's why she never spoke to you about it. She would never have wanted you to sacrifice yourself to advance the family's social status. She would have wanted you to be happy, wouldn't she?'

'Well, yes, but…' It seemed Nellie Regan wasn't the only one who was making Dominic question everything—his sister was starting to do the same.

'You've been moping around for the last week and I know it's got nothing to do with Lady Cecily breaking off the engagement.'

Dominic was not going to discuss such things with his sister, so he gave a *hmmph* in reply and took a sip of his coffee.

'You're miserable because of Nellie Regan.'

Dominic spluttered on his drink and stared at his sister, too shocked to speak.

'Don't look so surprised,' Amanda said as Dominic tried to compose himself. 'I'm not entirely blind as to what's been going on in this house. I saw the way you looked at her when she was here for the ball and it started to make sense. You'd changed since you came back from your time in London and I don't just mean because of your injuries. So, I asked my lady's maid for the gossip from below stairs. You know how the servants know everything. Well, she told me that there was indeed something between the two of you, that you'd actually rushed after her in the early hours of the morning when she left for London.' Amanda smiled, her eyebrows raised, her eyes shining. 'You rushed after Nellie Regan, not Cecily Hardgrave. That sounds like there's definitely something between you and Nellie.'

Dominic released his held breath. Thank goodness his innocent sister hadn't been told about the intimacy that had taken place in the library and hopefully that was also something that had escaped the notice of the ever-observant servants.

'All right, now you know I acted like a fool. But

fortunately, Miss Regan was more sensible and she rebuffed me. Now, let's say no more on the matter. What time will Lord Westcliffe be joining us?'

'Don't change the subject, Dominic. Nellie rebuffed you because she thought you were still engaged to Cecily. The ending of your engagement changes everything. You're now free to do what makes you happy, not what you think you're supposed to do, but what you want to do.'

'It's not as simple as that.' He took a sip of his coffee to underline that the conversation was over.

'Yes, it is. It's very simple. You're sacrificing your happiness because you want to elevate our position in society. You think it will make me and my sisters happy, but it's not what any of us want. We don't care about society. We don't care about making so-called good marriages. We want to marry for love, just like our mother, and be happy. We want that for you as well, Dominic. And you should want it for yourself.'

She smiled at him. 'Follow your heart, Dominic, do what makes you happy, not what you think society expects you to do.'

He stared at his sister as she continued to smile at him.

Was it really that simple? Could there really be a simple answer to such a complex problem? *Follow your heart.* It seemed far too easy.

Dominic looked down at his coffee. Had he been making things more complicated than they needed to be? Was his sister right?

He raised his head and nodded. 'All right, Amanda.

I will.' With those few words it was as if an enormous weight had been lifted off Dominic's shoulders. He would do something completely outrageous—he would follow his heart back to Nellie Regan.

Once he had spoken to Lord Westcliffe and given his blessing to his courtship of Amanda, he would take the next train up to London.

Chapter Nineteen

Throughout the train journey Dominic rehearsed what he was going to say to convince Nellie that marriage to him would be perfect. She had sounded so resolute at the train station when she had told him there could never be anything between them, but that was when she thought they could never be man and wife. Without that, she had quite rightly said she wanted nothing to do with him. But that was no longer the case. Now they had a future together.

And her actions when he had kissed her in the library had shown him that, despite her words, there *was* something between them. There was passion, there was fire, there was intense desire that had brushed aside all reason and had consumed them both.

She had also accused him of behaving like so many men of his class before him, of taking advantage of a woman from the servant class, but he knew that, too, wasn't true. He was certain that Nellie also knew it wasn't true. He was not the type of man who would do something so despicable. And even if he was, no one would ever take advantage of that lovely little minx. Any man who tried would be taking a mighty risk. He smiled to himself as he remembered her confronting him the first time they had met, with her eyes flashing, her hands defiantly on her hips. That was not a young woman who anyone would be able to take advantage of and he pitied the poor fool who tried.

The fact that he wanted to marry her swept away those objections. He could hardly be accused of taking advantage of her now. Not when he wanted to marry her. Contentment washed through him. Amanda was right—once you followed your heart everything became much more simple, everything started to make sense.

He looked out of the train window and watched as the view turned from green rolling countryside to small villages. The train would soon be entering the edges of London, taking him closer and closer to Nellie.

He smiled to himself. He would soon be marrying Nellie Regan, a former lady's maid who was now in trade. Who would have ever thought his life would change this much in such a short time? Who would believe that he could change so quickly from being completely opposed to people who let their hearts rule their heads to someone who was more than happy to do exactly that? But it was true. He was now being driven by his passions and throwing all caution to the wind, and all because of Nellie Regan.

He looked back at the empty compartment, pleased that no one could see him smiling to himself like a demented fool. He picked up the folded newspaper he had planned to read on the train, then put it back down again and looked out of the window.

But then, why should he be so surprised at the change that had come over him? Nellie Regan was more than capable of changing anything, including him. How could he have ever resisted her charms? Not when she was simply that, irresistible. He didn't have a chance. From the moment he had seen her standing in the kitchen at Hardgrave Estate he had been smitten. And every time he had seen her from that moment onwards, he had become more entranced until he could no longer think straight. But now he was thinking straight. Now he knew what he wanted. He wanted Nellie Regan to be his wife.

Arriving at the station, he hailed a hansom cab to take him to Nellie's hairdressing parlour. Impatience got the better of him. He tapped his cane on the roof and urged the driver to make all haste. Now that he had made up his mind, he could hardly contain himself, he wanted to propose immediately.

He had never noticed before just how congested the London traffic was as the cab jostled between omnibuses, trams, carriages and carts. It was as if this infernal traffic was trying to deliberately thwart him from reaching his goal. But now that his mind was made up nothing, not even the London traffic, could stop him. Despite his irritation he was still smiling. He patted his top pocket, which contained a beautiful diamond and ruby ring. It had belonged to his mother and was so appropriate. His mother was a woman who had given up everything for the man she loved. And now Dominic was doing the same, giving up everything for Nellie Regan.

Finally, after a seemingly interminable amount of time, the cab pulled up outside Nellie's business premises. He paused outside the door to try to get that foolish grin off his face. And he *was* a fool, a fool for Nellie Regan, a fool for love. But that didn't mean he wanted to look like an idiot, not when he was about to do something so serious. He took a few deep breaths and tried to compose his face.

The door opened and the jingling bell announced his arrival. She was standing alone in the empty shop, her account ledgers open in front of her. He had timed his appearance perfectly. It was past closing time. There would be no distraction from clients or staff. He had her to himself and that was what he wanted, to have her to himself, for the rest of his life.

She looked up. 'I'm sorry, we're close—' She stopped mid-sentence. Her cheeks exploded into a blushing red, her eyes narrowed, her expression wary.

'Nellie,' he whispered.

She coughed lightly. 'Mr Lockhart, this is unexpected.' That had to be the understatement of the century. Her face looked completely surprised, but she was about to receive an even bigger surprise when she heard why he was here, standing in her shop.

'I was just about to lock up for the day.' She picked up a large key and clutched it as if her life depended on it.

'I need to talk to you, Nellie.' As eager as he was to say what he had come to say, he wanted to do this properly. He wanted his proposal to be something she would never forget and would one day tell their children and grandchildren about.

'All right, but I just need to lock up first.' With shaking hands, she tried to lock the door. He took the key from her. Their skin touched and Dominic had to fight himself to not just pull her towards him and kiss her there and then. But he could not do that. He had to do this right. He turned the key in the lock with a satisfying *thunk*. They were completely alone. They would not be disturbed. He now had time to propose to her in an unhurried manner.

She took the key from him and turned it over and over in her hand.

He smiled in reassurance. 'I'm not sure if you've heard, but Lady Cecily and I are no longer engaged. In fact, she's run off to America with her footman, the man she plans to marry.'

She nodded. 'Yes, I'm sorry about that, Mr Lockhart. You must be very disappointed and your sisters must be upset that their futures have been affected.'

Dominic almost laughed. That no longer mattered. That was no longer important. 'Disappointed? No, of course I'm not disappointed. You know what this means now, Nellie, don't you?'

She shook her head, her expression still wary.

'It means I can marry you.' It was not how he had intended to propose, but in his excitement the words seem to tumble out before he could stop them.

Her hands shot to her mouth in a failed attempt to stop a gasp escaping and the key she had been clasping so tightly clattered to the floor. Her startled look of surprise made him smile even more. He took a step towards her. Now was the time to take her in his arms, to kiss her. Their first kiss as an engaged couple.

'You can what?' Her lovely voice was uncharacteristically high.

'I can marry you, Nellie.' He placed his hands on her arms, desperate to hold her close, to seal their engagement with a kiss. 'I know it wasn't what I wanted a few weeks ago, but everything has changed since I met you. You've changed me. A few weeks ago, I would have laughed at the idea of me marrying an ex-lady's maid, a woman now in trade, but that is exactly what I want now.' He laughed lightly, his heart so full of joy. 'Lady Cecily isn't the only one who can ignore what society expects.'

She was still shaking her head and he could see her doubts. She still needed reassurance that he meant every word he was saying.

He dropped her arms. Now was not the time for kisses. She needed an explanation. 'I know I said it was important for my sisters to make good marriages and ideally for the two younger ones to be presented at court when they came of age, but that is all taken care of. Lord Westcliffe is courting Amanda. He's the son of a duke. They're so in love I'm sure it will soon result in marriage and, when they do, she will be the daughter-in-law of a duke. Eventually she'll be a duchess. My family will have reached the pinnacle of society, and my sisters will indeed be presented at court. So that leaves me free to marry you. So, will you marry me, Nellie?'

She continued to stare at him with that delightfully dumbfounded expression on her face. For once, it was Nellie who was taken aback by his surprising actions, not the other way around. But he knew he was doing this all wrong. He had rehearsed what he wanted to say when he was on the train, but in his haste it had all come out wrong. He should have made a formal proposal of marriage, not just blurted it out in such a haphazard way.

It was time to make things right. He dropped to one knee in the middle of the shop and took her hand in his.

'Nellie Regan, will you do me the honour of becoming my wife?' He looked up at her and smiled. 'I promise I will do everything in my power to make you happy. I will give you everything you could ever desire. I'll endow you with all my worldly possessions. Nellie, will you marry me?'

She continued to stare down at him, still with that delightfully shocked expression. She blinked a couple of times and drew in a deep breath. Dominic also drew in a deep breath and held it as he waited for her reply.

'No, Dominic, I will not marry you.'

He must have heard wrong. Either that or she had misinterpreted what he had said.

'Nellie, I'm offering you marriage. I'm offering to take you away from all this.' He released her hand and waved his arm around her small shop, to encompass her living quarters and the entire neighbourhood. He took hold of her hand again and looked up at her, beseeching her to understand. 'You'll live a life of luxury on your estate in Kent and in your town house in London.'

Her expression did not change, but she pulled her hand out of his clasp.

'You'll be able to have your own lady's maid if you want and never have to work again.' He was desperate to make her understand. 'I want to marry you, Nellie, and I'm prepared to ignore whatever society says, because for the first time in my life I want to follow my heart, not my head.'

He continued to smile up at her, but his smile was starting to fray at the edges.

'Dominic, please get up off the floor and leave. I've given you my answer. I don't want to marry you.'

'Nellie… I…' She was no longer looking at him, but staring straight ahead. He rose slowly from the floor.

He had heard correctly. She really had said she didn't want to marry him. That was a possibility he had never considered. He had been so certain of himself, so certain of her, and certain that this was the right thing for them both.

He had imagined her crying with joy when he proposed, of falling into his arms, of kissing him with abandoned passion. He had also hoped she would invite him upstairs and they could continue what they had started at Lockhart Estate. He had hoped they would seal their engagement by consummating it in her bed. He had never expected this. Rejection.

Slowly he rose from the floor. She remained staring off into the distance, her jaw clenched tightly, her face resolute.

She reached down and picked up the abandoned key and handed it to him, never once meeting his eye. 'Please let yourself out.'

He looked down at the key, as if unsure what it was that she was giving him. He looked back at her. There must be something he could say to convince her to accept his proposal, to make her change her answer. But his mind was blank. All he could think was that she had refused his proposal of marriage. He had offered her everything and she had said no.

'But, Nellie, I...'

'Please, Dominic. Leave.'

She turned her back on him, returned to the counter and stared down at the accounts' ledger.

It seemed there was nothing more for him to say. He turned the key in the lock and left the shop. Without knowing where he was going, he walked off down the street and out of her life.

Chapter Twenty

Dominic hardly registered the journey home. He must have hailed a hansom cab at some point because he was sure he hadn't walked all the way to the station. And he must have taken the return train journey back to his estate. Then he must have summoned another cab from the station, otherwise he wouldn't be standing at the bottom of the steps, staring up at his house as if unsure what it was and how he had got there.

She had said no. She had said she would not marry him. He had never considered the possibility that she would turn him down. He loved her. He had assumed she loved him. He had been prepared to sacrifice any possible advancement in society by marrying a former servant, something that once would have been so unlikely it would have been ludicrous. But the ex-lady's maid didn't want him. Unbelievable.

Had he misjudged her feelings for him? Had he seen what he wanted to see? Had he been so sure that she loved him because he loved her? She had given him every indication that her feelings for him were as strong as his for her. From the moment they had first met there had been something intangible between them, as if they were made for each other. Hadn't there? Every moment he had spent in her company had reinforced that belief. He might not have admitted it to himself at first, but from the moment he saw her he had wanted her and he was sure she shared those feelings. Could he really have been so wrong?

When they parted at the train station, she had said she did not want to see him again, but he had assumed that was because she saw no future in their relationship. But he had offered her a future. He had offered her everything, but it wasn't what she wanted. She didn't want him. Didn't want to be his wife.

He shook his head and began walking up the stairs. How could he have got it all so wrong? But it seemed he could. He had based so much on one kiss. Too much. He had been prepared to change his life because of one kiss. There was no doubting it was a passionate kiss. Nor could he deny he wanted so much more, but that's all it was, just a kiss.

He halted halfway up the stairs. Was Nellie Regan right when she said it was just a fumble between a wealthy man and an ex-servant? That it meant nothing? It hadn't been how he had felt at the time and it wasn't how he felt now. It had meant something to him, a lot, but perhaps he was wrong about what it meant to her. To her was it *just a fumble*? Had he foolishly thought it meant so much more? Perhaps he should be grateful to

Nellie for setting him straight. She was more sensible than him, she could see that kiss for what it really was.

He dragged his feet up the last few steps to the house. It seemed he was going to have to face facts. He would not be marrying Lady Cecily and he would not be marrying Nellie Regan, two women at opposite ends of the social strata. He had wanted to marry one to advance his family's position in society and was willing to throw away any chance of advancement to marry the second, but he would be marrying neither. It was almost laughable, but the last thing Dominic felt like doing was laughing.

He walked into the house and handed his hat and gloves to the footman. But one good thing had happened this day and he was determined to focus on that, Amanda's happiness. If he thought about that, and that alone, he would forget his own problems.

After he had told Lord Westcliffe that he had no objections to him courting his sister, Amanda had burst into the drawing room, having been listening at the door. The love that had sparked between the two of them was a delight to see and their courtship would hopefully be a straightforward one that would end in marriage. Unlike himself, Amanda hadn't fallen for the wrong person. She hadn't fallen for someone who came with a raft of complications. Dominic should be amused by the irony of the situation. He had always prided himself on being the serious one in the family, the one who was never driven by passion, but always made sensible, rational decisions. Instead he had allowed his passions to drive his behaviour and fall for the wrong woman, while his sister had made a sensible choice. What a joke that was. What a joke he was.

Once he had given his blessing, the happy couple had rushed off to talk to his parents. They would be staying at the Westcliffe family estate for the rest of the week and thank goodness for that. He did not want to endure questions from his excitable sister. Nor did he want his own gloom to put a damper on her happiness.

He paused in the hallway, pulled back his shoulders and lifted his head high. He would not be the cause of anyone's misery. He would not ruin his sister's or anyone else's happiness. It was time to put this entire episode behind him. Nellie had given her answer. There was nothing more to be done or said on the matter. He resumed walking, increasing his pace as he headed straight to his study. The time for all this self-pity was over. He would throw himself into his work. Running the estate required his full attention and that's what he would do. He would not be sidetracked by any of this foolishness. After all, hadn't he disapproved of his parents because they had let their passions rule their heads? Now, for one foolish weak moment, he had done the same. Well, he wouldn't be making that mistake again. He did indeed have a lot to thank Nellie Regan for. She had mocked the upper classes for their lack of passion and he had been equally critical of her friends at The Hanged Man for putting too much emphasis on immediate pleasure and letting their passions dictate their behaviour.

But it seemed Nellie Regan was the one who was ruled by her head and he was the one who had let passion get in the way of making a sensible decision. That was not a mistake he would be making ever again.

He summoned his land steward so they could discuss the improvements Dominic wanted to make to the estate's farmlands. Nellie had taught him a valuable lesson, one he thought his parents had taught him, but he had so easily forgotten. His mother had let her heart rule her head and thrown everything away for love and he had almost done the same. Thank goodness for Nellie Regan and her sense and dispassion.

The land steward arrived and Dominic got down to business. It was time to put all thoughts of love aside and to concentrate on more important matters.

Taking afternoon tea with Arabella Huntsbury, the Duchess of Somerfeld, at London's swanky Claridge's hotel should have been fun. Nellie knew she should be enjoying herself. But it was hard to pretend you were full of the joys of spring when your heart thought it was deepest, darkest winter.

The Duchess had booked an appointment with Nellie, but instead of having her hair styled she had insisted on taking Nellie out for tea. It was a rare treat to be away from the parlour in the middle of the day and to be taking tea in such beautiful surroundings should be a joy. Nellie admonished herself to cheer up and looked around the room, determined to be impressed. She admired the ornate twinkling chandeliers, the exquisite arched windows and the enormous bouquets of out-of-season spring flowers.

She removed a delicate cucumber sandwich from

the three-tiered stand and placed it on her bone-china plate, although the last thing she felt like doing was eating. Instead she took a sip of her tea, forced herself to smile pleasantly, and looked at her fellow guests. The elegant ladies were adorned as beautifully as the room, wearing stylish gowns, and large fashionable hats, bedecked with feathers, flowers and ribbons. They were all enjoying a leisurely afternoon tea. Presumably they had just finished a busy day's shopping and needed to recuperate. Perhaps after tea they would return to their country estates, or maybe they were staying at their London town houses and tonight they would take in the opera or a play.

That was a life Nellie could have had if she had accepted Dominic's proposal. It was a life she didn't want. She would be miserable doing nothing but ordering her servants around, changing from her morning gown to her tea gown, then dressing for dinner, every day, day after day. She'd go mad making idle chit-chat with other idle ladies. She loved the life she had made for herself. Loved being independent, loved being busy. Unfortunately, she also loved Dominic Lockhart.

Dominic had said he wanted to marry her. He had also made it clear how much he would be sacrificing for her when they married. Instead of marrying someone who would elevate him up the social ladder, like Lady Cecily, she would be dragging him down. He said he didn't care, but how long would that last? How long before he looked at her and all he saw was the sacrifice he had made in marrying her. How long before he resented her? That was not a risk Nellie was prepared to take. Nor did she want to marry someone who thought she was beneath him, just because she hadn't been born into money. Nellie was beneath no one. She wasn't beneath all these wealthy, idle women and she was not beneath Mr Dominic Lockhart.

She picked up her cucumber sandwich, determined to enjoy this afternoon tea and not think about Dominic or anyone else who considered themselves better than her. Then she put the sandwich back on her plate. She just wasn't hungry. Instead she took another sip of her tea and smiled at the Duchess. The Duchess was one person who had never treated Nellie as if she was inferior, despite the vast gulf between their positions in society.

'So, how is the latest play going?' Nellie asked, determined to make polite conversation, despite that annoying pain gripping her heart. A pain that would not go away no matter how hard she tried to ignore it. 'I hear you got rave reviews, once again.'

'Mmm, yes, it's going very well. But I don't want to talk about that now. I want to know what's wrong with you, Nellie.'

'Me? Nothing. I'm fine. I'm always fine.' To prove the point Nellie sent the Duchess her sunniest smile. 'The business is going well. Very well. I'm busy every day. Booked solid most days.' Instead of the reassured nod she expected back, the Duchess rose her eyebrows and looked sideways at Nellie.

'When I entered your parlour this afternoon you looked completely miserable and that's not like you. I had a quick word with Matilda and she said it was man troubles. That's why I whisked you away here. So, are you going to tell me what the problem is, or do I have to grill Matilda some more?'

'I'm going to have to have a word with that Matilda about her tendency to gossip.'

'No, you're not. You're going to have to talk to me. So, what is this man trouble?'

Nellie looked across the white-linen tablecloth at the Duchess. She had that defiant look on her face Nellie had seen so many times when they were growing up. She was not going to let this drop until she knew every detail. The Duchess already knew about her first encounter with Dominic at Hardgrave Estate. She had helped engineer her escape, so Nellie filled her in on everything that had happened since, taking in the brawl at The Hanged Man, the assault in the streets, him recovering in her rooms, that fateful kiss, Lady Cecily running off with her footman, through to the proposal. Unlike every other time Nellie had recounted the tale of her encounter with Dominic Lockhart, this time she did not edit it to avoid any of the embarrassing parts. She just told it as it had happened. She even told the Duchess just how intimate that kiss really had been.

The Duchess laughed through the early stages of the story, when Nellie was playing games with Dominic. But then her face grew serious when he was beaten and recovering in her rooms. And once she got to the part where Nellie had kissed Dominic in the library and had been caught in an extremely compromising position by Lady Cecily, her brow furrowed and she nibbled on her bottom lip in concentration. But her smile returned when she told her about Lady Cecily crediting Nellie with the decision to run off to America with her footman, even though Nellie had no recollection of advising that and suspected it had all been Lady Cecily's idea.

When she got to the part where Dominic proposed, the Duchess beamed with happiness, then her smile suddenly died. She furrowed her brow and looked sideways at Nellie, as if trying to work her out. 'But that's good, isn't it? The man you've so obviously fallen in love with wants to marry you. So why do you look so miserable?'

'I said no.'

The Duchess's cup clattered back into its saucer and she stared at Nellie as if she had just sprouted wings. 'You did what?'

Nellie shrugged. 'I turned him down.' She looked at her cup, picked it up, then put it back in the saucer. 'It wasn't right. I'm not right for him. He's not right for me.'

Arabella folded her hands in front of her on the table and leaned forward. 'Look at me, Nellie.'

Nellie raised her eyes and sighed. The Duchess just didn't understand. She was a lovely woman, but she would never know what it was like to be Nellie, to have had to struggle for everything she had achieved, then for some man—well, Dominic Lockhart—to throw that all in her face and assume that all she'd ever really wanted was for some man—well, Dominic Lockhart—to take her away from the life she'd created for herself. A life she loved and was very proud of.

'And why did you say no, Nellie?' She waited for Nellie's answer. None came.

'Is it because he's rich? Is that why you said no?'

'No, it certainly is not,' Nellie shot back.

Arabella sent her a knowing look. 'That's it, isn't it? Oh, Nellie, you're such a snob.'

Nellie felt her eyes grow wide in disbelief at what she had just heard. 'Me? A snob? How can I be a snob? How can someone from my background, with my position in society, ever be called a snob?' She laughed to emphasise just how ridiculous that suggestion was.

'You are. You always look down your nose at people who were born wealthy.'

'I do not,' Nellie gasped out, barely able to contain her outrage.

Arabella tapped her lip with her forefinger. 'Well, let's see. When you first saw Dominic, you made fun of him because he was awkward with his fiancée. Is that right?'

'Well, yes, but…'

'If you'd seen one of the local lads and his fiancée dancing awkwardly down at The Hanged Man, would you have made fun of them for sport?'

'No, but that's different.'

'How?'

'Well…well…'

'Because Dominic Lockhart and Lady Cecily are rich and the local lad isn't.'

Nellie crossed her arms, refusing to accept that was true.

'And if you had offended one of the local tradesmen by doing a rude impersonation of him in front of his employees and he wanted to reprimand you for it, would you make him do it in a place where he felt uncomfortable and out of place, liked The Hanged Man?'

'No, I suppose not,' she mumbled.

'But you did that to Dominic Lockhart. Why?' The Duchess held up her hand before Nellie could explain. 'Let me answer that for you. Because he's rich and you wanted to put him in his place.' The Duchess picked up a scone and, smiling smugly, smothered it in jam and cream. 'See, Nellie, you're a complete snob.'

'Oh, all right, perhaps I was a bit hard on him because I saw him as someone from a privileged background. But that's not why I don't want to marry him.'

'So, what else do you object to about Dominic Lockhart apart from his excessive amount of money?'

Nellie shrugged. 'There are lots of other reasons.'

'Are you not attracted to him? Well, we know that you are. You're so hopelessly attracted to him that you kissed him and came very close to making love to him when you probably shouldn't have. So, is he not clever enough for you?'

Nellie gritted her teeth together, reluctant to answer, but the Duchess continued to stare at her, her eyebrows raised as she waited for an answer.

'It's not that. Yes, he's definitely clever enough.'

'Oh, so is he not the one person whose company you prefer to all others? Is he not the man you constantly think about, dream about?'

Nellie shrugged again. 'Well, yes, he's attractive and I do enjoy his company.' Despite herself Nellie smiled at just how much she *did* enjoy his company. 'And, yes, I suppose I do think about him all the time and wish I could be with him.' With each word she heard her voice grow softer.

She looked up at the Duchess and forced that soppy smile off her face. 'But that's not why I can't marry him,' she said, her voice once again becoming firm.

The Duchess turned her palms upwards and shook her head as if waiting for Nellie to explain why she wouldn't marry a man who she was so obviously in love with.

'I can't marry him, Arabella. I just can't.' She looked around the room, then leaned forward to talk quietly. 'I can't be like these women. I don't want to have servants and be an idle display case for my husband's wealth, dripping with jewels and filling my days with pointless activities to stave off the boredom, while downstairs battalions of servants slave away from morning to night.'

'Then don't be.' The Duchess shrugged as if it was all so simple. 'I married a duke, but I don't live like an idle duchess. I have my career. I still have the life I love along with the man I love. Did you tell Dominic that you wanted to keep your business, that you didn't want to change your life?'

'No, but he said he wanted to take me away from my life and give me a life of luxury. He told me I'd never have to work again, as if working is such a shameful thing that no one would want to do it.'

'But did you tell him you didn't want that sort of life?'

Nellie shook her head defiantly, causing the Duchess to sigh with exasperation.

'Nellie, he fell in love with a strong, independent woman.' She leant forward. 'He didn't fall in love with a woman who wanted to be waited on day and night and lead a life of idleness.'

'Well, that's not what he said. He reminded me of our class differences, as if he was doing me a big favour by dragging me out of the gutter. He was talking as if my business and my little home were something to scorn.'

'Oh, so he's a snob as well, then.' Arabella laughed. 'It looks like you're well matched.' Her face became more serious. 'Did you tell him any of this?'

'No, but he should have known.'

Once again, the Duchess crossed her arms in front of her, as if about to deliver a stern lecture. 'And if you'd been in love with a local lad, would you have said a flat out no, or would you have explained yourself? Would you have told him that you wanted to keep your business, you wanted to carry on working after you married? Or is it only rich men who are supposed to know exactly what you want and what you are thinking without being told? And is it only rich men who are never allowed to make mistakes?'

'Hmm,' was all Nellie could answer. Perhaps she had been consistently rude to Dominic and it had continued right up until he had proposed to her. Why on earth he wanted to marry her after the way she'd treated him she could hardly understand. 'Well, it doesn't matter now, anyway. He proposed, I turned him down, it's all over.'

Arabella rolled her eyes and laughed, as if Nellie had said something outlandishly funny. 'It's not a business negotiation, Nellie. It was a proposal of marriage. He's hardly likely to have taken the offer off the table because you said no. Perhaps you need to swallow your enormous pride before it chokes you, stop judging him so harshly just because he has the misfortune of being fabulously wealthy and go and tell him how you feel and what you want.'

Nellie looked across the table at her friend and now adviser.

'Well?' the Duchess asked.

Nellie nodded and smiled, then picked up her cucumber sandwich and started eating, suddenly feeling very hungry.

Chapter Twenty-One

Dominic stood on the steps of his house and watched the carriage as it travelled up the long tree-lined drive. It pulled up in front of him. The door flew open. Amanda all but jumped out and embraced him in a joyous hug. She had been excited when she had left for her visit to Lord Westcliffe's family, and was even more excited now, if that was at all possible.

'I take it the visit went well?' he asked, her beaming smile telling him the answer.

'Oh, it was perfect. His parents are wonderful. And they are so happy for us.' She all but danced up the steps beside him as they entered the house.

She shrugged off her coat and handed it to the footman. 'Thomas's parents gave us their blessing straight away. They didn't even ask about my family or my background. All they care about is that Thomas is happy with his choice of bride.' She gave him what could only be described as a pointed look. 'And *they* don't care about social advancement.'

Dominic chose to say nothing to dampen his sister's excitement. The Duke of Castlemere was at the pinnacle of society. Of course he had no need to care about social advancement. Unless his son married into royalty there was nowhere for them to advance to.

'But what about you, Dominic?' Amanda clasped his arm. 'Do you have some happy news to tell me?'

He forced himself to smile. 'You know I'm very happy for you, Amanda.'

Her smile faded and Dominic inwardly groaned. He had done what he told himself he would not do. He had ruined her happiness.

His forced smile started to become painful as she stared up at him, her brow furrowed. 'And I want to hear all about your time with the Westcliffe family,' he asked with false joviality. 'Have you already started to make wedding plans or is it too early yet?'

She raised her eyebrows and gave him a disbelieving look. He had tried too hard. When had he ever been interested in anyone's wedding plans?

'What happened when you went to London?' Amanda placed her hand gently on his arm. 'What went wrong? I want you to tell me everything.'

'There's nothing to tell. Now, you must be very tired after your journey. I'll leave you to your rest.' He turned to leave and she grabbed his arm, halting his progress.

'Nonsense. I'm not the slightest bit tired.' She signalled to the butler and asked for tea to be served in the drawing room. 'And I'm not going to rest until you tell me what happened in London.'

Dominic was about to inform her he had no interest in taking tea, but he saw the defiant look on her face as she continued to grip his arm and changed his mind. It was plain to see that he was not going to escape, so he might as well get it over and done with. The sooner he told her what had happened between him and Nellie the sooner they could put it all behind them. He escorted her through to the drawing room and waited until she had seated herself. Then he took a seat and wondered where he was supposed to begin.

She looked over at him, her face a mixture of concern and curiosity. 'Well, what happened?'

He stifled a sigh. 'I went up to London to propose to Nellie Regan and she said no.' Now that she knew what had happened, he hoped Amanda would leave it alone, although, knowing his sister as he did, he doubted that would be the case.

She chewed on her top lip and drew her eyebrows together. 'Oh, Dominic. I'm so sorry. Why did she say no? From what my lady's maid said, the servants were convinced she was completely enamoured with you. So, what did you say to her? What did she say to you? What happened?'

The door opened and the footman entered, bearing a tray containing a teapot, milk jug and two cups and saucers. He placed the tray on the table, placed a silver strainer on one cup and began pouring.

'Leave it, please, James,' Dominic said. He did not want his sister asking him questions in front of one of the servants and he most certainly did not want to become an even greater topic of gossip below stairs than he already was.

James bowed and departed, shutting the door quietly behind him.

'Well?' Amanda asked as she poured both teas and added a splash of milk to her own.

Dominic took the cup from his sister and placed it on the side table. 'It seems your lady's maid was wrong. Miss Regan was not enamoured with me. I asked her to marry me and she said no. Even after I offered her everything—a new life, one where she would never have to work again, where she could live in luxury rather than those tiny two rooms above her shop— she still said no and all but threw my proposal of marriage in my face.'

Amanda's eyebrows knitted tighter together and she frowned at Dominic. 'So, what exactly did you say to her?'

'I've just told you. I asked her to marry me.'

'And?'

He shook his head. What more did she need to know?

'What else did you say?'

'I don't remember the exact words, but I promised her everything, offered her everything, but she said no.'

'Did you tell her you loved her?'

'What?' He nodded, then shook his head. 'Yes...no. I don't remember, but surely that was implied anyway. After all, I was offering to marry her.'

Amanda picked up her cup, took a sip and looked at him over the rim. 'If what you've told me is correct, it sounds to me more like you were offering her your homes and your money, not your love.'

He picked up his own teacup, then returned it to the side table. 'It hardly matters, does it? I asked her to marry me, she said no, that's the end of the matter.'

Amanda took another sip of her tea, put the cup back on the table, and sat up straighter, staring firmly at him, as if he was a child in need of instruction. One would think she was the elder sibling about to explain the ways of the world to her younger, less knowledgeable brother.

'I've only known Nellie Regan for a short while, but I think I got to know her quite well while she was doing my hair. And there's a few things you should realise.'

Dominic sighed in exasperation. It seemed now that his sister was being courted by a duke's son she had assumed the role of family matriarch.

'Even in that short time I could tell she is an independent woman and proud of the life she has made for herself,' Amanda continued, ignoring his loud sigh. 'But when you proposed to her, it sounds as though you forgot all about that. You effectively insulted her life by assuming she wanted to be taken away from it. That this is what she wants.' She raised her hands and looked around, to indicate the surrounding drawing room and Lockhart Estate. 'And you're surprised that she rejected you?'

'Well, surely she could see the advantages of living here.' He followed her example and waved his arm around to encompass the large, elegantly furnished drawing room, the even larger house, which was one of the biggest in Kent, and the extensive lands that surrounded it. 'And surely she could see how much I was giving up for her. If that's not an expression of love I don't know what is. I was prepared to marry an ex-lady's maid. To give up the possibility of making an advantageous marriage and of elevating the family's position in society. Instead I was risking our family being further shunned by society. And all because of her. Surely that shows how much I love her.'

Instead of the expected nod of agreement, Amanda's eyes grew wide and her mouth fell open, before she recovered and quickly shut it. 'Did you say that to her? Please tell me you didn't say that to her?'

'I don't remember. Yes, I suppose so. Something like that. I wanted her to see how much I was prepared to sacrifice for her. How much I wanted to marry her.'

'Oh, Dominic. You're hopeless. You proposed to her by insulting her and the life she had made for herself. Then you went on to further insult her by telling her just how much you were prepared to demean yourself by marrying someone who was once in service. I don't blame Nellie one little bit for turning you down. You're a complete snob, Dominic.'

He stared at his sister, too stunned to answer.

It was her time to sigh loudly. 'You think everyone wants to be rich, everyone wants to be titled, everyone wants to advance their position in society, just because you do. But Nellie wants something different. She's good at what she does. She's building up her business and wants to succeed in an area where she excels. She doesn't care about status and I very much doubt she wants everything handed to her on a platter.'

Dominic needed something stronger than tea if he was to be forced to continue with this infernal discussion. He strode over to the sideboard, poured himself a large brandy from the crystal decanter and took a long, fortifying drink.

'She made it very clear to me she doesn't like being treated like a servant, that she expects people to respect her.' He poured himself another drink and returned to his seat. 'Well, if she was the wife of a wealthy man, she would never be treated like a servant again. Nor would she be treated like someone in trade. She would get all the respect she deserves.' Dominic sent his sister a grim smile. He had proven his point.

Instead of accepting that he was right she shook her head slowly, as if surprised by his lack of intelligence. 'She wants respect for who she is, what she's achieved, not because of who she's married to, who her husband is.'

Dominic swirled the brandy round in his glass. 'Well, if she had married me, that would be who she was, my wife. She'd be Mrs Lockhart and she would get all the respect she deserves.'

Amanda raised clenched hands to the sides of her face and grimaced. 'That's not what Nellie wants,' she said, slowly enunciating each word. 'She wants to succeed on her own terms. She doesn't want to get respect through someone else. And all you did was show her how little you respect what she's achieved, what she's done with her life. How little you respect her.'

'That's not true,' he said, his voice rising. 'That's not true,' he repeated, his voice lower. After all, he was not arguing with Amanda, just explaining what had happened and why he and Nellie would not be marrying. 'Of course I respect her. I admire the way she is so independent and so determined to succeed. I admire the way she has made a life for herself, built up a business.'

'And did you tell her any of this?'

He stared at his sister and she raised her eyebrows, knowing the answer.

'No.' He absorbed the implication of what he had just said. 'You're right, Amanda. They are qualities I admire about her. If she wasn't independent, if she wasn't doing things her own way, then she wouldn't be the Nellie I fell in love with.'

His sister sat back in her chair, picked up her teacup and smiled in satisfaction.

'Nellie's business is important to her,' Dominic said as much to himself as to his sister. 'Succeeding is important to her.' He looked over at Amanda. 'But if she doesn't want my money, my houses, my estate, then I have nothing to offer her.'

Amanda's eyes grew wide again and she looked as if she was tempted to throw her cup at him. 'Dominic, you are hopeless. You have something very important you can offer her. Your love. If you love Nellie Regan, then that is what you should have told her. You should have told her why you loved her. You do love her, don't you?'

He flicked his finger against his brandy balloon. *Wasn't that obvious? Hadn't he already said that?*

'Well?'

'Yes, of course I love her. With all my heart.'

'And do you want to live without her?'

'No, of course I don't.'

'And do you want to marry her?'

'Yes, of course I do. I've already asked her and been turned down.'

'Well, ask her again. And this time tell her how much you love her. Let her know all the things about her you love, all the reasons why you fell in love with her. Even a dunderhead like you must be capable of doing that.'

He stared at his sister. She glared back at him, her expression uncompromising. 'What's the problem, Dominic? Are you too proud to ask again? Are you too proud to admit you got it wrong and your last attempt at proposing marriage was worse than bad, it was awful? If she had said yes to that preposterous proposal, she would have been saying yes to your homes and your money, she would be agreeing to a business proposition, not a marriage proposal, not a declaration of love.'

He continued to stare at Amanda, weighing up her words.

'So, this is what you are going to do. You are going to go back to London and you're going to propose to Nellie again. And this time you're going to do it properly.'

Dominic drew in a deep breath, exhaled slowly, then smiled at his sister. 'How did someone as young as you get to be so clever?'

Her glare turned into a gratified smile. 'Oh, it's

very easy to be clever when it's someone else's love life you're trying to sort out. Now off you go.'

Dominic stood, kissed his sister on the top of her head and departed for London.

Chapter Twenty-Two

Nellie knew what she had to do, but was unsure how she was going to do it. What do you say to a man who you've told you don't want to marry and you never want to see again? How do you say that, um, you've changed your mind, and if he's still interested, then, yes, you would like to marry him after all?

Should she write him a letter? Spill out her heart on paper? Should she take the train down to Kent and burst into his home, or should she lurk about outside his town house and wait till he came up to London so she could accost him? None of these options seemed particularly appealing as all of them involved Nellie admitting she was wrong, something she was unfamiliar with doing.

But she had to do something. She had to let him know how she felt. Of all the options she had available, writing a letter seemed like the least difficult to do. Well, it was the easiest from an organisational point of view, but it was hardly easy. Seating herself at the counter, she placed a clean white sheet of paper in front of her, uncapped a bottle of ink and dipped in her pen. Then she stared at the blank page, her pen poised above it, her mind equally blank.

Why was this so hard? All she had to do was tell him how she felt. She wrote *Dear Dominic* at the top of the page, then stared at it. Should she have started with *My Dearest Dominic*? Yes, that would be better.

She screwed up the piece of paper and threw it on the floor, took another one from the pile and wrote *My Dearest Dominic*.

Then what?

She chewed the end of her pen. Suddenly, the idea of lurking outside his town house or surprising him by turning up unannounced at his estate was becoming more appealing.

The bell above the door rang. 'I'm sorry, we're closed, you'll have to…' She looked up and the words died on her lips. 'Dominic. I was just…' She looked down at the page bearing just three words, then looked at the man standing in the doorway. 'What are you doing here?'

He stepped into the shop, closed the door, then stood in the middle of the room looking uncharacteristically awkward. 'Nellie, can I have a few minutes of your time to talk to you?'

Nellie nodded, climbed down off the stool and went around to the other side of the counter. It looked as if Dominic had made the decision for her. She did not have to write him a letter or stalk him in London or Kent. She could now tell him in person how she felt.

She clasped her hands together, then released them. It was now her turn to feel uncharacteristically awkward, to be uncharacteristically tongue-tied.

But they could not just stand in the middle of the shop, staring awkwardly at each other.

'Please, come through to the back room, it's more comfortable there.' Her voice came out surprisingly calmly, despite the frantic words spinning round in her head. Words that she was going to have to get into some sort of order before she would be able to say them to him.

He followed her through to the parlour. She took a seat, but he remained standing, so she stood up again. 'Please, Nellie, sit down.'

Nellie sat and gestured to the other armchair. He sat down, then immediately stood up again, so Nellie followed his example and also stood. Now they were standing in the parlour staring awkwardly at each other instead of in the shop. It wasn't much of an improvement.

Nellie knew she should say something. She just wished her brain, which could be so quick when she was being rude to people, could be just as quick when she was trying to tell the man she loved how she felt.

'I came to apologise,' he finally said, breaking the awkward silence. 'I believe I insulted you the last time we spoke and I'm profoundly sorry for that.' He paused, looked down at his hands, clenched in front of him, then back up at Nellie. 'No, that's wrong. I *did* insult you the last time we spoke and for that I am profoundly sorry.'

'No…' she shook her head '…you have nothing to apologise for.'

His face scrunched up into a pained expression and he closed his eyes. He opened them and took in a deep breath. 'I'm doing all this wrong again and sounding pompous. I had a speech prepared and now that I've started to say it, I realise it's not what I want to say at all. All I really want to do is tell you how I feel, what's in my heart.'

'Oh?' Nellie gasped.

He turned his hands palm upwards. 'I love you, Nellie. It's as simple as that. I think I fell in love with you that first time I saw you in the servants' hall at Hardgrave Estate. I know you were making fun of me, but you were so funny and so risqué. How could I not be captivated? I knew I should have been offended, but if anything I was envious of all the servants who were watching you, laughing and enjoying themselves. I also envied the man who would some day have you in his life, a woman who could make him laugh and make him laugh at himself.'

'Oh?' Nellie repeated, still tongue tied.

'Then my love continued to grow. When we spent those days together in your room, despite my pain I couldn't remember the last time I had felt so comfortable, so at home. But I'd also never met a woman who affected me so deeply. And I don't just mean…' He waved his hand in the air, causing Nellie to smile.

'Oh, you mean that standing ovation you gave me when you saw me in my nightdress.' Nellie bit her tongue. Once again she'd slipped into being cheeky and now was not the time for that.

He smiled back at her, that lovely smile that lit up his dark eyes. That smile Nellie had feared she would never see again. It seemed her comment hadn't offended him. It seemed he was telling the truth, he enjoyed being teased by her.

'Yes, that.' He laughed lightly. 'My standing ovation. But it's not just that you're the most beautiful woman I have ever seen.' His face became more serious. 'And you are beautiful, Nellie, you have a beautiful soul, a beautiful mind.' He smiled, that lovely warm smile. 'As well as a beautiful body. And when I finally did have you in my arms, I knew that was what I wanted, what I had to have. I realised I wanted you in my life, that I loved you.'

He looked down at his hands, clasping and unclasping in front of him. 'Then I made that stupid, clumsy proposal, which you were right to turn down.'

'Oh, yes, that.' Nellie nodded. Now was her time to tell him what she felt, but her annoying brain was still blank.

'I'm not surprised you said no,' he said before she could formulate the words she was so desperate to say.

'You're not?'

'No. I insulted you with my proposal and I'm sorry.' He paused and drew in a deep breath. 'What I should have said was, Nellie, you are a beautiful, clever, talented, funny, delightful and wonderful woman. I admire your talents. I admire the way you have made a successful life for yourself. I admire your way with people. After just one meeting with my sister you transformed her, made her see the joy in life, and that's what you do with everyone. That's what you've done with me. You make the world a joyful place with your fun and your laughter.'

He looked down, drew in a deep breath and looked back at her. 'Nellie, I'm sorry I insulted you with my proposal. My mother married for love and I had never understood it. I thought she had thrown away everything she had, but now I realise how wrong I was. When I judged her harshly it was because I didn't know what love meant. Now that I do, I realise that it is worth more than titles or property. My mother gave up her position in society, but she gained so much more. For you Nellie, I would give away everything, my wealth, my position, even the clothes off my back.' He shrugged off his jacket and threw it on the chair, then crossed the room and took both her hands in his.

Tears sprung to her eyes and she held her breath as she looked up at his tense face.

'I know I'm not worthy of you. I know that a man like me has nothing to offer a woman like you. But all I *can* offer you is my undying love. Nellie, will you let me love you, cherish you, honour you? Will you make me the happiest man who ever lived by consenting to be my wife?'

Nellie nodded quickly, wanting to drive away the anxiety gripping his face. 'Yes, yes, I will, yes.'

'You will?' His eyes grew wide. 'You will?'

She continued nodding vigorously.

He took hold of her hands, his face no longer tense,

his lips and eyes smiling. 'Oh, Nellie, I love you so much and I will do everything in my power to make you happy. Truly happy. Whatever that takes. I know you don't want to live at my home in Kent. If you want us to live here, then I'm happy to move in with you. Anything you want is what I want as well.'

Nellie looked up at the ceiling and thought about her small rooms, rooms barely big enough for herself, never mind two people, particularly a man as energetic and vigorous as Dominic.

'Well, let's not be too hasty about that. I'm sure I can cope with living in your town house.' She laughed, her happiness bubbling out of her. 'Oh, Dominic, we can work out details like that later. As long as I'm with you I don't care where we live.'

She forced herself to be serious. She had promised herself she would tell him how she felt and now was the time. 'I have to tell you that I have fallen in love with you as well. I didn't want to. I tried not to fall in love with you, but I failed, miserably.'

'Well, I'm pleased there's one thing you failed at,' he said, still smiling.

Part of Nellie wanted to just smile and leave it at that, but he had been honest with her, so it was her turn to be honest with him. 'And I also want to make an apology. I have been rude to you, made fun of you, put you in a compromising position, even caused you to be beaten up...'

'No, Nellie, you...'

She squeezed his hands and shook her head. 'I did. And all because I judged you harshly, because you've got money, because you mix with aristocrats. I've been so rude to you I can't believe you could fall in love with someone like me. I'm sorry, Dominic, and I promise to try to change, to not be so rude in the future.'

'No, no, no, Nellie. Don't change a thing.' He pulled her hands up to his lips and lightly kissed them. 'I love your rebelliousness. I love the way you can be so cheeky and, yes, I love the way you can mock people who deserve to be mocked, especially me. I was a pompous buffoon when I met you and you taught me to laugh at myself. Being cheeky when people deserve it is part of your spirited nature, it's part of what caused me to fall so hopelessly in love with you from the moment I saw you.'

'Oh, is it, really? You like it when I'm rude to you? I'll hold you to that one.' Nellie smiled back at him. 'Well, I also have to confess that I started falling in love with you the first time I saw you as well, when you were dancing at Hardgrave Estate. I think that's why I made fun of you, because I knew you were a man I could never have. I could never be the one you were gliding across the floor in your arms. I could never be the one you were holding. Deep down, that was what I really wanted, but couldn't even admit to myself, so I did what I always do. I made jokes. Then when you were in my rooms, in my bed, I wanted you so badly it was almost painful. But I still knew you weren't for me. But even though I knew that I still stole a kiss from you that first night when you were sleeping because I just couldn't stop myself.'

'You did?' Dominic threw back his head and

laughed out loud. 'Why didn't you wake me? Then the kiss wouldn't have had to be stolen, I would have gladly given it to you for free and given you much more into the bargain, as you well know.'

Nellie bit her lip, remembering how the next day he had unintentionally shown how he would indeed have given her so much more. 'Well, you're awake now, aren't you?'

Still laughing, Dominic drew her towards him. 'I am indeed.'

As his arms encased her and his lips found hers Nellie could hardly believe such happiness really existed. She was being kissed by a man who loved her, who she loved with her heart and soul. Breaking from him, she took his hand. 'Well, you've promised me much more. Was that just an idle promise or are you going to make good on it?' She raised her eyes towards the ceiling, indicating her rooms upstairs.

'You're damn right I am.' Scooping her up in his arms, Dominic carried a laughing Nellie up the stairs and into her room.

Epilogue

There was laughter, there was dancing, there were toasts. Guests were hugging each other and even occasionally breaking into song. It was just how an engagement party should be. It should be a celebration of love, with the happy couple surrounded by friends and family. And that was exactly what the engagement party of Mr Dominic Lockhart and Miss Eleanor Regan was.

Dominic had originally said he'd be happy to host the engagement party at The Hanged Man, so all Nellie's neighbours and friends could join in on the celebration. As he had said, they owed a debt of gratitude to The Hanged Man. After all, if it hadn't been for Dominic nearly getting into a bar room brawl on the premises, they might never have spent time together, might never have had the chance to fall in love. Although both suspected it would have happened anyway. How could they not fall in love with each other? How could two people who were perfect for each other not meet and fall in love? Those were two questions they were pleased they would not have to answer.

While Nellie appreciated Dominic's gesture, she had convinced him that the ballroom at Lockhart Estate was a better venue for an engagement party. As she had said, it would make a nice change of scenery for Matilda and Harriet and all Nellie's friends from the neighbourhood. Especially as many of them were staying overnight at the estate. Dominic had rightly pointed out that some might not be able to afford the train fare, but then he had come up with the perfect solution. He included train tickets with the invitation. Nellie had felt so pleased with him for making such a tactful gesture and so proud of herself for agreeing to marry such a man as wonderful as Dominic.

She was prouder still when he relented under her determined insistence that they hire staff for the day so the household servants would be able to join in the festivities, along with the tenants who lived on Lockhart Estate.

One thing they did agree on immediately. Inviting Patrick Kelly and his friends would be going a bit too far, even though they admitted they also owed them a debt of gratitude. If it wasn't for their fists and boots Dominic would not have had to recover at Nellie's home. That was time they treasured as it was when their love first began to blossom. But instead of an invitation, they decided a more fitting way to repay that particular debt was not to press assault charges.

The Duke and Duchess of Somerfeld, along with the Duke and Duchess of Knightsbrook, also attended the engagement party and both dukes had offered to walk Nellie up the aisle. Nellie hadn't mentioned it yet to Dominic, but as she had two friends who were duchesses, Dominic would be marrying a woman who could easily arrange for his sisters to be presented at court.

Amanda no longer needed to ask the Duke of Castlemere to arrange this, as Nellie could now make it happen. She knew she shouldn't be looking forward to telling Dominic, but she was. It meant that she, little Nellie Regan, the ex-lady's maid, would be the one who elevated the Lockhart sisters to the loftiest of heights on the social calendar when they made their debuts.

Not that either Violet or Emmaline seemed to care one fig whether they were presented at court or not. Like their older sister, Amanda, they seemed like very sensible young women who would marry for love and not for status. Just like their mother did before them and just as their brother was about to do.

Nellie looked around the ballroom, smiled and saw her handsome fiancé making his way towards her. 'May I have the honour of this dance?' he said, giving her his most formal bow.

'Indeed, you may, sir,' Nellie replied, making an equally formal curtsy. Dominic's arm wrapped around her waist and he glided her across the parquet floor, while everyone watched. Nellie was sure she must be glowing she felt so radiant with happiness. How could she not be? She was dancing with the man she loved, the man who loved her.

And when Dominic ignored all protocol, all ideas of what constituted proper behaviour, and kissed her on the dance floor to the enthusiastic applause of all the guests, Nellie's happiness reached a level she would have once thought impossible.

'Who said the upper classes lacked passion?' Dominic said, laughing, as he lifted her up in his arms and twirled her around.

'Some fool who didn't know what she was talking about.'

'A beautiful fool who unlocked this fool's heart and showed him what love and passion really mean.' With that, Dominic lowered her to the floor and kissed her again.

* * * * *

If you enjoyed this book, why not check out these other great reads by Eva Shepherd

Beguiling the Duke
Awakening the Duchess